Karamea House

Karamea House

Anne Keen

BELBORA MOUNTAIN PRESS

Paperback: ISBN 978-0-6456153-0-2

Ebook: ISBN 978-0-6456153-1-9

Edited by Lu Sexton

Cover Photo by Anne Keen

Cover Desgin by Jen Dusseault

Typeset by Jen Dusseault

Bebora Mountain Press

Belbora, NSW, 2422

Australia

www.annekeen.com.au

Thank you to all of those people in my life who read my work, encouraged and supported me, listened and laughed alongside me, and helped me get this far. I could not have done this without you.

Chapter 1

I can't remember why I wasn't in the car that night. I'm not sure if I was being punished or if I was just sick. I should have been in the car. Maybe I had broken one of the rules. I can't remember. Mother would tell me it was just God's will, but I can't for the life of me understand how something like this could happen. I should have been with them. Why didn't I go? I normally go with them. Maybe if I had, none of this would have happened.

These are the thoughts that consume my mind every time I close my eyes. It's no wonder I can't sleep. Once the clock strikes five, I decide to get up. It's the last morning I'll wake up in my own bed. They allowed me to stay here until the funeral, but after today this will no longer be my home.

My shoulders are heavy as I drag my tired body towards the bathroom. I can't get there without passing their room. I stop at the door that has been closed since they left. I haven't been able to bring myself to open it. Part of me wants to believe that they are both still in there, making me feel a little safer in this old creaky house. I never really noticed how much noise it makes in the middle of the night. It's funny really, considering I've lived here all my life, you'd think I would have known that the weatherboard pops and cracks as the cold night air rustles across it.

I place my hand on the faded, chipped eggshell paint of their door where my mother would hang a prayer wreath on sacred days. The coldness of the wooden surface sends a shiver down my spine. I still can't find the strength to enter the room.

I've cried so much. I don't think there are any more tears left inside of me, so instead my heart aches.

The elders are coming to the house this afternoon to take care of my parents' possessions. It gives me some sense of relief knowing that it's not up to me to pack up the house. The night of the accident, Mr and Mrs Edwards told me they would take care of everything. At first, I thought that perhaps the Edwards would ask me to come stay with them. They were the closest with my parents, especially Mr Edwards and my father. They've been elders together ever since I can remember. I've never lived with anyone other than my parents. The idea of going somewhere I've not been before with people I've not met before is making me feel nauseous.

I peel my palm from the closed door and head into the bathroom.

After the shower, I put on my best dress – the one my mother bought me for special occasions – and make my way downstairs to the kitchen. My movements are robotic as I open the cupboard to get out the same box of cereal I've been eating from every morning since they left. I take little notice of the sour scent of the milk. It's not until the clumps of clotted cream tumble into my bowl that I realise it's well past its prime. Doesn't matter though, I'm not hungry anyway. I'm just trying to keep myself busy as I wait. This waiting has been going on for a fortnight and the agony of my grief has shifted to a dull hum of nothingness. The lounge room wall clock chimes to mark the new hour. Seven strokes before the silence of my solitude returns. It's almost deafening, so much so that I don't hear the door. The numbness consumes me. It's not until Mrs Edwards places her hand on my shoulder that I even notice that other people are in the room.

'Sara, dear, have you said your morning prayer?' Her voice is soft and smooth.

I nod my head. I know it's a lie, but I don't feel much like praying. What kind of God takes both parents and leaves a child alone?

'Have you packed your things?' Mr Edwards asks.

I nod again. There isn't much for me to take. Just a bag of clothes and my favourite stuffed toy. Possessions have never really been a thing in my family. I was never permitted to keep up with all the latest trends like the other kids at school. That's just something my parents would not allow.

'I'll go put them in the car. We'll take you out to Karamea House after the service,' he says before heading upstairs to get my things.

I'm torn about leaving my home. On one hand, I don't know what to expect having to integrate into someone else's way of life. It makes me feel uneasy and nervous. On the other hand, staying here is just a constant reminder that I'm alone.

But Karamea House isn't your typical foster home. And Del Moon isn't like anyone I've ever met before. My parents would not approve of me living with her.

My mother had issues with her the moment she arrived in town.

It's a day I'll never forget. There was just something about Del that was so different from what I was used to. I'm not sure if it was the way she seemed to demand the attention of everyone around her or if it was more about the feeling that you get when she catches your eye. My mother noticed it too. And not just Mother, Del seemed to make quite an impression on the whole town.

Gloucester is a small place. It's proud of its country virtues and has no plans to change or progress ahead of its own schedule. Everyone knows everyone's business and people like it that way. So when Del drove into town that morning, she sent a shock wave through the main street.

Being a Sunday morning, most people were lingering in town after church. They habitually gather in clusters dotted along the footpath to catch up on their weekly gossip. Not only did lots of people see Del when she first arrived, they also witnessed the incident that occurred shortly after.

It all started with the type of vehicle Del was driving.

Now I don't want to mislead you, Gloucester isn't so small that it's never had visitors passing through in vehicles that stand out and catch your attention. It's seen plenty of cars in all shapes and sizes creeping over the speed bumps as they pass through town. There's even been a couple of beat-up old classics floating around the neighbourhood from time to time. But I guarantee you that no-one had ever laid eyes on the creative setup Del arrived in.

She was behind the steering wheel of a weird looking, multi-coloured Kombi ute. The sight was so unusual that people found themselves staring. Perhaps, if she'd just been driving the thing on its own, the town curiosity may have been short lived. But the fact that she was towing a trailer loaded with furniture stacked almost as high as the pile of crumbled boxes in the tray of the ute made the sight more intriguing. Not to mention the fact that the precarious mountain of belongings in the tray rose over the roof of the cabin, where a mattress was strapped down with ropes running through the windows. Everyone on the street stood frozen, watching as she negotiated the raised pedestrian crossings. It's no wonder she did what she did.

I was standing pretty close to Mrs Vale at the time – one of the women in the hierarchy of the town – and I could hear her talking to Mrs Munn – one of the primary school teachers. She was making comments about how a lady shouldn't be driving such a monstrosity. That it wasn't proper. Now I don't know if Del heard her or not but, she stopped right there in the middle of main street, stuck her head out the window, and hollered to Mr Vale, who was standing right beside Mrs Vale.

'Excuse me!'

Mr Vale walked straight over to the ute.

The two had a brief conversation, much too quiet for anyone to hear, except at the end when Del was laughing and saying how funny he was.

When Mr Vale walked back over to Mrs Vale, he had a grin on his face. Mrs Vale, on the other hand, wasn't smiling. Although, I reckon her hair was pulled back so tight she couldn't have been able to manage one.

Del stuck her arm out the window and waved to Mr Vale as she continued on her way.

'Thanks darl!'

Now I know that I've been raised in a pretty conversative family, under the watchful eye of numerous crucifixes on the walls, but I could see that Mrs Vale didn't like that Del had spoken to her husband. A bit of jealousy, I suspected.

'What do you think you were doing?' Mrs Vale demanded.

'Just helping that nice lady with some information about town.'

'What kind of information did she want?'

'She wanted to know where to get a cold beer after her long drive on this hot day.'

'Beer? On a Sunday morning?'

'Well, it's almost midday.'

Mrs Vale was so angry she didn't respond but instead stormed off towards their car. Mr Vale tipped his hat and winked at me before following along behind her.

As if nothing had happened, Mother, Father, and I simply continued our journey to the pub like we always did for lunch on Sundays. They didn't say much about what happened on the street, except Father did say something to Mother about the ute being a 'hippy drug den'. I didn't really know what he meant by that, and I wasn't brave enough to ask him.

When I think about that now, I regret not asking. In the fortnight since the car accident, I've run through moments like this over and over, wondering what he would have said. At the time I was scared of him, but now that seems so silly.

As the memory swirls through my head, tears return, stinging my swollen eyes. I'd give anything to have them back with me just so I don't have to live through today.

I stay seated at the table in the hope that time will also stand still, but the commotion continues to build around me. Mr Edwards returns from putting my bag in the car with several other elders and I can hear them shuffling their way upstairs. Mrs Edwards grabs hold of my arm and lifts me from the chair. She's mumbling something inaudible as she directs me outside. My head is heavy and full of fuzz. All I want to do is go back to bed and hide under the covers. But instead, I'm placed in the back seat of the Edwards' car and chauffeured to the church.

I can see the two hearses parked out front of the small, white chapel. What was once a shining beacon of hope, now appears more like a horror house I desperately don't want to enter. Maybe if I stay in the car this whole nightmare will simply disappear. If I don't attend the funeral then they won't be dead.

I press my head against the cold window and watch as the two caskets are wheeled into the chapel. I struggle to breathe with the pressure of loss on my heart.

'I think I'm going to be sick,' I manage to say just before my stomach begins to wrench. I open the car door and vomit into the gutter.

As Mrs Edwards rushes to my side, I stare through the water in my eyes at the mess I've made on the street and all I can think of is how it reflects me.

'I don't think I can do this,' I confess to Mrs Edwards.

'Of course you can, my dear,' she says gently as she helps me out of the car, making sure to avoid the pool of vomit. 'It's your duty to see your parents off on their eternal journey.'

I know her words are coming from a place of kindness, but I can't see how my parents' death should be celebrated. I've been to funerals in this church before and I know how it all goes. We're told to pray to the Lord for guidance and support knowing that our loved ones are going to a better place in the Kingdom of God. It's all meant to make us not fear death and to embrace the afterlife that comes complete with shining glory. But I'm just simply not ready to say goodbye. To do that means that they aren't coming back and that is just too hard for me to swallow right now. I'm still hopeful that it's a bad dream and I'll wake up to my normal life any minute.

My parents never prepared me for life without them. I haven't been taught all the things I need to know to survive alone. They were supposed to be with me until I met the man I was to marry and I was ready to move out to start a family of my own. This was the path they had told me I was to follow. Them dying wasn't part of the plan. This wasn't meant to happen.

I stand frozen beside the car watching as members of our small church community make their way towards the tiny white building. Two black crows caw as they tussle mid-air above the church. One seeks refuge upon the arm of the cross at the top of the steeple while the other beats its wings in frustration. The noise of their disagreement echoes through the air causing the mourners to look up and watch as the one still flying attempts to knock the other off the cross. Its aggression is duly met by the other who refuses to leave its post. Finally, the aggressor abandons its mission and settles on the other arm of the cross next to its nemesis.

And just like that, the pair stand side-by-side in silence. I can't help but think about the times my parents would argue and Father would become so angry that he'd start slamming doors as my mother persisted on loudly voicing her point of view. To think that they continue to squabble in their afterlife makes me smile. The irony of them taking that kind of angst with them to paradise causes me to quietly giggle.

'It's time,' Mrs Edwards whispers.

I take a deep breath and follow slowly behind her. My gaze drifts back up to the crows who seem to be watching me. Their tiny heads moving with me as I get closer and closer to the entrance. I'm not sure if I should feel scared or secure under their watchful eyes.

As I reach the door, they both let out a loud caw before launching from their perch.

Chapter 2

Back in the Edwards' car, the blur of the funeral lies on me like a weighted blanket. I rest my head, tilted to the side, watching the smear of the town pass by as we start our journey towards Karamea House. I've never been out this way before and I have no idea where the place is. I only know that it takes some time to get there. I've been told that the bus ride to school will be close to an hour long. While the thought of going to school is normally the last thing that I look forward to, after having been so isolated for the past couple of weeks, I'm kind of missing it. My stomach is tight with nerves as I think about what it's going to be like in my new home and the possibility that Del might not be the only one living there. Being a foster home, it's likely she'll have other kids coming and going.

My heart begins to race as I think about living with strangers, then it occurs to me that Del isn't actually a stranger. This isn't the first time I've met her.

It was at the pub that first day Del arrived in town. When my parents and I walked in, Del was leaning against the bar wearing blue jeans with her hair swept up into a loose bun right on the top of her head. My mother always told me that it wasn't right for ladies to hang out at the bar. She said that it was a place for tradies and farm hands. But that's where Del was that day, standing right in between Mr Moore, the plumber, and Mr Stevens, the electrician, drinking beer straight from the bottle.

I'd never seen anything like it before – from a woman, I mean. My mother's friends are way more uptight and rigid in their behaviour. I've not once seen them drink alcohol, let alone beer from a bottle. Wine is consumed during our Friday night prayer sessions, but that is only for the men.

The sight of Del blatantly standing there in a public space drinking and chatting with people she'd just met was like watching a movie. Not that I've seen very many movies. Only the ones that are approved by my parents, and they aren't really that interesting. I remember being enamoured by Del that day. I couldn't help but watch her. It was hard not to mimic her motions as she flicked her head back when she laughed. Mother kept telling me to stop staring, but I couldn't help it. There was just something about her. I was drawn to her. So much so that I literally ran into her, and I mean that quite literally. Our first meeting was so sudden and unexpected that I was almost knocked to the floor.

I had to go to the toilet, but I didn't want to be gone very long, as I didn't want to miss anything, so I was rushing out the door as Del was coming in. The shock of my downturned head contacting her body caused me to pull back so quickly that I lost my balance. She caught me with both hands.

'My goodness young lady, are you ok?' she asked as she pulled me back onto my feet.

The blue of her eyes made me think of the ocean on the clearest summer's day. I was stunned.

'Are you in a hurry?'

'I…ah...I…'

'Gave yourself a bit of a scare, did ya?'

'No…ah…I'm ok.'

'Excellent,' she stated, releasing me from her grasp. 'I'm Del Moon. I'm new in town.'

'I'm Sara Johnson,' I managed, finally regaining some self-control. 'I've been here my whole life.'

'Well Sara Johnson, it's very lovely to meet you,' she said, putting out her hand.

'It's nice to meet you, Mrs Moon,' I said as I shook it.

'Call me Del.' She smiled with a brief flash of her stunning blue eyes. 'All my friends do.'

I felt my cheeks go hot.

'Now that we are friends, can you tell me where I can buy some groceries?'

'There's a place up the road from here. You would've passed it on your way in.'

'You saw me come in did ya? I caused quite the stir, didn't I?' she laughed.

'People 'round here aren't used to seeing the kind of ute you're drivin'.'

'Really?' She seemed genuinely shocked. 'Kombi's have been around since the late 60's.' She leaned in a little closer. 'Not that popular around here?'

'Not really, Del. This place is more used to the traditional varieties of utility vehicles,' I responded quickly with a tinge of sarcasm.

It's not like me to make cheeky comments like that. If my parents heard me, they'd be very angry and the punishment would be pretty severe. They would say that I was being disrespectful for speaking to an adult in such a loose manner, and then they'd go off about my lack of appreciation for my community. But it just slipped out so naturally with Del. She immediately made me feel at ease.

So much so in fact, that I had no issue continuing my banter. 'This place isn't good at accepting things outside the norm.'

'They're not so good at accepting change, eh?' Del laughed. 'Well, I guess this town is in for a real treat.'

The bathroom door opened behind her.

'There you are Sara.' My mother seemed relieved. 'I thought you'd fallen in.'

'I'm afraid I've been keeping her, Mrs Johnson,' Del apologised. 'I'm Del Moon and I'm new in town. Your daughter was helping me with directions to the grocery store.'

'Welcome to Gloucester, Mrs Moon. Now if you'll excuse us.' Mother was using her not-so-friendly tone as she grabbed me by the hand.

'Of course.' Del's response was gentle as she stepped out of the way.

Without another word, Mother grabbed my arm and pulled me out the door.

'See you later friend,' Del waved.

'Bye,' was all I managed to say before the door slammed closed behind me.

'I've told you not to talk to strangers.' Mother's voice was low and angry.

'Sorry Mother,' was all I said. I knew it was best not to argue with her when she was using that tone.

I didn't get in trouble that night which surprised me. I was expecting to be given a long list of chores to be completed to the highest standard in a ridiculously short amount of time. Instead, Mother just told me to say extra prayers before bed so that Jesus would help me make the right decision next time. I suppose she decided that a dose of guilt would do the trick instead.

It didn't take long for Del's arrival to consume my mother's gossip sessions. And not just her, but the rest of town as well. Everyone was talking about it. At the grocery store, Mrs Montgomery told Mother that she had heard that Del had bought the old Winchester's farm. Mother figured that must be true because

Mrs Montgomery's son was the real estate agent who sold the property. Up at the post office, Mother was told that Del's husband had kicked her out for not being enough of a lady and that's why she decided to move here. It was Mrs Pritchard who told her that, and seeing how Mrs Pritchard was married to the only solicitor in town, Mother was pretty sure that was true as well. But then some of the women at the Country Women's Association – a group of women that Mother believed lived their lives as close to God as any person could – told Mother that Del was not able to have children and that's why her husband kicked her out. Given how much faith Mother had in those CWA women, she started to wonder if what Mrs Pritchard said was true. Then she heard some of the women at church talking about how Del had been under investigation for the death of her husband and that she moved to Gloucester before they could find out the truth. The rumours were going around so fast and fierce that Mother really didn't know which story to believe. Although, she said she knew for sure that the one she heard from my father, about Del being a lesbian, was definitely not true because Mother thought she was simply too pretty to like other women.

After a while, the talk of Del simmered down and the town found a new thing to gossip about. I never knew that Del turned old Winchester's farm into a foster home. I only learned about it after the accident when those government people came by. And now I'm on my way to Karamea House, and it's to be my new home. I suppose knowing that Del is going to be there gives me a little bit of comfort, but my world is so jumbled and twisted it's hard to see any positives.

We've been driving for a while, and I'm so caught up in my memories, that I'm not paying attention to the murmurings of the Edwards in the front seat. I'm not sure how many times Mrs Edwards has said my name before I finally hear it.

'You okay, my dear,' she asks softly.

'Uh-huh,' I mutter.

'We were just saying that we don't want you to think that we are abandoning you,' she continues, having turned in her seat to face me. 'You will still continue to come to our house on Friday nights.'

I nod my head. Knowing I can return to my church community each week provides some sense of normality.

'If you continue with your prayers, Jesus will guide you along the right path,' Mr Edwards says, flashing me a glimpse through the rear-view mirror.

'Thank you, sir,' I respond as our journey takes us up a long gravel road.

We are so far from town I wonder if there is even electricity out here. We pass large sections of bushland interlaced with vast portions of barren farmland. Occasionally I see herds of cattle huddled together in meagre spots of shade cast by the pockets of trees. It makes me wonder why the farmers cut down all the trees if that's where the cows want to be. Every so often there is a hole in the ground with a shallow pool of water resting at the bottom.

Before my parents died, I heard them talking with the Edwards about the lack of rain over the winter. Mr Edwards was telling my father how difficult it had been on the land as the summer season rolled in and there was still no rain. I now understand what they were talking about as each patch of pasture we pass is scorched from sun and lacking any sort of nutrient-rich green grass. I'm just about to ask Mr Edwards how his cattle are going when he starts to slow down.

The road is blocked by a gate housed at the bottom of an enormous wooden frame. Hanging from the top is a large wooden slab with the word 'Karamea' burnt into it. As we approach, I see a billow of dust coming towards us with a swift moving vehicle at the front of it. The ute is unmistakably the one Del was driving eighteen months earlier when she moved to town. Del reaches the entrance just as we do and comes bounding out of the driver's seat. She's waving as she proceeds to unlock the gate. Mrs Edwards rolls down her window to greet Del.

'You're here,' Del announces, sticking her head in the window in order to direct her enthusiasm to me. 'I'm so excited to have you come to stay with me.'

I muster up a weak grin. I want to get caught up in her positivity, but my stomach remains a pit of anguish.

'I can take her from here,' Del says. 'No need for you to venture much further than you already have.'

'It's not trouble,' Mrs Edwards says, although she seems a little tense.

Her demeanour has changed in Del's presence. Her back has stiffened and she's leaning away from Del.

It strikes me as strange that neither Mr or Mrs Edwards have got out of the car. It's the polite thing to do when greeting someone. That's what my parents taught me. You should get out of the car and shake the person's hand. But instead, the Edwards remain seated.

'Let's grab your stuff,' Del says directly to me.

I suspect she also finds the situation uncomfortable and is trying to get things moving.

'Of course,' I respond as I get out.

I meet Del at the back of the car and she offers to take my bags so I can say goodbye.

'Thank you for the ride,' I say through the open window.

'Not a problem my dear,' Mrs Edwards says as her shoulders relax and a smile returns to her face. 'Mrs Moon will make sure you get to our house on Friday.' She pats my hand, but her glare is fixed on Del.

'I certainly will,' Del chimes.

Mrs Edwards leans in closer to me and whispers, 'Jesus is watching over you.'

A moment later they are gone and it's just me and Del. It's the first time I've been alone with her since the day we met. I've seen her around town and at the cattle sales, but we've not spoken since that day. My mother would always pull me closer or make an excuse to leave if we were ever near enough to Del for a customary conversation.

I take a moment to breathe in my surroundings, leaning back to look up at the impressive sign above me.

'It's an Aboriginal word meaning 'Welcome here', she explains as she heads towards her ute. She throws my bags into the back and waves me over. 'Pull the gate closed behind you.'

I obey her request, clipping the latch before I make my way to the vehicle. I take a deep breath as I open the door and jump in.

The emotion of today has been immense, but somehow getting into this techno-colour vehicle that smells like fresh flowers seems to lift my spirits.

'River's up a bit high for crossing at the moment, we'll need to use the bridge,' Del explains as we approach a shed about a kilometre down the driveway. 'We had a heavy downpour up on the catchment last night and it's just making its way down here now. Let's hope it's the start of lots of rain to break this damn drought.'

As she parks the vehicle around the side of the shed, the expansive view of the property begins to reveal itself. The road we are on continues ahead of us into the river, where I can just make out the concrete treads beneath the water leading to the other side. By the looks of how quickly the water is flowing, I'm relieved that she has no intention of attempting to cross. My eyes follow the road through the dotted line of gum trees that opens up to a neatly manicured lawn. Perched on the top of the hill at least a hundred metres away, I can see a slightly rusted green tin roof that seems to dwarf the whitewashed walls below. The homestead looks huge, even from this distance. My eyes continue to scan, but I can't see the bridge Del is referring to.

'You ready?' Del asks as she comes up beside me with my bag in one hand and a box of groceries in the other. 'We'll need to carry one thing at a time. Not enough room to carry more than that.' She smiles as she passes me my bag.

I stand for a moment longer, trying to figure out what she's talking about before I hustle to catch up with her. She's heading straight for the river following along a narrow dirt track. I can hear the roar of the water. It sounds like the freight train I could hear from my room some nights as it travelled through town. The pace of my heart quickens before it stops altogether when I finally spot the 'bridge'.

Obviously, Del and I have very different opinions of what a bridge was. For me, a bridge was a sturdy structure made of large wooden trusses and secured with lots of steel bolts, like the large bridge on the highway we'd driven over on the way out here. For Del, it's a series of half-metre wide wooden planks held together by a few cables suspended over the raging river below. And suspended is a key term, the whole thing begins to bounce and shake the moment Del sets foot onto it.

'Don't worry,' she shouts back at me without turning her head. 'It's perfectly safe.'

I swear I can hear her laughing as the water rushes over the rocks below. I wait until she's all the way across, trying to work up the courage to make my first move. I have to sling my bag over my shoulders like a backpack in order to fit. I slip one foot in front of the other, inching my way across the bridge, working hard not to make it move too much. I can feel the chill of the water below. I hold my breath, not willing to let it go until I reach the other side. Del is almost at the steps of the house when I finally make it across in one piece. I stand still for a moment appreciating the solid earth under my feet.

'Come on now,' I hear Del holler from the front verandah before disappearing into the house.

'What kind of place is this?' I mutter to myself, frustrated by her lack of compassion.

I've just come from burying my parents and she doesn't even have the decency to wait for me. I stand in my stubbornness not wanting to go any further. Tears gently roll down my cheeks as the realisation that I'm now an orphan washes over me. I don't want to continue on this journey, I just want to go home. The ache in my heart causes my knees to buckle and I collapse into a sobbing mess on the perfectly mowed lawn.

'Hey there,' Del's voice ripples through my ears. 'Mind if I join you?' I hear the crinkle of the grass as she sits beside me. She places her hand on my back with a soft caress. 'It's going to be okay,' her tone is soothing.

'I don't think I can do this?' I sputter.

'Course you can,' she says gently, handing me a handkerchief. I place it on my eyes and breathe in the sweet smell of lavender as I pull myself up to sit next to her.

'Crossing that bridge is symbolic,' she says. 'It represents the start of your journey.'

I stare at the bridge trying to understand what she's implying. *Does the bridge represent my unstable future?* I bury my face in lavender. *Maybe if I'm quiet, she'll just leave me be,* I think.

As the moments pass, I start to wonder if she's already gone, but I'm not ready to look.

'Nothing more soothing than the sound of water rippling over the rocks,' Del breaks the silence.

I slowly lift my head and peel the handkerchief from my eyes. The movement of the water below catches my gaze and I'm fixated.

More time passes in silence, and the longer I'm with her the calmer I become. She isn't pressuring me to talk or confess my emotions, we are just sitting there getting lost in the movement of the water. The sound of the rushing river fills the space.

'The salmon that swim in the rivers of Canada spend their lives fighting to prove themselves,' her tender voice raises above the noise. 'They defy all odds by swimming upstream, against the current. In order to make the journey, they must leap through the air, all the while avoiding the deadly jaws of awaiting grizzly bears.'

My mind wanders to an image of an enormous brown bear frantically snapping its jaw as rainbows of flying fish soar through the air in front of it. I can't help but laugh at my cartoon reconstruction.

'When I was a girl, my mother used to take me to the botanical gardens in the middle of the city,' Del continues. 'We'd spend hours there together exploring all the different types of gardens, learning about plants from all over the world. No matter how many times we'd go there, I'd still be amazed at how this little oasis could be nestled within the bustle of a big city. It was like our own slice of paradise that we could escape to when things were getting too tense.' We continue to stare at the water as the cool air rises up, causing my skin to prickle. 'That's why I bought this place. I couldn't continue in the city any longer. I reckon I was allergic to the place. It used to make my skin itch and I'd find it hard to breathe. Living there was like wearing a dress when all I wanted was a pair of comfy jeans.'

I look down at the ankle length, navy sundress that lies upon me like a potato-sack and I can't help but smile. I hated this dress from the moment my mother picked it off the rack. I've never liked wearing dresses or skirts, but that never seemed to matter to her. She wasn't really interested in my opinion or thoughts. She made it clear that I was just meant to exist as her daughter, follow the rules and be thankful for all I had.

'She told me that this is what proper young ladies wear,' I blurt, tugging at the edge of the dress. 'It's more like a parachute than a piece of clothing.' Laughter begins to tumble out of my belly as I realise how ridiculous I must look.

Del just smiles. 'Are you ready to come home now?' She reaches out her hand as she stands up next to me. I nod and accept her help. She slings my bag over her shoulder and starts leading the way.

With the tears gone from my eyes and the fear dissipating, I take a moment to survey the house. It looks like it's over a hundred years old and hasn't been touched much since it was built. Although it does have a distinct charm about it. There's a wide verandah wrapping the whole way around offering shelter from the sweltering heat.

'I plan to spend the next year or so renovating the place,' Del says as we make our way closer to the building. 'I'm planning to knock out a few walls to make it a bit more open plan. You know, drag it into this century without completely removing its kitsch-style. There are some fabulously tacky tiles embedded around the fireplaces that simply must stay,' she laughs, flicking her hair off her shoulder while switching my bag to her other side. 'But I guess it all comes down to how bad the termite issue is. These types of buildings weren't really designed to withstand the little borers. Who knows, maybe it'll all be in vain and it'll be best just to push the damn thing off the cliff. But you've gotta try right.' Del winks at me as she opens the creaking screen door.

The moment I set foot inside, I'm taken in. The smell of freshly baked bread is like a warm hug and I instantly hope she doesn't change anything. The place has a certain feel about it that makes me really comfortable, and given the uncertainty of the past few weeks, it's a feeling I'm really in need of.

Chapter 3

I don't get much sleep. There are lots of sounds lurking around outside the house and some coming from within. In the beginning, as the sun went down, it started with the high-pitched buzz of hundreds of cicadas rippling like crashing waves around the house. As they began to fade for the evening, the crickets started chirping almost in time, like a well-rehearsed ensemble, accompanied by the deep rhythmic popping sounds made by the band of frogs. This extraordinary symphony, tied together by the distant rumbling of the river, is merely a backdrop for the fierce hissing of the quarrelling possums and howling dingoes. Each noise, new to my town-dwelling ears, makes my mind race with images of the beasts from *Where the Wild Things Are* prancing through the bush.

The mere thought of the old children's book strikes my heart with guilt. I used to spend as much time as possible reading it in the library at my primary school, despite knowing my parents would never have approved. It's the first memory I have of disobeying their rules. As a tear rolls down my cheek, the outside noise seems to make its way inside the house. The tiny pitter-patter in the ceiling above my bed causes me to grab hold of my stuffed bear, Paulie, pull the sheets up over my head and pray for the sun to rise.

'Antechinus,' Del explains as we enjoy a delicious cooked breakfast early the next morning. 'They're marsupial mice. Pesky little things, they shit everywhere.' Nothing to worry about, she assures me. Just part of living in the bush. She says the same about the orchestra of creatures outside. 'They won't bother you, as long as you don't bother them.' She smiles.

After breakfast, Del invites me to help her with some farm chores.

'If you're going to be living here for a while, it's best you learn how it all works,' she says, handing me a pair of work pants and an old flannel shirt. 'Bush life is a beautiful thing, but it takes a bit of work to keep it all going.'

'I'm not afraid of a little hard work,' I let her know as she places a wide brimmed hat on top of the pile of clothes in my arms.

'Good to hear,' Del winks.

Once I'm dressed, we head straight to work on fencing in one of the paddocks. I'm a bit astonished to see that Del knows exactly what she's doing. In my family, the women are preordained to work within the home, with allowances made for light garden work. I would never have seen my mother cutting and twisting barbed wire. When I told Del that I wasn't afraid of hard work, I meant within the home, which is what I thought she meant when she said 'farm chores'. I assumed we would be scrubbing toilets and waxing floors. I'm prepared for that type of labour. I'm not even sure my body is equipped to do the type of work Del needs done.

I can hear my father telling me that a woman is responsible for keeping the home. *'Your role is making sure the men are fed, the children are tended to and the house is kept clean and tidy,'* he used to say. He'd said it so many times, it sometimes sits on repeat in the back of my mind. Being out in the paddock with Del, makes it come forward and thump against my temple.

'I grew up on a farm in Queensland and ever since I was big enough to help carry the tools, my father would take me out with him,' Del explains as she pulls the wire through the holes in the fence post.

Her hands are buried in enormous leather gloves that make her appear cartoon-like. She continues to talk about how her father taught her everything she knows about running a farm. Especially how important it is to fasten the wire correctly to ensure it will last longer than the wooden posts it's attached to.

'No girlie knots in my fencing,' she says with a laugh.

I try to imagine what she was like as a little girl, and how different her childhood was from mine. It's almost like we're from two different planets.

'He let you help him?' I manage to mumble.

'Oh dear child.' Del stops and turns her face up towards mine. 'What kind of place have you been living in?'

I don't know how to take her comment – is she being endearing or demeaning? Her eyes appear to be full of warmth, but her words cut me. A swell of embarrassment brews in my belly and I'm not sure if I need to run or vomit.

Before I can make up my mind, Del is standing square in front of me, her hands on each of my shoulders and her eyes piercing mine. 'You are safe here,' she whispers, pulling me into her. She squeezes her arms around me and I feel myself go limp. Confusion swirls in my brain, pushing tears from my eyes. I rest my head on her shoulder and stay in her secure arms, not wanting her to ever let me go.

'I've got an idea,' Del's voice is like a spark. 'How about we get ourselves a little morning tea? I reckon I could scrounge up a bickie or two. A little sugar might do us both a bit of good, what do ya say?'

With a hot cup of tea in one hand and a freshly baked chocolate chip biscuit in the other, I sit with Del on the verandah enjoying a rest. She starts telling me more about her decision to move away from the city.

'I was always getting sick, but my husband didn't understand.' It's the first time she's mentioned a husband. Despite the rumours that had been floating around town, I haven't really imagined her married. She just seems too carefree. 'When I turned sixty, I decided that I'd lived my whole life for other people,' she continues rather nonchalantly. 'I ate what other people wanted, I dressed how other people wanted and I went where other people wanted. So, I decided for the next sixty years I was going to live my own life,' she laughs.

'What did you do?' I ask as if she were one of my best friends. There's just something about the way she talks to me that makes me feel so comfortable in her presence.

'I bought this place.' She smiles. 'I'm still feeling fit enough to keep it going for several years, so I figured, why not?'

The separation was quite civil according to Del. They both seemed to know the marriage had disintegrated and agreed to go their own ways.

'It's not something I did lightly,' she confesses. 'It's just something I had to do.' She takes a sip of her tea and a munch on her biscuit before continuing. 'Having this place, and opening it up to others who need healing, helps me stay healthy.'

I've been so caught in my own situation and entranced by her, that I'd completely forgotten about this place being a foster home. Before I moved here, I was consumed with anxiety about having to live in a house full of strangers, but so far, it's just been me and Del.

'Have you had many kids like me come stay here?'

'There's been a few children who've needed to seek refuge at Karamea, and none of them are the same,' she says softly as she turns to face me. 'You all have your own stories and travel your own journeys. This place just helps keep things calm.'

After we finish our tea, and I enjoy a few more cookies than I care to admit, we return to work. Once Del ties off the last bit of wiring, we move onto digging post holes. Del gets to work on the tractor burrowing deep wells in the land, while I stand to the side clearing out any rocks that roll back into the holes.

It doesn't take me long to get into the swing of things and I'm starting to feel comfortable with this new style of chores. I can't remember the last time I'd spent all day outdoors. My mother and I would sometimes do a little work in the garden, pulling weeds, and planting flowers, but mostly my parents preferred me to stay indoors, where they could keep an eye on me. They kept telling me it was for my own protection.

'*The devil lurks in many places and you never know when he's going to strike,*' my father would tell me.

But as I stand here on this foreign piece of land, far from my old home, with the wind in my hair and the sun on my face, I'm filled with a sense of freedom. I wonder if this sensation is the work of the devil. The thought lingers only for a speck of time before it's washed away by a feeling of euphoria. My body tingles.

'*Pleasure is only found with the Lord.*' I hear my mother's words echo in my mind, and just as quickly as the sense of glory had filled me, I'm overcome with a rush of guilt. My knees quiver with shame.

'How about we stop for lunch?' Del calls out.

I haven't noticed that she already stopped working. I look up to see her standing across the newly dug post hole staring at me.

'Best we take a break from the sun for a while. We can get back to this after the heat of the day passes.'

After lunch, Del sets me the task of shovelling the loose soil and rocks out of the post holes. As I'm digging, I notice an unusual looking rock. It's a different colour from the other rocks I've come across, more of a dark grey instead of the brownish-red ones. It's flat and fits comfortably in my hand. But what strikes me most about it is how the edge comes to a point along one side, looking almost like a knife blade.

'Could be an axe head,' Del says from over my shoulder as she approaches me admiring it.

I pass it to her to examine. She runs her fingers along the smooth surface bringing it close to her face.

'Why don't we call it a day,' she says, slipping the stone in her pocket. 'I think we should go visit a friend of mine.'

We trade in the tractor for a quad bike and ride off towards the neighbouring bushland. It's not long before we are in the thick of it, driving slowly along an overgrown fire trail. Tree branches scratch along our bodies from head to toe as we move deeper and deeper into the scrub with the path closing around us. I shut my eyes as Del begins to jerk the bike bit by bit through the undergrowth.

'Doesn't take long for this stuff to take over,' she shouts over the groaning engine. 'I swear it was only the other day that I cleared this trail.'

When I feel the bike finally break free from the stranglehold of nature, I open my eyes to see a house in the clearing in front of us. We make the rest of the way on foot, heading towards the smoke that's floating up from a fire pit near the building.

'Aww, Del,' an elderly woman emerges from inside. 'I'm just about to put the billy on,' she announces, carrying a metal kettle over to the fire and setting it on top of the coals.

'Aunty Bev,' Del says as she wraps her arms around the tiny woman. 'This is Sara.'

'Sara, my child,' Aunty Bev smiles, walking over to greet me. 'I've heard so much about you.'

She places her hands on my shoulders, drawing me deep into her brown eyes. Wisps of white hair accents her weathered face, her smile giving way to tea-tinged teeth. Although she appears old and frail, I can feel her strength as she embraces me.

'Come sit with me, my dear,' she says, waving her hand as she moves to a wooden bench near the fire. 'Let me have a look at you,' she insists, clasping my hands and gently pressing her thumbs along my palms. 'Tell me about your mob?' I sit frozen, unable to find words. I don't fully understand what she's asking me. 'Don't be scared, child,' her voice is comforting. 'Tell me about your family. Where you come from.'

I'm not sure what to say, I've never been asked about my family before. But for some reason the words in my mind just start to tumble out.

'The only relatives I know of are my parents – I mean, were my parents.'

'No aunties? No uncles?' she enquiries, softly. I shake my head. 'No brothers

21

or sisters?' Her gaze is locked in mine as though she's searching for more than I can offer.

'It's just me,' I mumble, biting my lip to hold back the urge to cry.

'That won't do,' she sits back, the flare of the fire reflecting in her eyes. 'No one is alone. Family is more than bloodline. Family is all who share a connection to Country.'

She tells me about her connection to the region, explaining that the land around Gloucester and far beyond is part of her Country. She tells of her many aunties and uncles, brothers and sisters who have helped guide her and teach her from when she was a little girl.

'Your mob is not just mother and father. Your mob is all the people who help make you who you are,' she says as the kettle begins to boil. 'Now it's time for tea.'

As Aunty Bev moves to the fire to make the tea, I wonder about my mob. Those people who have been a part of my life for as long as I can remember. I think about the Edwards and the rest of our church community. I haven't ever thought of them as my family, but I guess that's what they are. I know they were close to my parents. That was very clear at the funeral, when several of them shared stories of Mother and Father when they were younger. I heard things about them that I never knew before. There were stories of a time when they must have been truly happy and in love. They were not stories of my parents as I knew them. It makes me wonder if I really knew them at all. Maybe they changed after they had me? Maybe I wasn't what they expected? Father regularly made comments about what it would have been like to have a son, especially when he had outside chores to do. There had always been a part of me that felt like I was the wrong child for them. That I didn't really fit in. Maybe that's why Aunty Bev's question about family was so hard for me to answer.

While we all have a cup of tea, Del pulls the stone from her pocket and shows it to Aunty Bev.

'Oh my,' her eyes tear up a little. 'I haven't seen one of them in a long while.'

Aunty Bev takes the stone, cupping it in her hands, she closes her eyes and takes a long deep breath. After a moment, she speaks. 'My people would collect rocks like this. It's the flat oval shape that makes 'em best. Only found in some rivers but they knew where to get 'em.'

'Lots of history buried in this land,' Del says to me. 'It's important we take time out to acknowledge those who came before us.'

We sit around the fire for a while longer, three generations of women from backgrounds worlds apart. The distance in age vanishes like a puff of smoke that rises from the coals as we laugh and learn from each other; me learning more from them than them from me. But I don't feel out of place. For the first time in my life, I feel like I belong.

Later that night, when I try without success to get some sleep, I notice there is a different tone to the sounds around me. The intoxicating aroma of the fire clinging to my hair ripples through the visions in my mind as I try to imagine what this place looked like when the first peoples roamed the hills. I wonder what it was like to feel so connected to a place that you could feel your ancestors inside of everything around you. Aunty Bev never spoke of God or how He created heaven and earth, but I could feel her spirituality through her connection to the stone. I envy her sense of belonging and wish I hadn't felt so lost within my own family. I'm beginning to feel safe in this place.

The rest of the week with Del is exhilarating and exhausting with each day filled to the brim with projects around the property. I'm learning farming 101 – how to grow nutrient-rich grass and the importance of rotating cattle around paddocks to ensure the grass has time to regrow, never being eaten down so low it can't recover. Del even let me drive the tractor, which is much harder than it looks, but I managed to get the hang of it. My hands are becoming calloused and every muscle in my body aches, but I feel so alive and in touch with the land. By the time Friday rolls around, I'm dreading heading back into town.

Chapter 4

As promised, Del gets me to the Edwards' house on time, dropping me out front and waving goodbye as she continues on her journey into Forster. She said if she needs to drive somewhere to kill a few hours, then she may as well grab some fish and chips and head to the beach. It's a stunning summer evening, and as I watch her drive away, I wish I was going with her. I know I've been coming to these Friday night events since I was born, but it's never really been something I've felt a part of – not even when my parents hosted them.

I drag my ragged body towards the house, mentally preparing myself for the hours-long sermon, disguised as bible study, that awaits me. The driveway is filled with the usual array of cars. I reluctantly make it to the front door and wrap the scarf around my head before I ring the bell. It's the same scarf I've been wearing to these prayer nights for the past several years. It's beige to match my prayer dress.

'*The scripture says that a woman praying with uncovered head causes herself shame,*' my father told me the day my mother gave me the scarf. It's the same reason he gave me for why the women in our church wear ribbons in our hair when we leave the house. '*We are always under the eyes of the Lord*', he told me. I suspect this logic also extends to why the women aren't permitted to cut their hair, but I never worked up the courage to ask him about that one.

'Blessed be, it's lovely to see you, Sara,' Mrs Edwards greets me. 'Come, come, you're just in time.' She shuffles me into the living room where everyone else is already congregating. With my bible tucked under my arm, I find a place to sit on the floor just as Mr Edwards tinks the ceremonial chimes.

Normally, I sit at my father's feet, but since the accident, I've been shifted to the back corner. Without a family of my own, the elders decided that it was best for me to sit just behind the other daughters and wives. It's to best make sure that I don't drag any evil spirits into another family's circle.

Mr Edwards scans the room to confirm that everyone is in their correct place, then begins the Lord's Supper.

As I sit in silent contemplation, my mind wanders back to Del and the farm. A warm rush of happiness fills my body as I picture her friendly smile and hear her gentle voice telling me what a good job I'm doing around the property.

This moment of joy is shattered when James Harrigan is the first to be led by the Holy Spirit.

'No one can serve two masters,' he bolts straight up. With his eyes closed his body convulses slightly as he is overcome by the voice inside him. 'For either he will hate the one and love the other, or he will be devoted to the one and despise the other,' he preaches as though he is Jesus, himself.

The other men in the room mutter in agreement.

Without skipping a beat, James opens his eyes to indicate the return to his body. 'You cannot serve God and money. Matthew, chapter six, verse twenty-four.' He sits back down.

'James, tell Jesus why you call to him tonight,' Mr Edwards's tone is encouraging.

'I have seen the light,' James confesses.

As is customary, only the men are allowed to speak, while the women silently pray for each man's revealed weakness. As James begins to divulge his recent bet on a horse race, I stop listening altogether. I wonder if Del is at the beach yet and imagine her wiggling her toes in the sand as she munches on hot chips.

I must have been completely lost in my thoughts because before I know it the prayer is over. Mr Edwards has already given thanks for the bread and everyone is making their way to the table. The bread is torn and shared among the group. I continue to stay at the back as thanks is given for the wine. I'm so bored at this stage I don't even notice which elder did the blessing. After the cup makes a pass around the room, I sneak away. Children aren't expected to give an offering, so I'm not the only one who ends up in the backyard as the collection plate is handed to each member with the expectation of depositing at least one paper note.

John is already sitting on the backstep by the time I make my way outside. I would have thought he'd be more involved in the ceremony seeing as his dad is running things, but it appears he's just as keen to get out of the room as I am. We sit in silence, staring out into the darkness of his yard as the voices from inside raise in a hymn of praise.

'Do you ever wonder what it would be like to leave Gloucester?' John Edwards is a couple years older than me and left school in year ten to work on his family farm.

'No.' My response is quick. I've never wondered what it would be like. I guess I never thought that leaving was a choice I could make.

'There's got to be more to the world than this place.' He continues to stare straight ahead.

I'm not really sure if he's talking to me, so I don't say anything. Instead, I just sit there and wait with him as he returns to silence.

It isn't long before Mrs Edwards calls out to let me know that Del has returned. I swiftly make my way through the lounge room, which is now almost empty. There are only a couple families left behind, mainly to help the Edwards clean up. After saying the customary goodbyes, I slip out the front door to find Del sitting in her ute with the engine running.

I suppose I can't blame her for not wanting to come inside. I know that I feel really awkward entering a room full of people I don't know. Although, I am surprised that Mrs Edwards didn't insist that Del come in for a cup of tea. Everyone that comes to the house is offered one, and given Del is partial to a cuppa, it seems strange – just like when the Edwards dropped me off at Karamea House. I find the behaviour between these adults confusing as it goes against everything I've been taught about manners and social interaction. My parents told me that it's important to always open the door to strangers and make room for them in my heart. It was one of the teachings from the scripture. I don't blame Del. Given she isn't part of our church, she can't be expected to know the rules, but the Edwards have no excuse. The worry rumbles in my belly as I approach the ute.

'Did you have a nice time?' Del asks me softly as I slip into the passenger's seat.

I nod, looking at the floor mat below my feet.

'I bet you're tired,' she says. 'Let's get you home.'

Once we were on the open road, I let out a huge sigh of relief. I open the window and stick my head out, letting the wind rush over me. The sensation brings tears of joy, although it may simply be from the air rushing across my eye sockets. Del turns up the music so loud that the bass is shaking the inside of the ute. She starts thumping the dashboard in time with a thunderous beat and singing at the top of her lungs. Her thumping gets quicker, joining the pace of the drum beat bouncing through the speakers.

'*I'm on the highway to hell*,' she belts out, tilting her head back as if she's howling at the moon.

I've never seen anything like it, nor heard anything like it. My music experience is very limited – mainly focused on the hymns sung in church, with the occasional Christian artist permitted to be played at home in the presence of my parents. It's not that I'm completely naive about the range of music out there in the world. I've even heard a snippet or two over the years. But not the kind of music that is currently rattling the inside of Del's ute. This stuff is all new and it seems to be stirring something inside of me. Something that I suspect has been lurking there all along but that has been too scared to come to the surface. A smile sweeps across my lips as I stare down the long highway to Del's.

There is no conversation between us the rest of the drive home. We just listen to music. As I watch Del smiling and singing along, I wish I was more like her. She has no fear about facing the world exactly how she is. There is no pretence or posturing in anything she does. I've met people like her before, but they've all been men. In my world, only men have the freedom to behave without boundaries, and if they slip off course, they just simply repent and all is forgiven. It isn't the same for the women. Our path needs to be trod with purity and obedience. One wrong move and everything can be taken away.

As I lie awake in bed listening to the soothing sounds of the bush life around me, John's words return to me. Why hadn't I wondered what it would be like to leave Gloucester? It's only a few months until my eighteenth birthday and I've no idea what I'm going to do with my life. All these years have passed without any talk about it. Neither of my parents ever mentioned it, and now it's too late. I guess I just assumed that I'd continue to live at home until I met a nice boy who wanted to marry me. Then I'd go live with him. I haven't given much thought to what I want. It never seemed to be okay to think that way. All my life I have listened to my mother's story of her upbringing and righteous path to meeting my father. They had known each other pretty much all their lives, having grown up in the church, spending Friday nights together. I suppose you could say they were destined to be together, having been on the same journey towards God. My mother said that Father chose her because she worked so hard to be worthy. My father knew from a young age that he was meant to be an elder, and it was important he married the right woman.

These were the types of stories I grew up with, but when they would fight and Father's voice would shake the room, I wasn't sure if they actually liked each other.

I think about Del and how she just picked up everything she had and moved here all by herself, without knowing anyone. She seems so brave and wild at the same time. I'm not like that at all. I'm boring and dumb, and I always do what I'm told without question or complaint. I'm a good Christian girl, living my life under the watchful eye of Jesus.

I begin to wonder if Jesus exists outside of Gloucester. Is he really present everywhere or just in this town that has a church on almost every corner? Is John right, could there be more to the world outside of Gloucester? I mean, that's where Del came from. She's from the outside.

Chapter 5

I can't shake the thought all night and before I know it my room is flooded with sunlight. It's the first day of school and I'll be continuing the rest of year twelve. School has never been a source of joy for me. The work has always been a struggle, and so has making friends. Even though we all wear the same uniform, I've never really fit in. It's a pattern that started in primary school when my parents wouldn't let me go to birthday parties, playdays or sleepovers. The only other kids I was allowed to see outside of school were the ones from our church, and there weren't any girls around my age. My alienation was continually echoed in the classroom when other students argued with the teacher if they're ever forced to do group work with me, and in the schoolyard, with none of them wanting to be seen talking to me.

When I got to high school, things improved a little. Being at a bigger school meant I was able to fade into the background easier. Eventually the ones who went out of their way to make nasty comments about me lost interest, and I found solitude in the quiet spaces around the school. But every day is the same and I've got really good at keeping up with the pattern.

One of my teachers, Mr Cook, got especially annoyed with me at the end of last year. He would ask me questions and every time he'd catch me out not listening. I just find it so hard to keep my focus on what he's saying because it's so boring. But I guess he'd had enough of it by the end of term, as I found myself in the principal's office. I'd never been to Mr Martin's office before and I was really nervous. When I got there, both Mr Cook and Mr Martin were waiting for me.

'Miss Johnson, please come in and take a seat,' Mr Martin said.

I could hardly breathe as I moved ever so slowly towards the chair. I felt faint by the time I sat down.

'Now Miss Johnson, I suppose you are wondering why we have asked you here,' Mr Cook said.

'Yes, sir.' I barely managed to speak, my mouth was so parched.

'Next year is an exciting year for you and your classmates,' Mr Martin said, emerging from behind his large desk. His wide navy-blue tie flicked at me like the tongue of a snake as he positioned himself on the front edge of the desk.

With Mr Cook sat next to me, I felt trapped.

'Mr Martin and I have been talking about our year twelve students as we make plans for the year ahead.'

I could smell the gel in his shiny black hair and the faint stench of coffee on his breath.

Both of them were staring at me, their gazes coming at me from all directions. I felt dizzy.

'Did you know that you can apply for an apprenticeship straight from school, Miss Johnson?' Mr Cook leaned closer to me, the waft of coffee getting stronger. 'An apprenticeship will allow you to learn a trade and teach you the skills you need to find a job without having to finish year twelve.'

'Have you thought about what you want to do after school?' Mr Martin inquired as he also leaned in making the space between me and them smaller.

No one had ever asked me that before. I wasn't sure what the right answer was. The two men had boxed me in, I didn't know what to do, so I shook my head.

'You could learn to be a hairdresser. That's a pretty good career option, don't you think?'

I nodded hoping that was the correct answer. My head was swimming. I wasn't sure what they were talking about.

'Definitely Mr Cook, I do believe that would be a great option for Miss Johnson.'

Their faces were growing larger by the minute and I found it hard to swallow. Their condescending tone sat like a lump in my stomach. All I wanted to do was get out of there, but I couldn't leave without being excused, so I held my breath, praying that it would be over soon.

'But that isn't the only thing you can do,' Mr Cook continued. 'You could get a job with Mr Vale at the grocery store next year. If you have full time work, you don't need to attend school anymore. Did you know that?' His question was clearly rhetorical and he continued without so much as taking a breath. 'We could help you approach him for the opportunity.'

'Why yes, Mr Cook, that is a splendid idea,' Mr Martin said eagerly. It was as though they were having a conversation by themselves and there was no need for me to even be in the room. 'Miss Johnson, what a great opportunity Mr Cook is offering you. You must be a very hard-working student.'

There was barely enough air left in the room as the two of them seemed to fill the space. I could feel my eyes beginning to swell.

'Well, it's settled then,' Mr Cook declared as he stood up. 'We will make arrangements for you to be transferred to the transition classroom.'

'Excellent idea, Mr Cook,' Mr Martin said, standing up from the desk.

Caught up in their movement, I lifted myself from the chair and walked with them as they guided me out of the room.

'Don't you worry 'bout a thing, Miss Johnson,' I heard Mr Cook's voice in the distance.

I wandered outside. The bell must have rung while I was in the office. I was alone.

Almost all of these events had escaped my mind over the summer holidays. But as I sit on the bus, with plenty of time to kill before I get to school, it all comes flooding back. *Surely, they will have forgotten about it too*, I tell myself. And given that I lost my parents only a month ago, I'm hopeful that I can continue in school as normal. With that in mind, I decide to head straight to my favourite corner in the quad near the assembly hall. There's always an assembly on the first day back. The teachers like to tell us school rules for the fifteen-millionth time, like we'll have forgotten over the holidays. But mostly, it's a chance to let us know what homeroom we're in so we can collect our timetables, which will inevitably change multiple times over the next fortnight as they try to figure out the complex matrix of students versus teachers versus subjects. I'm almost in my safe haven when I hear Mr Cook call my name.

'A bit confused are you, Miss Johnson?' Mr Cook smiles smugly. 'You no longer need to attend the main assembly.' He steers me away from the hall and towards the library. I follow him like a lost lamb, having no idea where I'm meant to be going.

Mrs Thompson greets us at the entrance and without a word between them, Mr

Cook departs and I'm left to follow the librarian towards one of the glass-framed study rooms. It feels like I'm being sent to detention, especially considering the other students in the room are the ones who notoriously get in trouble. The room is filled with the buzz of a dozen kids all talking at once, which ceases the moment Mrs Thompson pushes through the door.

'Find a seat,' Mrs Thompson barks at me. 'And I don't want any trouble from you.'

Her beady eyes seem to be staring me down. She's a haggard, bitter little woman with short mousey brown hair littered with streaks of unkempt greys. Everyone at school calls her Mrs Thompson out of respect, but we all know her husband left her years ago. Poor soul, I bet he couldn't wait to get away from the miserable tyrant.

'But Mrs Thompson, I'm not sure what I'm meant to do?'

'Please child.' Her eyes seem to literally roll backwards in her head. 'You're meant to not give me trouble.'

She gives me a slight shove before closing me inside the room. I'm left standing there facing the solid wooden door with a lump of dread in my throat. I can feel all twenty-four eyes burning a hole in my back.

'*Now what,*' I think to myself. '*I could just stay here and not move. Maybe they'll lose interest.*'

'Hey Goldilocks, you scared to come in the big bad wolf's house?'

'That's Little Red Riding Hood,' I mumble.

'What's that?'

The voice comes from right behind me, so close I can feel their hot breath on my neck. I take a deep breath and spin on my heels.

'Goldilocks is from Little Red Riding Hoo....' I'm face to face with Charlie Baker. My heart skips a beat.

'You makin' fun of me?'

He's so close to me that I jump back and slam into the door.

'No,' I try to explain. 'I...I was just trying to tell you that Goldilocks was from the Three Bears. You got your fairy tales mixed up.'

'You sayin' I'm stupid?'

Charlie Baker is one of the most feared guys in school. Rumour has it he killed his neighbour's dog for looking at him the wrong way. He's also one of the biggest boys in my year and by far the scariest. I know I'm in for it. My whole life begins to flash before my eyes as I prepare for his flying fist. I squeeze my eyes tight.

'Leave her alone, Charlie. She ain't worth it.' It's like the voice of an angel, swooping in and rescuing me from the imposing threat. The words are enough to call off Charlie and he slowly returns to his seat, glaring at me as he goes. But then I see her, the angel, and she's making her way towards me.

Georgia Clement, I think as I hold my breath.

'What's your name?' Georgia asks. It's as if she's floating across the room.

'Sara,' I puff. There I am standing face-to-face with the prettiest girl in school and my palms start sweating.

'Come sit next to me,' she gestures with a sweep of her perfect hand, the light flickering off the gold polish on her perfectly manicured fingernails. 'If you're still standing there when the mole gets back, she'll be pissed off.'

I clumsily follow behind her, too nervous to argue.

The rest of the school day is a complete blur as I spend most of it locked in admiration. All I can think about is Georgia's amazing golden hair and how it seems to cascade like a waterfall down around her shoulders. She looks like a model from one of the magazines I sometimes secretly read in the school library. I imagine what I would look like if I was allowed to take the ribbon from my hair and let it rest around my shoulders. But mine is really long and not as shiny and pretty as Georgia's. It's rattier and more frayed at the ends, which seems to get worse the more I brush it. Thankfully, I can easily return my thoughts to her beauty instead of drowning in disgust reflecting on my own plain, boring exterior.

Thinking about her faultless face keeps me so completely preoccupied on the bus ride home that the driver has to call my name to let me know we've arrived at Karamea. My cheeks are flushed with embarrassment as I slink off the bus to where Del is waiting. The bus will only travel so close to the property and given it's a kilometre away, I need to be shuttled there. Del greets me with a huge smile.

'Looks like you had an exciting day,' she says as I jump into the ute.

I don't know how to put into words what I'm feeling. On one hand, I'm gutted that I've been moved into the 'special class', which is completely demoralising. While on the other hand, I seem to be forming a new relationship, which is something that is hard for me to do.

'It was definitely not what I expected,' I finally manage to say.

The only bad part about it, is that school started on a Friday, and now I have to wait all weekend before I can see Georgia again.

Chapter 6

I wake up extra early on Saturday morning, as it's the monthly cattle auction at the saleyards. Del is planning to attend, which is good news for me because it means I'll be able to continue my volunteer work with the Country Women's Association. Being a part of the CWA was important to my mother and she had made sure that the tradition continued with me. Knowing that I'm able to honour her wishes, gives me a sense of calm and helps me feel a little closer to her.

Truth be told, I like going to the saleyards. It's always full of interesting people from all over the place. Being one of the biggest sales around, it attracts a lot of buyers and sellers and gives me a lot of people-watching time. It's also where the CWA runs the canteen as one of their biggest fundraisers. The women start baking up a storm super early on the day of the sale to ensure they provide the best morning tea spread in the region. While the men spend the morning at the auction in the yards, the women are relegated to the kitchen preparing all the food. This type of hierarchy was exactly why my mother loved it so much. You would think it was Sunday the way they get all dolled up in their fancy dresses and curl their hair. Mother wanted to make sure we both fit in, so we'd spend an hour getting ready the morning of a sale.

To ensure I don't dishonour her, I make sure I wear one of my church dresses and give myself extra time to prepare.

As soon as we arrive, I make my way to the canteen where I will be expected to help butter the bread for the sandwiches. I've been hanging around the canteen for many years, helping place things where they're meant to be, and making sure the women have everything they need. A few months ago, the committee finally decided it was time for me to learn how to cook like a country woman and they trained me in the art of spreading just the right amount of butter on every inch of each slice of bread. They told me I was a natural, and pretty soon I didn't need supervision anymore. My mother was so pleased, she let me have an extra piece of cake that night for dessert. From then on it became my job at every sale.

'Hello my dear,' Mrs Carson greets me the moment I step through the door. 'We weren't sure you'd come today.'

'Was I not supposed to?' I question as panic strikes my chest. There's nothing worse than showing up at a place you're not wanted.

'Of course, dear,' she says softly, giving me a hug. It's a weird hug. Almost like she's not sure if she should touch me. 'It's just with everything that's happened, we weren't sure you'd want to.' After the awkward moment passes, I smile at her with the hope that she'll tell me to head to the kitchen. But she continues to hold my shoulders and stare at me with tears welling in the corners of her eyes. 'Your mother would be so proud of you.'

'Thank you,' I mumble as I tilt my head towards the floor. I'm struck with a strong urge to start praying for this moment to pass.

'That's enough dawdling ladies,' Mrs Vale calls over from the kitchen, breaking the tension. 'We've got lots of work to get done.'

Without hesitation, I grab an apron and a spreading knife, and make my way to my usual station where the stacks of day-old sandwich loaves sit ready for me. The ladies have taught me that it's important that the bread isn't too fresh, otherwise it will tear when you try to spread the butter. It is one of the secrets that I was taught early on, as well as the importance of using softened butter. The CWA women insist on using butter over margarine, even though margarine comes ready to spread.

'Butter just makes it better,' Mrs Carson had told me on my very first day of butter spreading. And who am I to argue with the vice president of the Gloucester CWA. Everyone knows these women know best when it comes to good, old-fashioned, wholesome country cooking.

I'm busy working my way through the stacks of bread when I hear Mrs Vale talking to the other women. As she's the president, the other women are always attentive when she speaks.

'I heard she went to the hardware store to buy a chainsaw,' she snickers. 'I mean, what type of woman buys a chainsaw.'

It's pretty obvious to me who she is talking about. Del has continued to be a hot topic around the CWA kitchen ever since she drove into town.

'Next thing she will be wanting to buy is a tractor,' one of the other women comments, perpetuating the snickering.

I can't help but giggle a bit myself but only because Del already has a tractor. 'Shows what you know,' I mutter to myself.

A group of men dressed in jeans, flannel shirts, and brimmed hats bound through the canteen door, breaking up the gossip circle.

'Crickey, I didn't expect she'd drive such a hard bargain,' one of the men says.

'I woulda thought ole' Jack Dwyer woulda got the price up a bit higher on her,' another one adds. 'She ain't messin' round.'

They make their way to the counter and order up a stack of sandwiches, and enough cups of coffee for all of them.

'She sure got herself a fine beast,' one says as they sit themselves down at one of the tables.

I can't hear much of their conversation after that as more people start pouring in. The sale must be over. It's about to get very busy in the canteen. It's all hands-on deck as we work our way through the sale of scones, slices, sandwiches and enough cups of tea and coffee to fill an Olympic-sized pool.

Almost as quickly as the canteen filled up with people, the crowd starts to dissipate and I find myself wiping down empty tables. People have been coming and going so much I don't take much notice when the door opens and Del walks in.

'Morning ladies.' She makes her way straight to the counter. 'I would love a cuppa and one of your wonderful, world-famous sandwiches.'

'None left,' I hear Mrs Vale snarl. I decide it's best if I just keep busy wiping tables and don't get involved.

'That's a shame. I'll come in sooner next time.' Del's voice remains pleasant and kind.

As she turns to leave, the women begin to whisper to each other, so she turns back. 'I beg your pardon. Were you talking to me?'

Mrs Vale steps out from behind the counter, placing her hands on her hips, tsk-ing as she surveys Del's faded blue jeans, rust and rose flannel shirt and a brown wide-brimmed hat.

'Ladies always wear skirts to a cattle sale,' Mrs Vale says.

'I'm not a lady coming to a cattle sale,' Del responds gently but firmly. 'I'm a cattleman buying cattle for my farm, and jeans are what cattlemen wear.' Del is smiling as she turns to leave, winking at me as goes. 'See you next month, ladies.' She waves her hand above her head as she walks out the door, allowing the flyscreen to slam shut behind her.

Mrs Vale's mouth is left hanging open and I can't help but giggle. It makes me think she's trying to catch flies, which isn't a hard thing to do at the saleyards. The place is full of them.

Thankfully, the CWA ladies don't take much notice of me as they are too busy gossiping about everyone else in town. They don't even miss a beat, the moment Del is gone, they are straight onto putting someone else down. After Mrs Vale recovers from Del's unexpected retort, she gets back into the swing of things as well.

Once my duties are finished, I catch up with Del at her ute, where she's chatting with a couple of young stockmen who've travelled in for the sale. As I approach, I take note of her open body language - the way she seems to sway slightly as she speaks and how she gently places her hand on one boy's chest while tilting her head back in laughter after he says something funny. It's mesmerising watching her interact with men. It's completely different to the way she is around Mrs Vale and Mrs Edwards. With them, she's more rigid and withdrawn.

I'm so captivated by her I barely notice the boys say 'hello' to me.

'Well don't be shy, Sara, say hello to Johnny and Paul,' Del teases.

'Hello,' I respond sheepishly, looking down at the road while digging the tips of my shoe into the gravel. I haven't had much practice speaking to boys outside of my church group and I'm really uncomfortable. I can feel my stomach turning.

'Don't mind her,' Del continues. 'She's been locked up in the kitchen all day. She's probably ready for a rest. We best be on our way.'

After she says a quick goodbye to the boys, she joins me in the ute.

'You aren't very good at chatting with strangers, are you?' Del asks.

'No one's ever interested in talking to me,' I blurt. I don't know why I can't hold things in around her, my inner thoughts just come tumbling out.

'Oh, that can't be true. You just need a little practice, that's all.'

Chapter 7

On Monday I can't wait to get to school. It's got to be the first time in my whole life that I have ever got up extra early to get ready. I can't wait to see Georgia and I want to look my best. I spend extra time brushing my hair so it will sit nicely around my shoulders. Instead of tying the ribbon around all of my hair making it into a ponytail, I decide to only tie the top half, leaving the rest out. I'm filled with a sense of excitement, partly due to the boldness of my daring move with my hair, and partly due to seeing Georgia again. The moment the bus arrives at the school, I hurry to the library to ensure I can plunk down in the same chair she had asked me to sit on the Friday before. Then I wait, very impatiently, for her to arrive.

Slowly the other students come banging into the room, throwing their bags down, slamming their books on the table, scraping their chairs along the floor. Their yammering is so loud I can't hear myself think, nor the bell ring. It's not until Mrs Thompson enters the room and tells us all to shut up that I realise the school day has started.

But Georgia still isn't here.

As Mrs Thompson prepares to leave the room, I hear myself say, 'Georgia isn't here.'

Mrs Thompson freezes with her hand on the door handle and her back to the room.

'Maybe you should call her house and make sure she's okay,' I continue to blurt as if possessed.

My request lingers in the silence of the room as all the students stare at me. The seconds pass, my heartbeat gets louder in my ears and the room gets smaller around me. Mrs Thompson slowly turns to face me.

'If I called a parent every time one of you little snots didn't attend school, I'd never be off the phone.' She rolls her eyes and leaves the room.

I continue to hold my breath waiting for a barrage of abuse from my fellow students. But no one seems to care, they all go straight back to talking. I start to panic. What if she's been in a car accident over the weekend and is in the hospital or lying injured in a ditch somewhere? What if she's been kidnapped on her way to school?

'Maybe she's just sick,' I think, trying to calm myself.

'She's probably wagging,' Maree, the girl beside me, says.

'Does she wag a lot?' I ask.

'Yep. That's why she's in here,' she responds nonchalantly.

When the door opens, I almost leap out of my chair in anticipation of Georgia's arrival, but instead I see Ms Davis. The moment she enters, the room goes abruptly silent.

'Sara,' Ms Davis says with a delicate wave of her hand.

I grab my stuff and follow her out of the room, my head hanging in shame. Ms Davis is one of the sweetest and most liked people in the school, but she isn't a teacher. She's there to support students with learning difficulties. And everybody knows it. As I follow her out of the library, down the stairs, across the lawn, and into her 'special room', I know my school days will never be the same. I expect to see some of the other students that Ms Davis assists; what I don't expect to see is Mrs Edwards.

'Hello Sara,' she says, smiling.

I've never had someone come to the school for me before. And I mean never. Not even my parents. They never attended any of the primary school assemblies or sporting events, and once I started high school, they seemed to become even less interested. It was like they were just sending me to school to appease the rules. They never asked me about school and I never talked about it. It was kind of an unwritten agreement in my family.

But seeing Mrs Edwards in the room is really confusing. Why on earth is she here? She hasn't really taken much interest in my life since I moved to Del's. I thought that she and Mr Edwards would be casting a more watchful eye over me to ensure I'm living to the correct standards, but since the funeral it's as though, in their eyes, I died as well. And now she's just standing in the room like she's meant to be here.

'Hello Mrs Edwards.' I swallow as a feeling of dread washes over me. I quickly pull my hair back off my shoulders and flick my bow so she knows that I'm still wearing it.

'Why don't you both take a seat,' Ms Davis offers. Her perfect chestnut-brown bob bounces on her shoulders as she pulls out a couple of chairs. 'Mr Charles should be here any moment.'

Mrs Edwards must have known she was coming to the school the whole time I was at her house on Friday night, but she didn't say anything to me about it. She also seems to be comfortable with the fact that we are waiting for the school's careers adviser. *Why hadn't she said anything to me about it?* I wonder.

It's not long before Mr Charles comes in. He introduces himself to Mrs Edwards, says hello to me and takes a seat.

Then the talking begins. And it's all about me, not to me. I may as well not even be in the room.

'Mrs Edwards,' Ms Davis begins, 'as I mentioned on the phone, we've noticed that Sara has been having some difficulties with her studies. She seems to be easily distracted and less engaged in the classroom setting, so she has been moved into a smaller, more nurturing learning environment.'

Nurturing learning environment, I almost choke. What is she talking about? Stuck in a room full of misfits and told to be quiet. There isn't any learning going on in there, the teachers just don't want to deal with any of us.

'But this is just a temporary solution,' Mr Charles interjects. 'We find that when students become disengaged at this stage in their school career that perhaps there may be better options.'

'Like an apprenticeship,' Mrs Edwards says as if she knows about the conversation in Mr Martin's office.

Then it hits me. Maybe my parents knew about the meeting with the principal. But if that's so, why didn't they talk to me about it. They gave me no indication that they knew. And what's worse is they must have told Mrs Edwards about it.

'It just so happens that Mr Edwards and I had spoken with Sara's parents about this matter before their untimely death,' Mrs Edwards says. I feel riddled with embarrassment and shame.

As I sit there, quietly listening to these adults make decisions about my life and my future, I start thinking about John. Is this what happened to him? Were his choices taken from him? Is that why he was thinking about leaving?

I tune out of the conversation and the next thing I know, Mrs Edwards and Mr Charles are gone, and I'm alone with Ms Davis. She's talking to me. I can see her red painted lips moving, but all I can hear are muffled noises. I can't make out what she is saying. My head is fussy and I feel faint.

'Sara, are you okay?' she asks. The touch of her hand on my shoulder brings me back to the room.

'Yes, Miss,' I mumble.

'Before you head back to the library, I want to talk to you about something.' The kindness in her voice is reassuring. 'Do you do much reading outside of school?'

The question seems weird to me and totally out of context. 'Not really.'

'Do you find it difficult to read? Like maybe the words get jumbled up?'

'It makes me feel dizzy and sick in the stomach'. I've never told anyone that before. It makes me sound like a freak. Who gets queasy when reading? I mean really, that's just nonsense.

'Interesting,' her smile is calming. 'Have you ever heard of dyslexia?'

'No.'

'It can explain why someone might have difficulty with reading, but there are techniques that can be used to assist. I've been learning about it and I'd like to see if I can help you. Is that okay?' Ms Davis asks, with what appears to be genuine concern.

It takes me a bit by surprise, given the past few interactions I've had with the adults around me. I'm having a hard time coming to grips with the idea that this one is actually trying to help me.

As I make my way back to the library the conversation with Ms Davis swirls around in my head. I'd walked into her room feeling like I had no control over my destiny, and that my thoughts and feelings didn't matter. But I now feel like there is someone in the school that actually cares about what happens to me.

Chapter 8

I have some time to kill after school as Del went down to Newcastle that morning and told me she'd pick me up on her way back through. I have about an hour before she's due to arrive, so I decide to head down to the main street. I used to walk to and from school every day from my parents' house, so I'm kind of looking forward to it.

It doesn't take long for me to start daydreaming about Georgia, her lips and her perfect hair. The moment is disrupted by the yelling coming from a car pulled over at the side of the road. The deep baritone of the man's voice rattles me. I can't make out his words, but I can tell that he's really angry. The vibration pulses through me causing a flashback to moments when my father had that same tone.

I put my head down and pick up my pace. As I'm passing the car, I can hear a girl crying. The fear echoed in her tears makes me turn and look.

My heart jumps into my throat and I stop dead in my tracks. I'd recognise that cascade of hair anywhere.

'You stupid slut,' the man yells. 'Get the fuck out of my car.'

Georgia gets out of the passenger's side, sniffing back her tears. He barely waits for her to shut the door before he squeals away.

Before I know what's happening, I find myself leaping towards her. I can't help it. I just want to make sure she's okay. Her back is to me and she jumps when I say hello.

Her eyes are red from crying and black from her running mascara. She still looks beautiful with the blue of her eyes piercing through the darkness. She tries in vain to wipe the smear, but it makes little difference.

'Are you ok?' I ask.

'He's such a jerk.' She tries to smile.

'You weren't at school today,' I blurt, my nerves getting the best of me.

I want to tell her I missed not having her there, but it just seems like another stupid thing to say, so I stop myself.

She giggles a little. It's nice to see a flicker of light in her eyes.

'Rodney took me to a doctor's appointment.'

'Are you sick?' I ask without thinking.

What an idiot I can be, it's none of my business if she's sick or not. My parents always taught me not to pry into other people's business, especially their health. Although my mother did seem to think it was okay to gossip about other people's business, especially their health. The standard didn't go both ways.

'Not sick, just stupid,' she says, starting to look like her old self again. 'I thought he loved me.'

'I'm sure he loves you. How could he not?' The question comes out of my mouth before my brain has time to think about it.

I'm like a child drooling over a doll. I'm struck with a sudden urge to ask her if she wants to be my friend and it takes all my strength to not let the words escape. I don't know what is happening to me.

'You're sweet.' Her voice is so tender, it makes me weak in the knees. 'Where ya headin?'

I'm scared to respond for fear of what I might say. I seem to have very little control over the words tumbling out of my mouth.

'Town,' is my simple response.

'You mind if I walk with you for a while? I'm not ready to go home yet.'

We wander the streets aimlessly. I don't want to find a destination because I don't want her to say goodbye, so I continue to chart us on a path to nowhere. She doesn't seem to notice. She's more interested in just talking about lots of little things, getting to know each other. We each share our lists of the things we like and dislike. Mine's mainly around food, as my scope of the outside world is quite limited.

After a while, she starts talking about Rodney. At first, it's just a comment or two tangled up in stories about fun things she's done in the past. But after a while, the topic dominates the conversation. Although I'm extremely curious about their relationship, I try really hard not to pry. She tells me how they met. He's a friend of her older brother and used to come around their house a lot when they were in high school. She had a crush on him for years. But seeing he's five years older than her, she reckons he never noticed her much. Her brother moved away a few years ago, but Rodney stayed in town after picking up a job at the coal mine. She didn't see him much after that, and had forgotten all about him until he showed up at her brother's twenty-first birthday party about a year ago. She'd not long turned seventeen and Rodney seemed to have noticed.

'We spent most of the night together just talking.' Her words are almost dreamy as she recalls the early days of their relationship. 'He was so sweet and funny, and he really seemed to be interested in getting to know me.'

I'm not sure at this point if she is trying to convince me or herself. After that night, he started to show up after school and offer her a lift home. They've been together ever since.

'And your parents were okay with you starting to date him?' I ask.

There was no way my parents would have let me do that. In my world, dating isn't permitted until you are eighteen, and even then, no one is allowed to date without a chaperone.

'They never really noticed. They're both so busy with their own stuff, they don't bother to ask me about mine. Besides, they're hardly ever home. Work's always more important.'

'Mine were the same.' I'm overcome with a need to speak freely. 'In my family, we never shared stories about our day. It was all up to my father, really. If he wasn't interested in talking to us, then we were all silent.'

Georgia looks at me strangely. 'What? You weren't allowed to talk to each other?'

'Neither my mother nor I were permitted to initiate a conversation.' As the words tumble out of my mouth, I realise how strange it sounds. 'What's your favourite colour?' I fumble in a desperate attempt to change the subject.

She stares at me blankly for a moment. A wave of guilt and regret rushes over me. If only I can take the words back, then maybe she'll stop looking at me like I'm from a different planet.

'Hey, aren't you part of that weird religious group?' Her question catches me off guard. I hear her words but I don't understand what she's talking about. 'You know, the one that gets together every Friday night. The one no one is supposed to talk about.'

I'm speechless. Weird religious group? Is that how people see us? I'm mortified. I can no longer breathe and I can feel the tears brewing.

'Sorry, Sara. I didn't mean to upset you. Sometimes I say things without thinking. It's the blonde hair, I think.' She nudges me a little with a smile gracing her perfect face.

How can I be mad at her? I try to crack a smile.

'I think it's time for me to meet up with Del.'

'Oh, come on Sara,' she pleas. 'I didn't mean to upset you. Please don't be mad.' She grabs my hands and pulls me to face her.

I take a moment to look in her mascara smudged eyes, my heart fluttering in my chest. It's as though I can see into her heart as she continues to beg me to forgive her.

'*Weird religious group?*' Her words reverberate in my ears. I had no idea that people in the town thought we were weird. I believed that we were the chosen ones and everyone else was jealous. But maybe that isn't true. My mind swirls with flashes of my parents and I start to feel dizzy.

'Are you okay?' Georgia asks, squeezing my hands.

The sensation of her touch breaks the cycle in my head and I'm able to refocus on her piercing eyes. I can see they are holding back tears and I'm filled with a warmth I've never experienced before.

'I'm okay.' I attempt a smile.

'Oh good. You had me scared there for a minute.' She spins around and loops her arm in mine. 'Now let's get you to Del,' she announces and starts leading me towards main street.

Chapter 9

About two weeks later, rumours about Georgia around school are rampant. She hasn't come back to class and everyone is saying it's because she's pregnant. I try to tell people it isn't true. She's so sweet and lovely there's no way she's pregnant, I explain to anyone who'll listen. But no one seems to believe me. It's so frustrating. I don't know where she is or how to contact her, and the fact that everyone is saying such a horrible thing about her is making me really angry. They all talk about her like they know her; like they know for sure why she isn't at school.

But I know better.

She's just going through a rough patch, that's all, I convince myself.

That's what my mother would have said. Whenever things weren't working out for Father, Mother or me, that was the explanation she'd give. '*All you have to do is sit tight and Jesus will help you find a way through.*' This was exactly what she had said when Father had trouble trying to break in one of the horses at the farm he worked at. It was also what she said when I struggled to read through some of the more boring sections of the bible that I was tasked with reading every night before bed.

So, I'm not worried. I know that Georgia will be okay. She's probably just trying to work out the issues that her and her boyfriend were arguing about the other day. She'll find her path back to the classroom, or back to the library, I should say.

I keep telling myself that everyday I'm at school and she's not. The term drags on and ends without me seeing her face again.

On the last day of term, I catch the bus to the Edwards' farm, like I do every Friday, but there seems to be a different feeling in the air when Mrs Edwards greets me at the door. Her usual routine is to give me an afternoon snack and leave me alone to eat it. Today, she wants to have a 'catch up' chat.

The conversation begins with a few simple questions about the daily business at Karamea House, like where I sleep, what I eat, and if I'm helping out enough with the household chores.

'Are you homesick?' she gently enquires.

The question throws me a little. To refer to my situation as homesick is weird. I don't have a home to return to, so I'm not sure how to answer her question. I politely say, 'Yes'. I think it's best to appease her, but the truth is that my days are so filled with new experiences that I haven't been giving it much thought. I know I can't be honest with her and tell her that I love it there. That I love the crisp mountain air and the continual hum of nature's harmony, which introduces me to new sounds every day. That most of all, I love the feeling of being treated like Del's equal – like my thoughts and ideas are valued and are always considered as part of our conversations.

I don't think that I can tell her that the only time I think about my parents is when I'm here. It's like stepping back into my old life. Everything that happens on a Friday night is the same as it has always been for as far back as I can remember, and sometimes, I almost forget that my parents are dead.

Hoping the awkwardness of the conversation is over, I dig into the vegemite sandwich.

'So,' Mrs Edwards continues. It seems that she has no issue with talking during mealtime, contrary to how my parents raised me. 'Have you met Del's husband?' Apparently, she has an agenda. 'I mean, she does have one, doesn't she?' The gossip trail on Del's life must have gone cold in town and they're looking for some new information.

'I don't know,' I lie.

'She hasn't said anything about why she's moved to a huge property, in the middle of nowhere, by herself?' Her tone is more accusing than enquiring.

I shrug and take another bite of my sandwich, keeping my eyes on my plate. I can feel her staring at me just like my mother used to. I refuse to look up. This lying thing is still very new to me. I only really started in the last year as a way of trying to get out of something that my parents wanted me to do. But with such little practice, and having been caught a few times in the past, I'm not sure I'll be able to keep it up if she catches me in her gaze. I find it hardest to lie when someone is looking directly at me.

'It's just that some of the elders are concerned about the example that Mrs Moon is setting for you,' she says firmly. 'They want to know what kind of marital situation she's in so they know that you are learning the value of a loyal marriage.'

As the conversation continues down this intrusive path, I struggle to swallow my food. My stomach starts to squirm with discomfort and I'm not sure how much longer I can hold myself.

'Divorce is not something that the elders support, you understand that, right?' She leans closer to me causing my heart rate to rise.

I nod and try to take another bite of my sandwich, but my mouth is so dry I begin to choke. The shock brings tears to my eyes.

'Now don't get yourself all worked up, Sara.' Her tone is patronising as she hands me a glass of water. 'Just relax and take a drink.'

I force down the swallow, wipe my eyes, and take the glass from her.

'That's better, isn't it?' The trademark sweet Mrs Edwards returns as she gently rubs my back. 'It's okay dear, you can tell me what you know.'

I'm paralysed, unsure of what to do. I feel like if I tell her what I know about Del then I'll be betraying Del, and if I don't, I'll be betraying my parents. It's an impossible situation. What Del has told me about why she left her marriage makes sense to me. I completely understand what it's like to feel like you're living a life you don't belong in. But I know Mrs Edwards will not understand, nor will any of the elders. For them, marriage is a contract under God that can never be broken for any reason.

If I tell Mrs Edwards the truth, I'm scared she won't let me go back to Karamea House, and I need to go back. It feels like the place I'm meant to be right now and that there is so much more I need to learn from Del. The weight of the passing moments presses on me and the room closes in. Just as I'm about to break, John enters.

'I can't find the prayer cloth,' he says.

'Jonathon, have you forgotten your manners? Sara and I are in the middle of a conversation,' she scolds.

'Sorry Mum, I didn't realise,' he apologises, bowing his head. 'Please excuse my interruption.'

'Better,' Mrs Edwards says sternly as she rises from her chair.

'You okay?' John asks quietly after his mother leaves the room.

'I wasn't expecting that,' I admit in a whisper.

John and I have made it a habit of meeting up on the back steps after every Friday prayer evening. And although we don't talk that much, there seems to be a sense of understanding between us.

'She can be pretty full on sometimes,' he tries to joke.

'No kidding.' I smile.

'It's almost time for people to start arriving, you might want to go and get ready.'

I wait until everyone is in the room before I slip into my designated spot. Being placed at the back has its benefits. It's easy for me to let my mind wander to help pass the time. I generally reflect on moments I've shared with Del and how I envy the way she lives life so freely. But today, I can only think about Georgia. My belly is filled with dread about her safety and the fear that I'll never see her again. Thoughts of her consume me, and the moment John and I are alone on the back steps, it all starts to spill out.

'I'm terrified something bad has happened to her,' I blurt.

'To who?'

'My friend Georgia.' It's the first time I've mentioned her to anyone. Although I don't know why I've kept her a secret, even from Del. 'She hasn't been at school for weeks and I don't know what's going on.'

'When was the last time you saw her?' John asks gently. His genuine concern is sweet.

I give him a quick summary of the incident with her and Rodney. 'But she seemed okay when we said goodbye.'

'You said she'd gone to the doctor…maybe she's just sick.'

'Maybe.' I can't bring myself to tell him about the rumours at school.

'She means a lot to you.'

I nod with the heat of embarrassment burning my cheeks.

'It's nice to find someone to care about, isn't it?' John's voice trails off as if he's wandered into his own daydream.

As the silence falls between us, there's a growing noise of a commotion inside the house. It's the sound of people leaving in a hurry. The disturbance breaks us from our trances and we bound into the house to see what's going on. Mr Edwards is the only one left in the room and he's standing, facing the front door. John starts to ask what's going on, when the door opens. Del enters the house with Mrs Edwards directing her in from behind.

'Good evening, everyone,' Del announces. She flashes me a smile.

'What's going on?' John asks with a sense of urgency.

Although John and I haven't had many in-depth conversations on the back steps, I have told him a bit about Del and the weird way his parents act around her. His protectiveness is endearing.

'Calm down, John,' his father bellows. 'I thought it was time I invited Mrs Moon in for a cup of tea.'

'That would be lovely,' Del says graciously.

'I'm not feeling well and was hoping we could just go home,' I say as an attempt to provide a way out. After the conversation I had with Mrs Edwards that afternoon, I feel like I need to warn Del.

'I'm sure you'll be fine for a little while longer, my dear,' Mrs Edwards's sweetness is tinged with condescension.

Without missing a beat, she proceeds to the kitchen.

Mr Edwards offers Del a seat at the table. John and I quickly find our own. There is no way I'm leaving Del alone. Mrs Edwards swiftly returns with two mugs of tea, placing one in front of her husband and the other in front of Del.

'So, Mrs Moon,' Mr Edwards starts the interrogation.

'Please, call me Del,' she says with that cheeky, overly friendly smile I've come to know so well.

Mr Edwards continues as if Del hasn't said a word. 'Mrs Moon, it's my understanding that you bought the Winchester's old place out in Giro, is that correct?'

'Yes,' Del retorts quickly.

'The whole six and a half thousand acres?' he fires again.

'Yes.'

'And you're there by yourself?'

'Yes.'

'In that big old house?'

'Yes.'

'I see,' Mr Edwards takes a moment to sip his tea. Del doesn't touch hers. 'And you're running cattle on the property?'

'Yes. I've got about fifty head at the moment, but I'm looking to grow the herd. Lots of grass to be mowed out there.' She laughs. Mr Edwards does not.

Del flashes me another smile as if to let me know that it's all okay. My stomach is in knots, I really don't like the way they are treating her.

'I see.' He takes another sip of tea. 'And what is Sara expected to do?'

'I'm not sure what you mean?'

'What is her role in your household?'

'Role?' Del looks completely confused.

'I presume you are teaching her the proper duties of a woman,' his voice is firm.

'Well, sometimes you just need another set of hands to help when you've only got two.' She winks at me. 'Nothing too strenuous. Just being there to help when it's needed.'

I can tell from her answer that she's acutely aware of what Mr Edwards believes a woman's role is. How can I not admire this woman? Under this type of pressure, she's not even breaking a sweat.

'I trust you'll teach her what it's like to be a single woman on a farm,' he says in a way that makes my stomach turn.

'Absolutely,' Del responds in a very respectful but smug way.

On the drive home, the conversation keeps rolling around in my mind.

'You know what I've learned about people over the years,' Del comments when we're about halfway home. 'When someone already has an opinion of you there is no need to try hard to change it.'

Del is the strongest person I've ever met. She handled every moment of his judgement with class and grace. And even after it was all over, she doesn't even say a bad word about it.

Chapter 10

It's about halfway through the school holidays, and Del and I are working together in such a good rhythm you'd think we'd been doing it for years. She no longer has to ask me to do things. I'm able to sense what she needs before she gets a chance. And our meal-time routine is almost like a choreographed dance as we float around the kitchen cooking and cleaning together.

One afternoon, she decides we deserve a break and declares an early mark on the farm chores. She suggests that we pack up a picnic and take a ride on the quadbike to find a pretty spot to relax. With the picnic backpack on my shoulders, I climb onto the seat behind her and we head off to a part of the property I haven't seen before. It takes us about twenty minutes to ride over the rolling hills, up and down until we reach one of the highest peaks at the edge of the neighbouring national park.

'It's so beautiful,' I say once the engine has stopped. 'You can see everything.'

We are on a point that overlooks the expansive valley below. There are stretches of farmland with different shades of green and brown, dotted with patches of blue-grey bushland. The blue, cloud-rippled sky seems to rest upon a ridge of jagged peaks on the horizon, with the glimpses of sun constantly changing the light and dark patches of the rock. I'm so taken by the view I don't notice that Del has already set up the picnic blanket and laid out the food.

'Come and join me,' she offers. 'The view is just as good from down here, I promise.'

I curl up on the blanket next to her, taking a deep breath to fill my lungs with the glorious fresh air. 'It's so peaceful up here.'

We enjoy our lunch in silence and just appreciate the beauty below us. I'm feeling so relaxed and content. I lie back on my arms and stare at the sky.

'Do you believe there's a heaven?' I ask as I wonder if my parents are looking down on me.

'To believe in heaven, you need to believe in a divine being who dishes out punishment and rewards,' she says calmly. 'I'm more of a karma-girl, myself.'

'So, if you don't believe in God, what do you think happens when you die?' I'm fascinated. I've never known someone who doesn't believe.

'I'm not really sure, but it's nice to think our soul simply passes on.' She ties her hair up in a bun and lies down next to me. 'I like to think we're on a never-ending journey.'

'Doesn't it scare you to not know what happens?' The idea of there being a heaven is very comforting for me.

'Not really. I don't really think about it. I'm more interested in enjoying what happens each day.'

The concept of no God and no rules is so foreign to me. Even though I've always struggled to feel like I fit in among my church, I've never considered that there may not be a God. As we lie in silence, I begin to imagine what it would be like without the rules.

'What happened to your parents?' Del asks quietly, as if she's scared to say the words out loud. We've never talked about it. And to be honest, I've tried really hard to not think about it.

'I keep telling myself that I don't remember.'

'Is that true?'

Her question triggers the horrific memory that I've been blocking and the visions of that night start flooding through. Tears roll from my eyes and a heavy weight presses upon my chest.

'Sorry, Sara. I didn't mean to upset you. You don't have to talk about it if you don't want to.'

'It's okay.' I take a deep breath. 'I want to tell you. I'm just scared.'

'Scared of what?'

'What you'll think of me.' Tears turn to sobs. I sit up and place my hands over my eyes.

Del joins me, placing her hand on my shoulder. 'I know your soul. I can see who you are deep inside. That will never change. Don't be afraid. Letting it out will help you heal.'

I take a moment to regain control over my emotions. I turn to face her. 'It's my fault. They were on their way to the Edwards' house to confess my sin when the accident happened.' I hang my head in shame, tears streaming down my cheeks.

'It's okay, Sara,' she says, rubbing my back.

'It's not okay,' I snap. It's like a tidal wave of anger has come rushing out of me. 'I stole. I went into the store. I took a phone and I didn't pay for it. I mean how could I pay for it? I don't have any money. But I really wanted the phone.' I can hear myself yelling, but I can't seem to stop. 'We aren't allowed to have phones. But everyone else at school has one. They already think I'm a freak 'cause of this stupid thing I have to wear.' I flick my ribbon to emphasis my point. 'And my hair.' I grab the end of my ponytail and show Del the coarse, broken, tangled tips. 'How disgusting is this? And I can't even cut it. Oh no, that would be a sin. That one they'd notice right away. But the phone. The phone I could hide.' I'm flooded with flashes of that night as they come bubbling up to the surface, with a stream of guilt along with it. 'I should have been with them in the car. I should have agreed to face my punishment, but I was so mad at them for making me different from everyone else that I refused. We had a huge fight. Father was so angry the walls shook. I was so scared of him that I ran from the house and hid in the bushes down the road.' I'm shaking and feel like I'm going to vomit. 'When they didn't come home, I was relieved. And when the police came to the house to tell me that their car had run off the embankment, I wasn't even sad. They told me that my father was driving so fast, he'd lost control. So, I blamed him.' My anger shifts to grief and the tears return. 'But it was my fault. It never would've happened if I had just got in the car with them.'

'It's not your fault,' Del whispers as she wraps her arms around me and lets me weep uncontrollably.

Her embrace holds me up while my insides fall apart. Saying it out loud makes it real and numbness that has possessed me since that night disappears.

'It's time to forgive yourself.'

Chapter 11

My return to school the next term is filled with mixed emotions. On one hand, I'm not looking forward to spending another term isolated in the library. The past couple of weeks with Del has been so therapeutic for me, I feel like I'm ready to start a new chapter in my life and would much rather stay on the farm to help. But on the other hand, I can't wait to see Georgia. I can barely contain my excitement when I see her sitting in the courtyard. I'm almost skipping as I approach her.

'Oh Georgia, it's so good to see you.' She doesn't even look up at me, but I continue anyway. 'I had such a great holiday with Del. I feel so energised.' She continues to stare blankly at the ground. It's like her body is there but her mind isn't.

'Great,' she mumbles.

She's so distant and vague, I decide I should try to cheer her up and continue talking about some of the projects that Del and I got up to, like making a riverbed in the garden near the house. But she doesn't seem to care.

I give her a bit of space while we're in the library, but once we're back outside at recess, I decide to try out a joke that Del told me.

'Why do you never see elephants hiding in trees?' I start. After I give her a second to think about it, I chime in with the answer. 'They can't climb the trunk.' She doesn't even flinch. 'Get it…they can't climb the trunk.' I even make the elephant trunk gesture with my arm, but still nothing.

So, I try another one.

'I was thinking of going on an all-almond diet.' I give time for a dramatic pause, 'but that's just nuts!' I'm hoping that laughing at my own jokes will get her going too, but she doesn't flinch. There could be tumble weeds passing by us, it's so deadly silent on her end.

I give up on cheering her up and spend the rest of the day just being there for her, in silence. She doesn't ask me to go away. I think she likes having me with her. There's been snickering from some of the gossip mongers, but she's far too vacant to notice. And I don't really care if she talks to me or not, I'm just so happy to be with her. To see her beautiful face again fills me with the same kind of warmth I have when I'm with Del.

I'm meeting Del in town after school, so I offer to walk Georgia home on my way. Actually, it's a little out of the way, but it doesn't matter. It's just an excuse to be with her. I have time to spare, so I suggest we stop for a milkshake.

As we sit with our drinks, mine chocolate and hers caramel, I realise I've spent the day rambling on so much that I've actually run out of frivolous things to say to her.

'My birthday's on Saturday,' I blurt.

I can feel the blood running to my cheeks and the shame of boasting rushing over me.

'What?'

My comment seems to have broken her trance and Georgia's shimmering blue eyes fall upon me for the first time today.

'It's my birthday on Saturday,' I repeat sheepishly.

'Are you serious?' She's bouncing back a little, sounding almost like herself again. 'I had no idea.' I notice a tinge of shame in her tone.

'Why would you? I've never told you when my birthday is.' I giggle.

Perhaps I should have opened with 'it's my birthday soon' at the start of the day. Maybe she would have snapped out of her funk earlier.

'But I should know. I don't even know how old you'll be.'

I start to feel bad that I hadn't told her sooner, she looks so hurt.

'Eighteen.'

'For fuck's sake,' Georgia says so loudly the rest of the conversations in the café come to a halt, not that she even notices or cares. 'We have to do something. We have to celebrate,' she announces.

'Oh, it's okay. I don't really celebrate my birthday,' I whisper.

'What?' Georgia's eyes are almost bursting out of her head with disbelief. 'What do you mean you don't celebrate your birthday?'

'I've never had a birthday party,' I confess. 'It's just not something we do in my family.'

Georgia sits back in stunned silence, her mouth gaping. I welcome the silence as it gives the people around us the chance to return to their own business.

'Well that's going to change,' Georgia says. 'We're going to celebrate.'

The idea of celebrating my birthday with Georgia completely consumes my mind for the rest of the week and before I know it, it's Friday and I'm on the bus to the Edwards'. The service will be focused on me. I'll be expected to talk about all the things I've done wrong under the eyes of the Lord and tell them all the ways I'm going to live as a better Christian until my next birthday. But I'm completely unprepared for my birthday confession. I've been far too busy fantasising about Georgia picking me up on Saturday night and taking me out to celebrate. She told me she would take care of everything and that all I had to do was be ready. Living so far out of town, I'm struggling with the guilt of her having to drive so far to get me, but she assures me she's been in touch with Del to sort things out. Del, on the other hand, has taken the silent approach and has not revealed one single detail about the plans. She was also a bit shocked when I told her that our church doesn't celebrate birthdays the traditional way.

'That's unthinkable,' Del exclaimed the night I told her. 'Everyone deserves to celebrate the day they were born. The creation of life is a wonder that requires recognition.'

I don't go so far as to tell her that I also have to confess my sins over the past year. The fact that I've already revealed my treacherous truths to her is enough. I don't want to take her down with me any further. My life is my cross to bear.

The bus is running a bit late due to engine trouble, so most people are already there by the time I finally arrive at the Edwards'. My heart sinks when I see all the cars outside the house. *What am I going to do?* My pace is slow as I walk the long driveway towards the farmhouse. I'm desperately trying to think of what I'm going to confess to.

The reality is my church group doesn't take kindly to members breaking certain rules. While the act of stealing is something that can be managed by a period of fasting or complete isolation, or maybe even both, the punishment for disrespecting my parents and causing their death is far worse. It's grounds for banishment. Even though I don't believe in everything that happens in my church group, they are the people who've helped make me who I am. Like Aunty Bev said, they are 'my mob'. So to be banished - to never be able to see them again - would be devastating.

'You okay?' John's voice snaps me out of my intense thoughts. He's come to greet me outside. My shoulders sink, giving away my inner feelings. As we stand face to face, I realise I have never noticed the unusual colour of his eyes; one azure and one emerald.

He places his hand on my shoulder. 'Just tell them that you feel like you didn't read enough of the bible and that you're planning to double your readings.' His ability to read my mind and offer a valid solution, puts me at ease. 'Your birthday confession. That's tonight, right?'

'Right,' I say.

The sound of tinkling chimes is our cue to head inside. John insists that I lead the way. 'Sometimes it's just better to face it head on.'

John's suggestion works a treat. When his father asks me the question as I stand alone in the middle of the group, I respond with my head appropriately hung in shame.

'Sometimes I get distracted,' I confess, which is actually true. What I don't say is that I haven't even looked at the bible since I moved in with Del. 'And I struggle to get through the pages.' It seems that digging deep into my cavern of convincing regret is giving Mrs Edwards a sense of self pride, as a tiny smile creeps upon her face. Given she thinks that living at Karamea House is like living in a lair of sin, my confession plays right into her hands.

'The devil has been lurking inside you, my child,' Mr Edwards says, placing his hand on my shoulder. 'You need to be strong and not let him lure you into temptation.' I nod my head in obedience. 'What will you do to seek penitence for your sins?'

'I will pray to Jesus to help me,' I say, keeping my head low. 'I will beg him to forgive me. Then I shall read twice as hard for twice as long.' I even manage to squeeze out a tear.

I learned at a young age the importance of showing a physical sign of sadness when confessing to a sin. So being able to shed a tear every now and then is something I have got pretty good at.

After the prayer session is over, John and I make our way to the backstep.

'Thanks for saving me.'

'Not a problem.' John smiles. 'I've been there myself, dreading what to say to these people.

'How can I ever repay you?

'Well, there is something that you could do to help me,' he says quietly, leaning in a little closer.

'Whatever you need.'

'I have plans tomorrow night that my parents won't approve of, so I'm wondering if the plans could be with you?' He winks. 'You know, for my parents' sake.'

'But I've got plans…' The look on his face helps me realise halfway through my sentence that he doesn't actually want to make plans with me. 'I see.' I try to recover gracefully.

'I'm thinking that it might be good for both of us, if we tell my parents that we'd like to start to get to know each other better,' he suggests. 'So in future, I can say my plans are with you, whether we have plans or not, if you get what I mean.'

'But dating requires chaperones.'

'It's all in the wording. If I tell my parents that I'm interested in getting to know you better as a potential future partner, then we are permitted to spend time alone together,' he explains.

I guess the benefit of being a male in this church group is that you get more information about how the rules go. It also helps that John is almost twenty-one. That's when he'll finally be treated as an adult and be expected to take part in more of the service.

I agree with his plan. Considering what he's done for me, it's the least I can do. Twice, he's come to my rescue.

John will tell his parents that he would like to take me to a bible study in Taree tomorrow night so he can help me get back on track with my readings. They'll be so thrilled that he's helping fulfil my birthday promise that they won't have a problem with it. I will continue with my plans with Georgia, as I'm certain that no one from our church group will see us. We aren't meant to spend too much time with people outside the group, so no one really goes out for leisure in the evenings.

Chapter 12

I awake on the morning of my birthday to a sweet aroma. It smells so good my stomach starts to grumble. I can't stay in bed a moment longer, so I jump up and head towards the kitchen.

'Morning birthday girl,' Del sings as she greets me with a big, warm hug. 'Perfect timing. I've just finished the first batch of pancakes, so tuck in before it gets cold.'

She moves to the side revealing a buffet of toppings on the breakfast bar like nothing I've ever seen before. Not only have I never had big, fluffy pancakes before, but I've never had chocolate sauce, ice cream, whipped cream, peanuts, cherries, and sprinkles on top of anything. Del encourages me to get so much of everything that it's near impossible to eat.

'Have you had enough?' Del asks after I manage to squeeze the last bit into my very full belly.

'I feel like I'm going to explode.' The pressure of my full stomach is making it hard to breathe.

'Perfect. First task accomplished,' Del says with a smile.

She disappears down the hallway and I think about laying down on the lounge. Gluttony isn't something I've experienced before. Being one of the mortal sins, I've never been encouraged to indulge in it. As I drag my engorged stomach towards the lounge, I begin to see why it's considered a sin. There was so much pleasure while I was eating, but now I just feel like a stuffed pig ready for the spit.

'I have something for you,' I hear Del say from behind me just as I reach the soft cushions that are beckoning to me. I spin around and plonk myself down. 'Happy birthday.'

The moment I see her standing over me with a wrapped present I'm overcome with emotion. Tears start flowing and I'm reduced to a blubbering mess. I try to thank her, but I can't get the words out. I don't know what triggered this ungraceful display, whether it was her words or the gift. Neither have ever been presented to me before. Del's taken off guard and she scrambles around the room.

'Oh honey, I didn't mean to upset you,' she says, handing me a jumbo-sized box of tissues.

It takes me a moment to pull myself together.

'You haven't upset me. I've just never been treated like this before. This isn't the kind of birthday I'm used to.'

Del sits down beside me and wraps her arms around me.

'This is the kind of birthday you deserve,' she whispers.

I lie in her arms, softly weeping away the guilt. She lets me stay as long as I need.

'It's okay to enjoy this.'

Her words echo in my mind, battling against the mantras my parents instilled in me from the moment I was born. My insides are twisted, confused and full of foreign food. The warm sensation of a sugar rush embraces me and a sense of excitement along with it. I'm dying to know what's in that wrapping paper. I sit back and let Del know I'm ready for my present.

My hands are shaking as I carefully unwrap the book-sized package. Tears crowd my eyes once more as I reveal a brand-new mobile phone.

'It's completely normal to want what others have,' Del says gently with her arm around me. 'Although your methods were not ideal, you were expressing yourself the best way you knew how. You are a product of your upbringing. You didn't choose it. And you're not responsible for what happened to your parents.' Her words are warm and comforting. 'In this place, you are free to become the person you are. There are no rules about exploring your interests, desires or curiosities.' Del pulls from our embrace and turns my face towards hers. 'This phone symbolises the next chapter in your story. If you take it, you must forgive yourself and let yourself continue to try new things and make mistakes. Do you understand?'

I nod.

'The choice is yours,' she smiles and stands up. 'Now I'm going to clean the kitchen, while you let that lovely birthday pancake nourish you.'

After she leaves, I look down at the box in my hands. My thoughts are awash with snippets of my mother, my father, Del, Georgia and John. I feel like a stranger in my own body. Although it's not a new feeling.

For eighteen years, I've felt like I didn't belong. Like I was a stranger in my family. Like I wasn't the child they were meant to have. Every time they would teach me something, it was a struggle for me. Deep down inside I was always questioning. I was always wondering why. But I knew I was never to speak my thoughts or feelings in their presence. And until I started spending time with John, I thought I was the only one in our church group that felt like an imposter. When the police came to tell me that my parents were dead, part of me wondered if I had wished for it to happen. There had been a huge part of me that wanted to run away from them and never return, and that night I'd started to. I'd had enough of their control and their unwillingness to learn about me.

And now they are gone and I'll never be able to talk to them again. I'll never know if they would have accepted me for who I want to be. This isn't how I wanted my freedom to come. But I'm still not free. I'm still a part of the church. I'm not ready to let them go. Living with Del allows me to explore things I would never have been able to do when my parents were alive. It's an opportunity for me to try without having to give up everything I know.

I open the box to find a card inside. *It's all set up and ready for you to use. Enjoy. Love Del*

A tinge of full belly pain strikes me and I decide it's best for me to have a little nap.

Georgia's timing is impeccable. She pulls up to the meeting point just as Del and I arrive. After a quick goodbye, Del heads off and I slip into Georgia's car. I'm barely in the seat when Georgia hands me a beer.

'Happy birthday,' she smiles. I take hold of the slightly wet, icy brown glass bottle, not sure what to do next. 'Well,' Georgia says, looking directly at me. 'Aren't you going to drink it?'

With Del's words of seizing the moment ringing in my ears, I bring the bottle to my lips, accidentally knocking the glass against my teeth. Georgia giggles a little but in a sweet way not in a way that makes me feel bad. I tip the bottle, letting the cold liquid fill my mouth. After a moment, I swallow, feeling the rush of bitterness drain into my stomach.

'Better,' Georgia says, putting the car in gear and pulling away from the curb.

She drives us into town and turns into the park, following the narrow roads snaking all the way down to the river. She parks the car next to a few others. I manage a few more swigs of beer, but I'm still unsure if I like the taste. Although, the warm sensation rippling through my body is making it hard to care.

After grabbing a small esky from the boot, Georgia leads me to a group of people sitting around a fire under the bridge. It's a collection of former high school students, some who've dropped out recently, and others who'd dropped out years before. They are gathered on the concrete slab that protrudes from the footing of the bridge towards the bank of the river. When the river is high, the slab is at just the right height for you to dangle your feet in the swift current. But at the moment, the river is low, resting peacefully a fair distance below, weaving in and out of the exposed rocks. The underside of the bridge is graffitied with random expressions, crude drawings, and illegible names, which seem to loom in the flickering firelight.

Georgia joins the group with ease, bringing me along to sit next to her. No one seems to notice, or perhaps care, that I'm there and the chatter continues relatively undisturbed.

'I'm tellin' ya man, it was crazy.' Pete Jones, one of the older ones, is in the middle of telling a very animated story. 'Angus Young is fuckin' amazing!' he announces as he stands up, playing air guitar against his AC/DC t-shirt while flipping his head forwards and backwards to the beat of the music playing only in his head.

His impersonation means nothing to me, as I've never seen a live band or been to a concert. But I do recognise the logo on his shirt, thanks to Del, and have some idea of what he's talking about. She told me that their music has been influencing generations of youth since the early seventies, and based on Pete's love of Angus Young, the influence hasn't wavered. Pete tells us he streamed one of the band's live concerts earlier that day and how he wants to show us what a great show it was. The group is laughing and cheering at Pete's impression, which seems to keep his energy going.

'It was mind blowing,' he proclaims as he collapses onto the ground, causing even more laughter.

Georgia hands me another beer. Apparently, she's noticed that I've finished my first one even before I have.

'How ya feeling?' she asks, her eyes twinkling in the firelight.

'Good,' I say with a flush of fake confidence.

Not only am I spending time with people outside my church group, but I'm drinking alcohol. I try to keep the guilt at bay.

'Here,' Pete's girlfriend, Karen, says to Georgia, holding in her breath as she speaks.

Karen passes Georgia a rolled cigarette as she slowly lets the smoke escape from her mouth.

Georgia brings it to her lips and inhales slowly, intensifying the burning amber glow. She holds her breath for a moment with her eyes closed, before repeating Karen's slow exhale. The smell that wafts over me makes it pretty clear that it isn't a normal cigarette, not to mention the fact that I've never seen anyone smoke in such a ritualistic way. Georgia gestures it towards me. The alcohol fuzz that fills my brain convinces me it's a good idea to give it a go. Besides, Del did encourage me to make mistakes. I take a puff and not so gracefully cough my lungs out on the exhale.

'You okay?' Georgia takes the joint from me and passes it along.

'Yep,' is all I can manage as numbness takes hold of me.

I can feel myself floating up out of my body. It's as though I'm as light as air and I'm watching the people around me through a television screen. The sounds of the night become more vivid and the flames of the fire more intense. Then the spinning starts. I grab onto Georgia wanting her to make it stop. I try to use words to express my feelings, but my mouth won't move. Everything else around me is in motion. My need to walk away from the group puts me in motion. Their laughter begins to fade behind me and a shiver from the lack of warmth jolts through my body. Sickness fills me in an instant and I can't control it. Tears fill my eyes as I seek stability from a nearby tree to throw up next to.

When it's over, I feel a lot better. The spinning has stopped and my feet are grounded. Georgia is behind me, rubbing my back, asking if I'm okay. Once I stand up straight, she walks me down to sit by the river a good distance away from the others.

'It's normal the first time,' Georgia tells me.

'I can't go home like this.' I can feel the panic swelling inside of me. 'My parents will never forgive me.' The moment the words leave my lips, I'm slapped back to reality. I'm struck with a wave of guilt and embarrassment.

'It's okay, it'll pass.' Her voice is tender. Her words, soothing. 'We can just sit for a while, till you feel right again.'

We sit in the low light of the moon watching it flicker off the dark river as the water majestically moves downstream.

'I was pregnant,' Georgia confesses. I continue to look straight ahead, not willing to move. 'He made me get rid of it. Drove me there himself to make sure I went through with it.'

After a few moments of awkwardness, I finally feel brave enough to face her. I see tears running down her cheeks and I'm desperate to comfort her. I put my arm around her, letting her head fall onto my shoulder. I let her stay there as long as she wants, content in our silence.

Every so often she says something, allowing a random thought to pass through her perfect lips. She talks about her parents and how little they know about her and her life. She can never tell them about her situation because she knows they'll only tell her it was her own fault.

It's a feeling I completely understand. Her story of living in a house where you are only meant to be seen and not heard is very familiar to me.

She tells me how angry Rodney was when she told him she was pregnant. At first, he insisted that it wasn't his and accused her of cheating on him. Then he blamed her for letting it happen. When he found out how much it would cost to get an abortion, he started looking for alternatives. He suggested she take a bunch of pills and even threatened to throw her down a set of stairs. She was so scared of him that she told him she would pay for it, so he made her book an appointment. Being eighteen, there was no need to get her parents involved.

'Truth is, I'm not sure I wanted to get rid of it,' she admits. Perhaps it was this hesitation that Rodney suspected because he picked her up for the appointment making sure she wasn't ever out of his sight. It was day surgery and Georgia was able to get down to Sydney and back without her parents knowing – not that it would have been hard for her to stay out all night without them noticing.

'When we got to the clinic, it was like a scene from a movie. There was a group of pro-life protesters with big signs on the footpath blocking the way in. They were yelling at me to not to murder my baby.'

Knowing she had to face that situation rips at my heart and I pull her into a tight embrace. Her body convulses as she weeps into my chest.

'I couldn't move. I couldn't go through with it.' Her voice is muffled. 'He grabbed my hand and pulled me through the crowd, yelling back at them to leave us alone.'

I wish with all my might to take her pain away.

'Everything happened so fast after that. The only thing I remember is seeing you after we got back. The next day, I was really sick and I didn't want to get out of bed. I just cried instead. I haven't heard from Rodney since.'

In my religion, you're not permitted to have an abortion. We are taught that it's a sin against God. But as I sit there, holding Georgia in my arms, I can't see any evil in her. I can only see the glow of her gentle spirit. If she were part of my church, I would be forced to banish her from my life, but no part of me feels like that I should. My anger lies wholly with Rodney. He guided Georgia down a path then abandoned her. He's the one that deserves to be banished.

We sit in silence for a long time after she stops crying. I'm not sure what I'm supposed to say or if there is something I'm supposed to do. I've never been in this type of situation before. My heart aches for her and all I want is to help take away her sadness.

My mind is flooded with lessons from the bible and I find myself telling her a story about my church group. I've never shared anything like this with her, but I can't stop the words from rolling out of my mouth. It's the story of how one of the young children in the group got really sick a few years back and could barely get out of bed. After months of her not getting better under the prayers of her parents, my father performed a healing ritual in the girl's room. As one of the elders, he was within his rights to make the decision to conduct a special prayer ceremony devoted to the child.

'The next morning, she got up, went into her parents' room and asked for breakfast,' I tell her with as much enthusiasm as the day I first heard the story.

Georgia lifts her head from my chest. 'So, your dad reckoned he had the healing powers of Jesus?' she questions with the hint of a smile growing on her face. 'Like the touch of God?' She giggles. 'Churchie people can be so weird sometimes.'

Her words hurt a little. I know she doesn't mean to make fun of me, but it's hard not to take it that way.

'Aw, shit, sorry Sara,' Georgia says, returning to some semblance of herself. 'I didn't mean anything by it. I just find it hard to wrap my head around. You know, the whole blind faith in God thing.'

Instead of responding, I just stare at the ground.

'Come on now,' she says. 'It's time to lift the beat of this party. Tell me more about Del. She seems like someone I'd like to get to know,' she smiles.

It doesn't take much more convincing to get me to change the topic and pretty soon I'm retelling funny stories about Del and me on the farm. The whole conversation sobers me up and after another hour or so, Georgia is dropping me off to meet up with Del. I'm exhausted by the time I crawl into the ute. Del doesn't ask me any questions about my night but instead lets me drift off to sleep.

Once I'm in bed, sleep eludes me as my mind tussles with thoughts about Georgia. All my life I've been taught that having sexual relations before marriage is a sin and is only something done by heathens and those controlled by the devil. For me to think of Georgia as one of those people means I can never break bread with her nor have her as a close friend. I'm permitted to be kind to her and exchange pleasantries, but I can never have her belong to my inner circle. And knowing that she fell pregnant out of wedlock – well that proposes a whole other set of issues that doesn't align with the guidelines that I've been taught to live my life by. Adding in the knowledge that she chose to abort her unborn child really sets my head into a spin.

I really care about her. She stirs emotions in me I've never felt before. She's exposed me to things about the world I didn't know and things about people I didn't know. To think of her as someone who is bad and as someone that I have to cut out of my life makes me feel ill. I don't want her out of my life. She makes me feel more alive than I've ever felt before and I want more of that feeling.

Hence the struggle in my brain. I know I can never tell anyone in my church about what Georgia did. Not only is it not my secret to tell, but if the elders find out that I'm even spending time with her, it puts my position in the church family in jeopardy. And I'm not ready for that.

I'm not getting much sleep. It takes a lot of energy to justify that it's okay to continue my relationship with Georgia. I work so hard at it that I even convince myself that my friendship with her is all about helping her on a pathway towards Jesus. That, by merely being around me, she'll be brought back on the straight and narrow. Then I seal the deal with a promise to myself to pray for her at church next Friday, which is enough to allow me to fall into a deep sleep just as the sun is starting to creep up over the horizon.

Chapter 13

Each day that I attend school, it's pretty hit and miss as to whether or not Georgia attends. I try not to let it bother me and keep my head down to avoid getting into any kind of trouble. So, when Ms Davis comes to get me from the library during the start of week three, I'm not as afraid this time. In fact, I welcome it as I figure it'll be a good distraction.

We're barely outside the library before she starts explaining to me how she's working on a program to help me get an Australian Tertiary Admission Rank or an ATAR, as long as I'm interested. It's not really something I've thought about it, which is exactly what I tell her. I just assumed that my path is to simply finish the year so I'll be out of their hair. But Ms Davis has other ideas for me and stresses the importance of sitting the HSC exams at the end of the year.

'When you were in year eleven, you had enough eligible units to permit you to sit the exams, but your unexpected transition into the learning assistance program has thrown a spanner into the works.'

I really have no idea what she's talking about. Pathways to university and higher education were never terms discussed in my family, nor within my church group. It's been more about a woman's pathway to being a wife and mother.

Ms Davis has made arrangements for me to have a meeting with Mr Charles to discuss career paths. Having never been a part of a 'future plans' discussion about my life, I don't know how to prepare myself for the meeting. Not knowing what to expect is stressful, but given she's taking me directly to him, I have little time to worry about it.

'Sara,' Mr Charles smiles as he welcomes me into this office.

Ms Davis says goodbye then disappears and I'm left frozen, standing in the doorway.

'There is no need to be nervous.' His tone is calm and soothing. 'We're just going to have a chat about things you're interested in to get an idea of what kind of work would suit you when you leave school.'

Sounds simple, so I follow him to the chair he offers and watch as he makes his way around the desk to sit across from me. He starts slowly, asking me if I have any hobbies, which I don't. He asks me if there are any professions in town that I think are intriguing, which I don't. He asks me if I like the jobs my parents had, which I didn't.

'And what about the type of work you're doing at Karamea House, do you enjoy that?'

'I don't like the farm work, but I like being there.'

It's hard to explain exactly what it is that I love about the place. The farm chores are hard but satisfying. Although I could easily go my whole life without doing any more of them.

'Okay, that's good,' he says. 'What is it about being there that you like?'

It's nothing like my parents' house was, I think. 'The quiet of nature,' is what I say.

'Anything else?' he enquires, making a few notes on his pad.

Having independence. 'Making plans for each day.'

'What do you mean?' He stops writing and looks up at me.

'After dinner, Del and I sit down together and discuss the best way to organise our time to ensure we get as much done as we can,' I explain.

A smile creeps across my lips as I think about spending time with Del.

'Working on project efficiency?' he says as he writes it down.

'I guess,' I respond, not having ever heard the term before. 'We also work out the cost of everything to make sure the farm is earning enough money to cover the cost of the upkeep.'

'Balancing profit versus loss?' He makes another note.

'Something like that.'

His note taking is making me uncomfortable. I feel like he's judging me.

'Interesting. Sounds a lot like business management.' He smiles as if he's discovered the cure for cancer. 'Based on your maths ability, this could be right up your alley.'

He tells me that he'll take his findings to Ms Davis, and that together they will work out the best strategy for a pathway to university.

Me? Go to university? No one has ever made that kind of suggestion to me before. Not once did the topic ever come up with my parents, so the thought of it has never really crossed my mind. Father had been pretty clear about wanting me to learn how to run a household so that I would make a good wife. And last year I was told by Mr Martin that the best I could hope for was an apprenticeship or a job at the supermarket.

The concept of furthering my education is foreign to me. To think that I may be able to study somewhere else, outside of Gloucester, is really exciting. I can't wait to tell Del. I know she'll be so happy for me. I know I can't say anything to the Edwards just yet. They'll only blame Del and say that she's a bad influence on me. Although, I'm pretty sure they aren't expecting this kind of news from me. It should be fairly easy to keep it a secret.

It seems to be a similar issue with breaking the news to Mr Martin, something Ms Davis is also avoiding. She insists we keep the plan between us, for now. But she is so confident in what she thinks I can achieve, it's infectious. I'm beginning to believe it's possible.

'Sara, I've been working on something that may help you concentrate better on your studies,' she explains once I return to her room. 'The exams are standardised across the state, but there are methods I can put in place that may assist you.'

By the way she explains it, we only need to make a few little changes to the way I study. She's broken down my daily lessons in a spreadsheet, outlining the amount of time I need to work on each subject, keeping the time periods short enough that I can keep focused. She tells me that I'm able to ask as many questions as I want and that I'm able to alter the schedule if I don't feel it's working. It also helps that the space I'm working in has very few options for distraction. Unlike the library or a typical classroom, Ms Davis's room is quiet and there are no windows.

As it gets closer to the end of term, Georgia has pretty much completely stopped coming and I'm spending all of my time in Ms Davis's room. Although Georgia isn't at school, I still manage to see her. As a result of John using me as an excuse to go out on the weekends and his parents blatantly encouraging it with the hope that John will keep me out of the devil's pathway, I manage to catch up with Georgia fairly regularly. In the final week of term, she tells me about her plan to move to Queensland to live with her cousin, Peta.

'She's got a place at Mermaid Beach and she reckons she can get me a job at the pub she works at,' Georgia says as we sit together, rugged up by the edge of the river.

My stomach drops. I can't imagine life without Georgia. 'Sounds really good,' I try to be supportive.

'You should come with me.' She smiles that beautiful, charming smile. 'You can share a room with me. We could find you a job at a takeaway shop or something.' Her enthusiasm is enticing.

'No parents?' I ask.

'No parents. Peta's twenty-five and lives alone.' Her answer makes me smile a little. The thought of her having freedom makes me happy.

'Amazing.'

I begin to fantasise about leaving Gloucester and what the world outside of it looks like.

'I'm leaving Friday.' Her words are piercing.

'This Friday?' It's so soon. I start to panic.

'I'll leave at night, so you can sneak out of your church thing. John'll help you get out, won't he?' I can tell by her tone that she's deadly serious.

If my parents were still alive, her offer would have a completely different meaning. My desire to break free was so intense that I would almost certainly have gone with her. But things have changed for me and I'm not sure how I feel about leaving right now. I really want to see what's outside of this town, but I can't help thinking that there is more I need to learn here. And then there's the whole church group thing. If I go, I can never return. I'm not sure I'm ready for that.

Despite all this, I can't shake the thought of running away with Georgia. The idea of being with her all the time makes me feel warm inside. I think about her during the drive back home with Del, and the beautiful images of being with Georgia stick with me throughout the week. Her plan starts to grow on me and I start packing my things, hiding the bag under my bed. I don't want to tell Del. It's not that she won't understand, it's just that I don't want to upset her and make her feel like I don't like living with her. I can't stand the thought of her being mad at me or disappointed. So, I keep Georgia's offer to myself. I told her that I don't have any money, but she said she'll pay for the petrol. Peta isn't expecting us to pay rent until we get jobs, meaning I only have to pay for my own food, which Georgia has offered to cover. Everything is set.

By Friday, the excitement is brewing inside of me, I can barely contain it through the church service. It's almost exploding out of me by the time John and I get to our usual spot out back.

I can't wait to tell him, but before I get the words out, I notice there's something off about his mood. 'Are you okay?' is what I ask instead.

No words, just tears. He slumps over with his face in his hands. His body convulsing with devastation. I place my hand on his back and tell him it will all be okay. It's the only thing I can think to do.

After a few moments, he wipes his eyes on his jumper, takes a deep breath and says, 'I got dumped.'

'I'm so sorry, John.' My heart is breaking for him.

'Over text.' His eyes are red. 'Didn't even have the courage to do it in person.'

'She's a coward,' I say. 'You deserve better.'

He looks at me and smiles. 'Thanks.'

'You're a great guy,' I announce, lifting my enthusiasm with the hope he'll come along with me.

'It's nice to have someone to talk to who understands,' he says sheepishly.

There's something about his tone that makes me feel like there is more to his story. And just like that, I know I can't go with Georgia. I've always been taught that Jesus works in mysterious ways. His voice is guiding us through our journey in life, helping us make the right decisions to live a virtuous life. Although I'm not sure if it is Jesus talking to me, I have a feeling in the pit of my stomach that makes me think that John needs me more right now than Georgia does. I can't really explain it, but the feeling is so strong, I know I can't leave him alone.

Being the amazing person Georgia is, she totally understands.

'Keep in touch.' She says, grabbing my phone from my hand. She spins around, pulls me towards her, and snaps a slightly-angled selfie of the two of us. 'Now that can be your wallpaper.' She grins as she taps her thumbs delicately on the screen of my phone. 'There, see.' She holds up my phone to show me the screen with a close-up photo of our faces. She's spent the past few days teaching me how to work my phone, installing apps, and making sure I have contact with all the people in my life – her included.

'I'm really going to miss you,' I say.

'Me too,' she says softly, pulling me in for a tight hug.

I can feel myself melting in her arms and my conviction starts to waver. I don't know if I can let her go.

'Will I ever see you again?' I mumble once our embrace ends.

It feels like my heart is being ripped out of my chest and I'm finding it hard to breathe.

'Let's make a plan to see each other in summer.' Her voice lifts with a wave of excitement. 'You can jump on the train to come and see me. What do you think?' The small pool of tears that fill her eyes makes them sparkle.

'Sounds great.'

'The offer still stands. If you ever decide you want to come live with me, you're always welcome.' She smiles and gets into her car.

I know she's only trying to make my choice less difficult, but it really isn't helping. It's tearing me apart to say goodbye to her. She's been such a big part of my life over the past few months and I can't imagine what it's going to be like without her. As much as it pains me to see her go, I know I can't go with her. There's a part of me that's too scared to leave. I may have convinced myself that my decision is because of John and a duty to our friendship, but deep down inside I'm worried that something bad might happen to me if I go. Leaving means that I'll never be welcome back in the family. They will banish me and I'll be on my own. My life with Del is only temporary. Now that I'm eighteen, she's no longer legally responsible for me. Although she's told me I can stay for as long as I like, I know I'm going to need my church family after I finish school. I'm not ready to be on my own yet. Maybe Georgia knows that. Maybe she senses it and that is why she's made it so easy for me to say no to her.

Saying goodbye to her, though, is one of the hardest things I've ever done. As I wave a final farewell and watch her drive away, I hope that it's not the last time I'll ever see her.

My disappearance from the house has gone unnoticed and I quickly return to sitting next to John on the back steps. I only have a few moments to fill him in on what happened with Georgia before Del's ute pulls into the driveway. I rush through the house, saying quick goodbyes on my way out the front door. I can hear the ute door opening as I pull my hidden bag from the front bushes, where I'd stashed it. I told Del that I needed to return a few things when she enquired about the bag, and now that she's possibly spotted me retrieving it, I will have to fess up.

I'm barrelling towards the ute with my head down, ready to explain when I notice the torso in front of me isn't that of Del. I look up to see a tall, slender man with neatly trimmed dark hair walking towards me. He introduces himself as Del's son, Ethan. She's never mentioned having a son. I'm a little confused and assume he means he's one of her foster kids.

Chapter 14

'Where's Del?' I ask as soon as we're on the road.

'I surprised her with a visit and she insisted on cooking a fabulous meal to celebrate, so I offered to come and pick you up.' Ethan flashes a smile in my direction. 'She's told me so much about you.'

I mumble, 'Thank you'.

I wish I can return the compliment, but I'm at a complete loss. I didn't even know he existed. It strikes me as odd that Del has kept a secret like this from me.

'So how often do you surprise her?' I ask, trying to change the topic.

'First time in a while,' he responds quickly, not even looking in my direction. 'But I know how it is living with her. There's always a lot happening, so I try to keep out of her way.'

As he focuses on the road ahead, I take the opportunity to get a really good look at him. I'm trying to figure out how old he is. I don't think he's much more than twenty, but I don't have the courage to ask. In the short time I've spent with Del, I've realised that she isn't as young as she appears, so I'm not so sure I'm any good at judging someone's age.

Our conversation turns to things we like and dislike. After having done this with Georgia recently, I opt to use a few from her list so he doesn't know how inexperienced I am. By the time we get to Karamea, I've managed to figure out that he's only just turned twenty and is attending his second year of university in Sydney.

Ethan decides to have a shower before dinner after having spent most the day driving. I take the opportunity to grill Del about him.

'Why didn't you tell me you had a son?' I waste no time.

'It's complicated,' she says dismissively.

'Not good enough,' I snap. 'This is a pretty major part of your life that you haven't shared and I want to know why.'

My new-found brashness may be a little too much, but I can't help it. I'm really hurt that she never told me about Ethan.

'And you packing up your stuff and not telling me why, is an okay secret for you to keep?' Her retort stings.

'I...I...'

'The reality is, no one ever shares every detail of who they are.' Her voice softens. 'It's okay to keep part of you a secret. It's what makes us human. Revealing all of who we are makes us completely vulnerable to others.'

I'm not quite sure what she's trying to say.

'Keeping things hidden is also part of the mystery, don't you think?' Her jest makes me think she's seeking my forgiveness, but instead I'm overrun with my own guilt.

'Georgia asked me to move to Queensland with her,' I admit.

'Why didn't you?'

'Not sure,' I shrug.

'Ethan came to me when he was five years old. He's the only one I've adopted,' she speaks tenderly. 'He came rather unexpectedly. He was so young, I felt like I had no choice. Me and my ex are the only family he's ever really known.'

Del is speaking as though she's mostly comforting herself, soothing away a sadness that lies underneath her tone. 'He hasn't spoken to me since I left Sydney. He didn't understand why I had to leave. He didn't understand that I was leaving my husband and not him.'

Del had intentionally stayed in her marriage until Ethan finished high school, determined not to disrupt his life again. Without going into any detail about his birth parents, she simply tells me that she's mindful of the turbulence he's already experienced and she doesn't want him to feel any more loss. She figured that once he started university, he wouldn't need her the same. It turns out she was wrong.

'I'll never forget the look he gave me the night I told him I was leaving.' Her voice is shaking. 'He told me I was dead to him. He was so angry and hurt.'

She tried to explain to him why she needed to leave and that it wasn't about leaving him, but it made no difference. Ethan left the house that night and didn't return before it was time for her to pack up and go. She thought that maybe she had underestimated the demons left behind by his birth parents, but she believed he'd get over it in time. She was so devastated that he'd shut her out, she couldn't bring herself to talk about him with me.

'I'd let him down and I didn't want you to think less of me.' As a tear rolls down her cheek, I wrap my arms around her.

'It's okay.' I try to comfort her. 'He's here now.'

'I know, and I can't believe it. He showed up this afternoon and I was a blubbering mess.' She giggles.

He told her that he couldn't stay mad at her and the thought of losing her for good was just too much. Apparently, Del spent a lot of time that afternoon catching up on his life and talking about me.

After a banquet feast and some reminiscing, Del heads off to bed leaving me alone with Ethan. He's sitting by the fire in the lounge room, gazing at the flames with a glass of whiskey in hand, the light flickering on his lightly tanned cheeks. It's the first time I've looked at a man and have thought him to be handsome. With a woman, beauty seems more straight forward: long flowing fair, flawless creamy skin, beautifully painted lips. With a man, I'm not sure what to look for. But as I sit there watching him watch the fire, his soft black hair framing his glistening forehead, his long black eyelashes accenting his deep brown eyes, yesterday's stubble beginning to soften around his lips, I begin to see it. He turns his eyes to meet mine. I'm unable to remove my stare. There's a sense of comfort about him. He seems to add to the feeling of this place being home.

'Are you going to join me?'

It's the same smile he flashed earlier, but this time it weakens my knees. My inability to move is painfully obvious.

'How about I get one for you.' He gestures with his glass as he rises from the armchair and goes to the buffet where the whiskey bottle sits next to an ice bucket.

The rattling of ice disturbs my trance and I manage to take a seat on the lounge.

'My mother is a fascinating woman,' he comments, handing me a glass half filled with ice and whiskey. 'As strong as an ox and as stubborn as a mule.'

'She's amazing,' I say quietly. 'I've never met anyone like her.'

'She's one of a kind,' he laughs as he sits down next to me. 'She seems to have taken a liking to you.'

I can feel the heat from his body. At least I think it's from his body but it may well be coming from me. I can feel it rising from within me and resting on my cheeks.

'You are as pretty as she said.' He brushes the hair from my burning cheek.

I don't know where to look, his chest, his cheek, his lips, his eyes. I hold my breath and close my eyes. I can smell the whiskey in the heat of his lips as he kisses my cheek.

'It's good you're here,' he whispers.

He retreats, returning to the chair where he'd been sitting before. The air cools around me and I release my breath. My heart is beating so loud it feels like it's in my ears.

When I finally open my eyes, Ethan has returned his gaze to the fire and continues to sip his whiskey. I bring the cold glass to my mouth hoping to chill the fire inside me, but instead, the liquid burns all the way from my lips to my stomach. A tingling sensation rushes through my body and it makes me feel good, so I take another sip, continuing until I drain the glass.

When he notices I've finished he asks me to top him up while refilling my own. Without too much hesitation, I leap to my feet. I'm shaking as I take the glass from his outstretched hand. His eyes are on me the whole time. I focus hard to steady myself while I pour more whiskey in each glass. Desperate to calm my nerves, I take a quick sip before turning around to face him.

'So, tell me more about growing up with Del,' I ask in a big attempt to exude confidence.

'Cheers to Del,' he announces, taking his glass and clinking it to mine.

He precedes to tell what I believe to be a story about their old farm near Sydney. As far as I can tell it has something to do with a horse and dam. But between his struggle to speak without slurring and the fuzz in my brain from my second glass of whiskey, I'm really unsure what he's talking about.

The rest of the evening slips into a blur. His voice fills my dreams, his lips warm every inch of my body, and at some point, I'm riding a horse into a dam with the splash of the water waking me up.

The sun drenches the room where I find myself sleeping on the lounge exactly where I'd been sitting the night before. I'm fully clothed with a very sticky mouth and furry teeth. I follow the smell of coffee and bacon wafting out of the kitchen to find Ethan getting ready to fry up the eggs.

'Morning sleepyhead.' There's that smile again. 'Breakfast is almost ready.'

'I'll go get Del,' I offer.

'No need. She's already in the shower.'

I set the table for breakfast instead, stealing glances of Ethan as often as I can.

'When do you think you'll come back?' I try not to sound desperate to see him again.

Over dinner, he'd mentioned that he's only staying a couple of nights but that he'd love to come back soon.

'That's what I keep asking him,' Del announces as she makes her way to the kitchen table.

'Morning Mother,' Ethan says as he walks over and gives her a kiss on the cheek. Without thinking I touch mine where he'd kissed the night before, savouring the memory. 'Maybe I'll come up during mid-semester break,' he suggests, looking at me. The temperature in the room rises. 'This place is more interesting than I thought it would be.'

Chapter 15

After breakfast, Ethan plans on heading into town to pick up a few supplies from the hardware store. Del has given him a list of little jobs that need to be done around the house. It all came about because he isn't so keen on the way some of the light fittings make sporadic zapping noises when the light is turned on. Not to mention that his visit has emphasised the need to put a new handle on the bathroom door as the current one doesn't keep the door closed. He thought it best to get these things sorted out as soon as possible.

As Del and I stand on the verandah wishing him a safe journey, I must admit I'm quite enjoying watching him walk to his car. There is something about the way he moves in his jeans that is mesmerising.

'Close your mouth dear,' Del says before she heads back into the house. 'You're going to catch flies.'

A short while later, when Del and I are splitting wood, I try to figure out a way to bring up Ethan. My hope is that she'll start talking more about him the way she spilled everything about me. I can't stop thinking about him and I want to know everything about him. Del happily obliges.

'I never wanted to be a mother,' she admits point blank. 'It's not that I don't like kids, it's just that I never saw myself as the nurturing type, you know, for the really little ones.' Her words make little sense to me as she's the most nurturing person I've ever known. 'But when Ethan came to us, I was hooked.' Her eyes light up as she tells me about how cute he was as a child and all the mischief he used to get into. Before she moved to Karamea they were almost inseparable, spending most weekends together on the family farm just outside of the city. They both enjoy the connection to the land and the animals, and working long hours side by side to keep the farm running.

'He considered a career in animal husbandry, but his passion is law,' Del explains. 'When he found out that he could have a career helping farmers protect their land, he knew it was the right fit for him. I'm so proud of him.'

'I bet he was impressed when he saw this place.' I smile.

'Blown away, he was.' She grins. 'Told me the moment he saw the sign, he knew why I came here. I think he's finally forgiven me.'

'How can he stay mad at you, you're amazing.'

'Aren't you sweet,' she says bashfully.

'I mean it,' I insist. 'You make a big difference in people's lives.'

My focus on her seems to make her uncomfortable and she turns her attention back to splitting the wood.

'I'd say he'll start coming up during his uni breaks.' Her tone shifts from sentimental to light-hearted. 'Which'll suit me just fine. It'll be good to have another set of hands to help us with some of the bigger projects.'

I understand what she means. It's a big property and the two of us can only get through so much. Although I'm not complaining, it's a lot of physical labour but incredibly satisfying.

Once we've finished with the wood, I offer to check on the cattle on the far edge of the property. I'm feeling pretty confident riding the quad bike these days and figure it's time to venture out on my own.

To get to the lower ridge, where the cattle are supposed to be, I need to navigate down a very steep hill on a very rough road. It's like travelling down the barrel of a gun. I've been on the road before with Del but only as a passenger. She taught me the best way to get down without burning out the brakes. Her lesson was very clear.

'*Keep control over your speed and the bike will follow suit.*' Del's lesson vibrates in my mind. '*The key is to not put too much pressure on the brakes, use the bike's gears to keep the pace.*'

As I begin my descent, I opt for second gear to help keep me in control. I know in my brain how to get to the bottom without any major issues, but it doesn't seem to minimise the fear brewing inside me. Being at the front of the bike makes this hill look a lot steeper than I remember it to be. Second gear is what Del uses, but for me, at this moment, it's still going a little too fast for my liking. I attempt to switch the bike into first gear. As I release the clutch, I realise that I've put the bike in neutral.

'Oh my God,' I yell as the bike lunges forward.

My heart is pounding so hard it's making my knees shake. My speed continues to increase as I try to shift back into gear, but I can't get it to hold. I keep pushing the gear lever, but it only grinds and pops back out. I have no choice, I have to use the brakes to try to slow me down. The roar of the engine is muffled by the thumping sound of my heart. I can smell the burning brake pads as I get closer to the bottom. Tears are streaming down my cheeks.

There is no good ending to this story, I tell myself.

I know what is coming. I know what is in store for me. Before I reach the lower ridge there is a sharp turn, and all I can do now is hope that the brakes hold. I take a deep breath as the bend quickly approaches, trying hard to keep my shaking nerves from loosening my grip. I'm squeezing the brakes as hard as I can, causing my hands to start cramping.

I'm going to make it. I encourage myself to push through the pain ripping through my tensed body.

I muster my last bit of strength to keep the brakes engaged, but instead of stopping me, they simply release and the bike surges forward. There is nothing I can do, so I brace for impact as the bike begins to roll.

I don't know how much time has passed when I finally come to. Every inch of my body is throbbing. My head is screaming. I open my eyes to find the bike on top of me. Without thinking, I push at the machine to free myself and scramble out from under it. I'm at least three kilometres from the house and I didn't bring my phone. I have no idea what time it is or how much daylight I have left, so I begin to make my way back up the road. With each step, my ribs feel like they are stabbing me. After a few minutes of barely getting anywhere, my head starts spinning and everything goes black.

When I awake, I decide it may be better to crawl. I awkwardly manoeuvre onto my hands and knees. I can use my right arm, but my left is in agony. I somehow find a way to start making progress up the first mountain, trying hard not to think about the many other hills that I'll need to climb and descend before reaching Karamea. I know I need to keep moving. I'm covered in blood and if I'm out here after dark, the dingoes are sure to find me. The pain is excruciating, causing me to stop numerous times to catch my breath. I just keep telling myself that I can make it and that everything will be okay.

Time seems to be passing as slowly as my movements and I try to distract myself with happy thoughts. I picture Del, Ethan and I sitting by the fire in the lounge room, laughing at something funny Ethan has said. The vision of his face makes me feel stronger and I start to stand up. I'm fuelled by a sudden burst of energy that quickens my pace. As I gain ground, I can see the house in the distance. Just one more ridge to go. I feel my legs begin to run. I'm struck with a bolt of pain through my entire body and everything is dark again.

When I open my eyes, I'm sitting by the fire. Ethan is next to me with his arm around my shoulder. I'm safe and warm. Del's in the middle of telling a story.

'Your biggest enemy in the bush isn't the dingoes,' she says in an intensely animated way. 'It's the goannas. They aren't frightened of you and if they smell blood, they'll attack.' She starts talking about the time she came across an injured kangaroo one afternoon near the vegetable garden. 'Its thigh bone was sticking out through its skin. Poor thing, all I could do was help put it out of its misery.' When she returned from the house with her rifle, she was confronted by a very large prehistoric beast of a goanna making its way towards the roo. The pair of them both raced towards the injured animal. 'When I saw it leap on its final approach, I pulled the trigger.' Her eyes were glowing in the light of the fire. 'I shot twice. Once for the goanna. Once for the roo.'

Her story is so vivid, the sound of the shotgun rings in my ears. I close my eyes and shake my head to try and stop the echoing in my mind. A bolt of pain rips up my spine and I open my eyes.

Aunty Bev is standing over me as I lie in the long grass at the top of the last hill before the house. I can smell her shotgun.

'Bloody thing was comin' right at ya.' She moves past me, reaches into the grass and pulls out a large goanna by its tail. 'Should make for some good tucker.' She smiles. 'You're looking a bit worse for wear, my dear. We should get ya looked at.'

The gun shot brings Del and Ethan running out of the house and before long, they've driven the ute up to collect me.

'You look like you've had quite the adventure darl.' Del smiles as she crouches down to check on me. 'How about we get you back in the house so Aunty Bev can have a good look at you?'

Ethan comes around behind her and scoops me up into his arms. Although he's being gentle, the movement sends another shot of pain ripping through me and everything goes dark again.

This time when I awake, I'm in my bed with all three of them surrounding me.

Aunty Bev is closest to my side. She's busy wrapping my shoulder after having slathered it with some kind of poultice. 'There ya are, sleeping beauty.' She smiles.

'How are you feeling?' Del asks, worry written all over her face.

I try to speak, but my mouth is so dry I can't get words out.

'Here, have a sip of this.' Ethan offers a glass of water.

He helps me sit up. My entire body aches. Any kind of movement is difficult and exhausting.

'Looks like you've broken a few ribs and cracked your collarbone,' Del says. 'You'll need to go to the hospital for a few x-rays to confirm. The ambulance is on its way.'

No sooner than she speaks, there's a knock at the door. She rushes off to let the paramedics in.

Before they move me, they check my vitals and give me an injection to help with the pain. Del comes in the ambulance with me and Ethan follows behind in the ute. It's not long before the drugs kick in and I return to darkness.

I come in and out of consciousness at various stages over the next couple of days. They keep me in the hospital to ensure that I'm on the mend before discharging me back into Del's care.

Every time I open my eyes, Ethan is sitting next to me. Sometimes he reads to me. Other times he tells me a story about growing up with Del.

Once I'm feeling a little better, I start telling him what happened to me.

'I knew what was going to happen as soon as I couldn't get it back in gear,' I admit. 'But there wasn't much I could do about it.'

'I'm just glad that you're okay.' He smiles. His concern helps ease my pain.

'Thank you for staying with me while I'm stuck in here.'

'It's all good. I've been able to keep up with my lectures online. But I do need to get back. I have an exam in the morning.'

'No worries.' I try not to sulk.

Having spent so much time alone with him has given us a chance to get to know each other and I really like him. He's so easy to talk to and isn't scared to share his emotions. Although I desperately want him to stay, I understand that he needs to go.

'I'll be back as soon as I can.' He seals the promise with a twinkle in his sexy eyes. My heart starts racing as he leans in closer to me. 'Can you try not to hurt yourself while I'm gone,' he teases.

His face comes so close to mine that I can feel his breath on my cheek.

'You're free to go.' Del comes bounding in the room, causing Ethan to jump back. 'Let's get you out of this place.'

She heads straight to the bag of clothes she'd brought for me and starts packing everything up. Leaving the sanctuary that I've been ensconced in for the past few days is hard only because it means I'll no longer have Ethan's undivided attention, but I must admit, I'm really looking forward to getting back home.

Chapter 16

When Saturday rolls around, I insist on coming with Del to the cattle sale. Del is looking to pick up a few weaners to help bulk up her stock and I'm desperate for some normality. Although my ribs still hurt and I'm a bit shaky on my feet, I'm determined to help out in the canteen.

We head into town first thing in the morning, Del dressed as a cattleman and me dressed ready to help the ladies in the canteen. It's nice to be heading into town for a bit of socialisation. As much as I dislike how people talk about each other behind their backs, there's also something enticing about it. Human nature, I suppose.

The gossip circle is in full swing when I arrive at the canteen, with Mrs Vale, as usual, leading the charge.

'I heard that she was half dead when they found her,' Mrs Vale is saying to the very interested ladies. 'She's lucky to be alive.' I know that she's talking about my accident, but for some reason, she's talking like it was Del and not me. 'Imagine, a woman riding a quad bike. For heaven's sake, that woman should know her place.'

'I heard her son came up to help her,' Mrs Mason adds, tweaking my brain to conjure up images of Ethan in his blue jeans. 'Maybe she should have him live with her all the time. You know, take care of the farm work,' she says, sneering through her slightly crooked teeth.

The other women join in with a chuckle as I start buttering the bread. I'm tempted to correct them. To let them know that it was me that almost died, but I can't bring myself to open my mouth. Since coming here, I've learned that these women thrive on the stories they bring to the room, and the idea of highlighting the inaccuracy seems like a mean thing to do.

Pretty soon the auction is over and the men start pouring in, Del among them. I catch a glimpse of Mrs Vale's disapproving look directed towards Del as she chats away with the other farmers. By the time Del reaches the counter, she's alongside Mr Vale. I watch intently to see Mrs Vale's reaction.

'Margaret, get this fine woman a sandwich,' Mr Vale briskly orders. Mrs Vale promptly reacts without a word. Del's attention is drawn behind her as Mr Smith asks her a question.

Mrs Vale's reaction isn't what I expect. She almost seems demure as she places a curried egg sandwich in front of her husband.

'What? Are we meant to share?' he snaps at her in a low, demeaning tone that I'm pretty sure only Mrs Vale and myself can hear. She quickly remedies the situation by bringing another plate to the counter, her eyes lowered. 'That's better.' He smiles condescendingly before taking the plates and turning to face Del. 'Come on my dear, lunch is on me.'

Del thanks him for his kindness and leads him to a table. Mrs Vale stands frozen for a moment, watching her husband walk away before she is snapped back to reality by Mr Smith asking her if there are any vegemite sandwiches left.

There is something different about Mrs Vale's behaviour. It's almost like she's scared, but of what, I'm not sure.

Chapter 17

Term three kicks off with a bang. My schoolwork is improving every day and I'm feeling more confident about my prospects of sitting the HSC exams. There is just something about having the support and encouragement of Ms Davis, coupled with my newly formed friendship with Ethan, that fills me with a confidence I've not had before. Ms Davis is really impressed with my results from trial exams, but she wants to make sure I keep my momentum. Although my marks are a definite improvement from my year eleven results, it's not enough to get me into university. At this stage, I'm too late to apply for early entry, so my results are all that matters. But Ms Davis is determined to get me there. Better results may not be enough to get me into a business degree, but they will get me into a pathway course.

'Our biggest challenge at this stage is getting Mr Martin to sign off on your course completion,' Ms Davis explains to me one afternoon. 'We need his tick of approval in order for you to sit the exams next term.'

Being stuck in the library for most of this year means I'm not eligible to sit the exams. Ms Davis has been working with my regular teachers to ensure I'm undertaking all the classroom work and the required assignments, but Mr Martin still has the final say. Ms Davis believes that my trial exam results are the ticket to getting him to agree.

'You have been working really hard and I have no doubt that he will see that.' She smiles reassuringly.

Her belief in me is uplifting and is starting to rub off on me.

With Georgia gone, I don't have much to distract me in the afternoons, so I've taken to studying. I want to make sure that Ms Davis's faith in me isn't wasted. Every day after school, I get straight to work on maths equations or rewriting portions of English essays that I've been given feedback on. After dinner, I go back to my room and work on any assignments I have due or I simply review the other subjects I've covered at school that day. It's become such a routine that I haven't noticed or missed the lack of social interaction with other people my age. Besides, it's not like I haven't already spent most of my school career being the odd one out. Returning to isolation comes naturally to me.

But I'm not completely socially cut off. I still spend every Friday evening at the Edwards' house, continuing the ritual of John and I sneaking out back after prayer. Now that his relationship is over, he no longer needs to use me as an excuse to get out of the house. Instead, we are spending the time getting to know each other better. We have a natural connection, a stillness between us that makes us both feel at ease.

Perhaps it's this feeling that possesses John to suggest that we actually try to date each other for real. It's about halfway through the term when he pitches the idea to me.

'So, I was thinking,' John says, awkwardly looking towards the sky. 'Maybe we should go on an actual date.'

'You and me?' I'm a little taken aback by the offer.

'Yeah.'

'Okay,' just pops out of my mouth. I'm so comfortable around him, it's an easy decision. I know it won't be a typical relationship due to the fact that we aren't allowed to date unchaperoned, but the idea of keeping another secret from the church is enticing. John, being quite skilled at spinning lies for his parents' benefit, makes sure that we can easily spend time alone together without raising suspicion. I honestly believe that his parents think of me as so unworthy of their son, that they can't imagine he's interested in anything more than a friendship with me.

John and I make plans to get together on as many Saturdays as possible. Sometimes we go to the beach or the cinema, both very new concepts to me. Other times, we wander around the park in town or have a milkshake at one of the local cafés. He's a very gentle and kind person. I've never heard him raise his voice, swear or speak badly about anyone. He keeps his hair neatly trimmed, always wears nice clothing and smells good. He's so different from the other boys around town who tend to look like they've just rolled out of bed, walking around the streets in stubbies and thongs. John has a kindness in his eyes that makes me feel cared for.

One Saturday, John's parents invite us to have dinner with them. John tried to get us out of it, but his mother insisted. There's something about the invitation that is making me nervous. Even though they aren't meant to know that John and I are actually dating, I'm worried they've figured it out. I half-expect that the evening is going to be more of an ambush than a friendly meal. I know how these people work. My parents were the same. It's always about having the upper hand and maintaining control over the children.

Del, on the other hand, is really supportive about the whole ordeal, telling me that everything is going to be okay.

'It's best you don't arrive empty handed.' Del smiles and offers to help me bake a sponge cake. 'Something simple with fresh cream and strawberries. It's hard to be aggressive when your belly is full of sweetness.' She winks.

Preparing the dessert is helping pass the time, but it's not doing much for my anxiety. By the time John arrives to pick me up, I'm in a pretty bad state.

'It's going to be alright,' he reassures me.

By the time we arrive at his house, I'm feeling much better.

'What a lovely cake, Sara, thank you,' Mrs Edwards says as John and I enter the kitchen. 'Look like you're learning some good skills from Mrs Moon.'

'Yes I am,' I say respectfully.

'Tell me about the accident you had a few weeks back.' She gets straight to the point.

The fact that I rolled a quad bike and ended up in the hospital isn't a secret, but I haven't been forthcoming about how it happened. They won't look kindly on the fact that I was undertaking chores they consider to be more suited for a man, not to mention the fact that I was on my own while doing them.

'I was on my way to Del's neighbour's house to get some more sugar. We'd run out and were in the middle of making banana bread,' I begin, taking a moment to settle into my lie. I can see a little smile curling up in the corners of her mouth as I proceed to tell her what she wants to hear. 'I hit a rock hidden under the grass and it caused me to roll over.'

'Sounds scary, dear.' She offers a bit of sincerity.

'It was,' I retort, trying to show a bit of vulnerability. 'Thankfully Del was right behind me and we weren't too far from the house.'

I can tell by the glint in John's eye that I've successfully killed any way for his mother to cast further judgement on me or Del in regard to the matter. With the topic put to rest, we all enjoy a pleasant meal, with mere discussions about school, work and how ridiculous the town is getting with its Christmas decorations.

Although Christmas was still a few months away, the chatter about how the town will present itself for tourists this year is already happening. Gloucester holds a fair bit of pride in how it embraces Christmas. It's really just an opportunity to dress the main street up for a few weeks. For years, the businesses placed large painted wooden cut-outs of Santa with a full sack of presents casted over his shoulder. But this year, some of the new, younger business owners want to get a little flashier, and modernise with a light display. We spend longer than necessary dissecting the fascination people have with Santa and how the spirit of Jesus's birth has been stripped from Christmas. So much so that Mrs Edwards is still going on about it while I help her clean up.

After I'm released from my post meal chore, John and I go for a walk. John suggests that it will be a good way to walk off the huge slice of cake he had. He justifies his outrageous portion size by telling me that it was all about making sure he got a really good taste of my baking. He barely managed to eat it, rubbing his belly, and taking deep breaths in between bites.

Part of me hopes that he suggested the walk because he just wants to be alone with me. Having never been kissed, I'm a bit nervous about the prospect, but knowing that it could be with John, makes me feel comfortable. He makes me feel comfortable. He has an understanding of me that no one else does. Since we've been spending so much time together - as a proper couple - I've been thinking about what it would be like if he kissed me. There's a part of me that really wants it to happen. And sometimes, when he looks at me, I think that it's going to happen. But so far nothing.

As we head outside, I convince myself that tonight is the night.

The Edwards' farm is over two thousand hectares of beef grazing land spread across rolling hills about ten minutes out of town. The farmhouse is perched on one of the ridges somewhere in the middle of it all. As we wander down the gravel road, the nearly full moon casts a light almost as bright as the sun over the peaks and valleys as far as I can see. The landscape is vastly different from Del's place, which has chunks of land bordered by dense bushland. The Edwards' territory is only spotted with occasional treelines giving way to views of land kilometres away. It has its own magnificence and richness – that of vastness and productivity. In the moonlight, its eerie beauty seems almost magical and I wonder if John wants to hold my hand as we walk.

'When I was a kid, I used to pretend that this road led to a new world,' he explains as we wander down the road. 'In my mind, I was able to walk out there and become whoever I wanted to be. I didn't have to be John Edwards, the farmer; I could be anyone else.'

His pace quickens as his excitement grows. Once he's a few paces in front of me, he spins around to face me, the moon lighting his face

'Do you ever wish you could be someone else?' he asks as he grabs both my hands.

My heart begins to race as he stares deep into my eyes. My thoughts are distracted as I feel the warmth of his body close to mine. His touch is like a lightning bolt straight through me. My mouth is so dry I can't speak.

Is this the moment? I wonder.

As he leans in, I close my eyes and hold my breath.

'I understand,' I hear him whisper in my ear. 'I never thought I could talk about it with anyone either.'

'John! Sara!' Mrs Edwards's voice ripples through the air. 'Time to come back. You should get Sara home before it gets too late.'

John lets go of my hands and the moment is lost.

John's mood has shifted and for the whole drive to Karamea he talks about random things like footy and what it would be like to go to a live theatre production. As he speaks, I realise that I was so caught up in the moment of a potential kiss that I wasn't paying much attention to what he said to me. I begin to ponder what it is he was talking about.

I never thought I could talk about it with anyone either, his words replay in my mind. I really have no idea what he means. Riddled by the mystery, I say a quick goodbye as he pulls up out front of the farmhouse. I can't shake his words as I'm waving him off, nor when I say goodnight to Del or while brushing my teeth. And the more I think about it, the more I realise, I have no idea what 'it' is he's referring to.

Chapter 18

It isn't until my alarm goes off that I realise I was dreaming. Before being startled from my sleep, I was in the school hall sitting my HSC maths exam. When I look at the test paper the numbers are written in Roman numerals and the words are in Egyptian hieroglyphics. I try to work out the answers to the questions, but my pen is a twig and I can't use it to write anything. When I try to raise my hand to ask the teacher for a new pen, my right arm is so heavy I need to use my left arm to lever it up. The teacher who comes to ask me what I need is Mr Martin, and when he demands to know what I need, I can't speak. Then he starts to yell at me, telling me my incompetence as a student is exactly why he wants me kicked out of the school. He gets so angry at my inability to speak that he grabs me by the arm and drags me out of the room just as the school bell rings, which was in fact my alarm. It takes me a few moments to convince myself that the dream isn't real. But it was so vivid that I could smell his cologne, a scent that still lingers.

The dream recedes to a faint memory by the time I reach school and it's completely gone from my mind when I arrive in Ms Davis's room.

Without much more than a smile and hello, I get straight to work preparing for the final exams. Given the exams start early next term, and I have much to improve on, there is no time to waste. To help with my success, we've been sticking to our routine of me working on set tasks with her being there to help when needed. It's shortly after lunch and I'm quietly working on a chapter of the maths textbook when Mr Martin enters the room. He walks directly up to Ms Davis without even acknowledging my presence.

'Ms Davis, I'll get straight to the point. After meeting with the head teachers, it has been decided that Sara will not be permitted to sit the exams.' His words are like a thousand tiny knives perforating my stomach. 'We will continue her on her path to achieving her finishing certificate, but we believe she has not met the requirements.'

As quickly as he entered the room, he's gone leaving Ms Davis alone with her silent, gaping mouth. I'm frozen not knowing whether to cry or feel relief from the stress of not having to sit the exams.

In my daze, I don't notice that Ms Davis has got up from her desk. It isn't until she's standing in front of me that I realise she's even moved.

'Don't worry about a thing, Sara,' she says, bending down and placing her hand on my shoulder. 'This isn't over. You keep working. I'll be back shortly.'

I really don't know how much time passes, but I'm struggling to focus. I keep staring at the same question with no real attempt to put pen to paper. Thoughts swirl across my mind as I think about what my life will be like as a farmer. *It won't be that bad*, I attempt to convince myself. The upside is the idea that I'll be able to spend every day at Del's place and not have to go to school. I like being there and working with her. I know how to muster cattle and chop wood for the winter months, surely, I can make a life for myself as a farmer. Maybe it's the life I'm destined for.

I'm no stranger to resigning myself to the fact that I have no real choices of my own in life. That my future path is to be determined by those around me. I suppose trying to fight it is futile. It's just that, over the past few months, Ms Davis got me believing that I can do whatever I want to with my life. That I'm smart enough to have choices for a future outside of Gloucester.

I've allowed myself to imagine a life in a city like Sydney, working in an office with people who respect me and my opinions. I've envisioned a life where I can choose what I eat, how I dress, and what music I listen to. It has taken many months for Ms Davis to finally convince me that I can have that life, and with just a simple sentence uttered by Mr Martin, it's all been taken away.

I can hear voices coming from the hallway growing louder as they get closer. Although I can't make out what they're saying, I can feel the tension of the tone seeping through the door. It's as though Ms Davis's anger forces the door open as she enters with Mrs Becker, the head English teacher, in tow.

'He told me the decision was made during a meeting with all the head teachers,' Ms Davis says.

'I wasn't part of any such meeting.' Mrs Becker clarifies as she closes the door behind her. 'No decision should be made until the student has had time to complete the required assignments. And that doesn't happen until the end of this term.'

The two women are facing each other, both seemingly unaware of my presence.

'He can't do this. He can't just make decisions based on his opinion alone. He's only worried about his precious school results. He doesn't care about what's best for Sara,' Ms Davis says, her arms flying up in the air in an expression of helplessness. 'She's been working so hard. I know she can do this. She just needs to be given the chance.'

'Her parents could appeal the decision with the board of education,' Mrs Becker suggests.

An uncontrollable noise slips out of my body, drawing the women's attention towards me.

'I'm so sorry, dear,' Ms Davis says, slowly approaching me. 'Mrs Becker didn't mean to upset you.'

'How insensitive of me, my dear' Mrs Becker's voice is shaking. 'I'm terribly sorry about your loss.'

'It's okay. Even if they were still alive, they probably wouldn't want to appeal the decision.'

'Do you think your foster parent would be willing to write a letter to the school board?' Ms Davis's concern for me is so sweet. I can hear the hopefulness in her voice.

'I'm not sure the board would accept that,' Mrs Becker says solemnly.

'I'll do it,' Ms Davis announces.

'What? You can't. If he finds out, you'll lose your job.'

The two women stand quietly facing each other. Although there are no words spoken, they seem to be communicating through their body language.

'Julia, no one believes in a student's ability more than you do,' Mrs Becker says softly. 'You're an inspiration to all of us who teach, but you know your voice will be lost on the board. None of them have any idea how important your role is in the advancement of our students' education.'

Mrs Becker steps towards me and says, 'You keep studying, Sara. You are going to sit those exams.' I nod. 'This isn't over,' she says to Ms Davis before leaving the room.

'I know you can do this Sara.' Ms Davis looks me in the eye. 'You've made steady improvements in English and your maths scores are outstanding.'

My heart swells with her care for me and my future. I can't help but wonder what will happen to me without her support. Will the teachers at university understand me and the weird way I learn? It's hard enough being considered 'special needs' by the other students at this school, I can only imagine what it would be like on a huge campus with hundreds of people. But all of these thoughts are pointless. I want to believe as strongly as she does that I'll be permitted to sit the final exams but it's difficult.

Chapter 19

I'm so caught up in the dramas at school that I've spent no time trying to figure out what John's riddle was all about the last time I saw him. Our Friday nights together are pretty ordinary with little to talk about after the service, and our Saturday's being somewhat the same. On the last Friday night of the term, John and I make plans to get together to celebrate the official end of my formal schooling. Next term will be filled with a couple of weeks of study in Ms Davis's room before the exam period. Although I haven't had the official word that my name will show up on the list of students taking part, Ms Davis is certain it will happen.

For now, I'm focusing on each day as it comes, so I'm really excited when John arrives on Saturday morning to pick me up. There's a rodeo in town. I've never been to one before and have no idea what to expect, but it seems to have triggered something inside of John. He's so excited during the ride into town that he's talking non-stop.

'It's hard to explain the feeling you get when you see someone enter the ring sitting on top of a very angry bucking bull with the sole purpose of holding on for as long as possible. It's a pure adrenaline rush to watch.' I try to visualise what he's describing, but the whole concept makes very little sense to me. 'It's not just the bull riding that makes a rodeo so special, it's the whole atmosphere. When I was a kid, we used to spend almost every weekend at a campdraft. It's not quite as extreme as a rodeo, but it was still lots of fun.'

'What's a campdraft?'

'Oh Sara, it's a big part of Australian farm life.' His tone turns nostalgic. 'Parents cart their children and horses all around the state to compete in events that showcase how they'll make excellent jack or jillaroos. It's really just a chance to hang out with other farm kids and show off your horse-riding skills.'

He continues to tell me stories of his campdrafting adventures as we make our way into the showground. The place is full of utes, horses, and people. There is a voice on the loudspeaker saying words I don't understand and the place smells like barbecued onions and cow manure.

Although John hasn't been a part of campdrafting for the past couple of years, he still knows people who take part. We make our way to the showring and join a group of his friends. It's like I'm seeing a whole new side of him. One that borders on childish but is definitely fun.

'So what happens is, the rider needs to single out one of the beasts and herd it out of the gate,' John explains as one of the campdrafting events begins. 'Then they have to herd it around the flags without it coming out of line.'

What's the point? is what I think; 'Interesting,' is what I say.

'It's all about the skill and being able to control the animals.' He speaks with such passion. 'Both the horse and the calf.'

'Is that how you wrangle cattle on the farm?'

'Kind of,' John snickers. I hope he's laughing at how cute my innocence is and not at my lack of knowledge. 'Don't you muster cattle at Del's place?'

'Not really,' I admit. 'If Del needs to move them, she jumps on the quad bike and I open the gate. They pretty much go where you ask them too.'

'Fair enough. This style of mustering is a little more old-school but is still used on cattle stations with really rocky terrain. Safer than a bike.' He winks. The burn of embarrassment rises in my cheeks. 'Even we rely on the dogs and a ute.' He laughs.

There is something familiar and safe about being with John. I know that I don't have to hide anything about myself when I'm with him. And the more I'm with him, the more I am sure that he is the one I'm meant to have my first kiss with. When he drops me off later that afternoon, any hope of that happening is squashed the moment I spot Del in the front garden. I try not to let it worry me. I know I'll be seeing him again soon, convincing myself that it's only a matter of time before it happens.

The next morning, I wake to the sounds of a car coming towards the house. My eyes are barely open as I make my way towards the front door. I'm not sure I'm ready to talk to anyone at this point, having not been able to sleep in. Without much thought, I open the door to find myself face to face with Ethan. My voice gets caught in my throat.

'Gday,' he says, the light dancing in his chocolate eyes as it always seems to.

He leans in towards me. I hold my breath, unable to move.

As he reaches for the door and pushes it wide open, he looks at me with a smile. 'Mind if I come in?'

He makes it halfway across the room before I expel the air from my lungs. I'm entranced as I watch him take the hoisted bag off his shoulder and place it on the lounge.

'Mum up yet?' His words jerk my arms into motion and I close the door.

'Nope.'

'Good.' He spins on his heels and heads towards the kitchen. 'I'll get cracking on breakfast.'

As he unpacks food from a cloth bag onto the kitchen bench, he starts telling me about his visit to Gloucester. He stopped into the grocery store to pick up a few things.

'I just thought I'd be in and out quickly, you know. Figured I'd be the only one there seeing as it's so early, but I was wrong,' he retells the story with dramatic emotion. 'Apparently, it's the place to be if you want to catch up on all the town's gossip. It's amazing how much information you can find out about the locals by simply meandering around aisles at six o'clock in the morning.'

He fills me in on a few little tidbits, but I don't have the heart to tell him it's stuff I've already heard. My regular canteen duty at the cattle sales keeps me pretty much across everyone's business in town. Ethan seems to be having so much fun recounting the stories, even interjecting with renditions of how people speak, I don't want to take away his fun.

'I hear you're in a very serious relationship with a farm boy,' he teases as he starts scrambling some eggs.

His words pierce through me. I don't know if I'm more upset about the fact that I'm part of the town gossip or the fact that he knows about John.

'According to Hannah-Mae, everyone's just waiting on a wedding date.'

'We're just good friends,' I snap. 'It's no-one's business anyway.'

'I didn't mean to upset you,' Ethan says softly.

'What did he do to you?' Del interjects as she comes into the kitchen. 'Only been here a few minutes and you've already upset my girl.'

'He did nothing,' I say, giving her a big hug. 'I'm just tired. It's been a long term.'

'I was only teasing her. I didn't mean anything by it.' I can hear remorse in his tone.

'Don't you mind him, dear. Boys can sometimes be a little insensitive.' Del's words help my anger melt away. 'As punishment, let us just sit at the table and he can serve us breakfast and clean up after himself.'

While we wait for our meal, Del tells me a story about her first attempt at preparing the property for the bushfire season. Aunty Bev had arranged for a couple of her nephews to come by and give Del a hand with some burning off.

'It's amazing how quickly a fire can get away from you. The blady grass burns hot and fast. Give it just a little bit of wind and it can spread like wildfire. When you see it happen, it's pretty clear where the expression comes from.' She laughs.

It turns out that one of the days they were burning, a bit of wind rustled up out of nowhere and took hold of the fire behind the house. The flames jumped up high and fierce towards the building.

'Thankfully, the boys knew what they were doing. One of them ran around to the front of the fire and lit a strip of grass to make a break. They told me to grab a shovel and scrape back a line of bare earth near the house so the fire would run out of fuel.' Her pace quickens. 'I got to the front of the garden beds and started scraping my heart out. The boys were yelling at each other across the fire, trying to keep a handle on it. Aunty Bev heard the hollering and came to help, a young tree branch in each hand. She stood between me and the fire, using the branches to smother any flame that came near her. It only took about twenty minutes to get the fire under control, but it felt like an eternity. My heart was pounding so hard I thought it was going to give out on me.'

'Mum sure has a flair for the dramatic,' Ethan comments from the kitchen.

'It was quite an exhilarating experience,' Del continues, not taking any notice of her son's tongue-in-cheek remark. 'The house smelt of smoke for days.'

Del asks me to update her on the school situation.

'Any news on the exams yet? Do you need me to pay that principal of yours a visit? Knock some sense into him?' Her protectiveness makes me feel loved and I seriously consider her offer.

'It's okay, Del.' I decide it best to leave it up to Mrs Becker. I'm not really interested in upsetting Mr Martin and having him dislike me anymore than he already does. I imagine a visit from a pissed off Del Moon would not tip the scales in my favour. 'I'm sure it'll all work out.'

'You're a smart girl, Sara. You can do anything you put your mind to,' Del says. 'Don't let anyone tell you that you can't. I mean, look at me, all of Gloucester thinks I'm mad for having bought this place on my own, but I'm managing. I do admit though, I need a little help from time to time.' She laughs. 'But it's still all mine.'

A short while later, for the first time in my life I'm served a meal cooked by a man, and it's the best tasting bacon and eggs I've ever eaten.

Chapter 20

The next day is unseasonably warm and, according to Del, lends itself well to chopping firewood. She tasks Ethan and I with the job of splitting some of the wood pile into smaller pieces.

'If you have too much big stuff, you've got nothing to get the fire going,' she explains before sending us off to the pile of wood.

We jump into the ute and make our way to the southern edge of the property. A couple of years ago, several trees had been felled to make way for a fence line and after having sat on the ground and been given time to dry out, they are ready for the fireplace. Del and I had already cut the tree into rounds and split it into large chunks, most of which we'd taken back to the woodshed near the farmhouse. But there is still a fair bit left there. The plan is for Ethan to chop and for me to load the split wood into the back of the ute.

On the drive over, Ethan tells me about some of his uni classes and how he's taking part in a mock trial as part of one of his law courses.

'The trial's based on an actual case where a Sharpies inter-gang rivalry resulted in several people getting badly injured,' he says.

'Sharpies? You mean like the marker pen?'

'No.' He laughs. 'Although, I did think the same thing at first. They were these gangs of kids in the 1960s and seventies who liked to look sharp.'

'And they liked to beat each other up?'

'Apparently.' He shrugs his shoulders as he gets out of the ute.

'Maybe it had something to do with all of them wanting to be the sharpest looking,' I joke as I grab a pair of gloves from the back.

'Nice one,' Ethan says, flashing me a smile.

I love the way he teaches me without judgement and the way he shares stories with me. My childhood was so sheltered from the outside world there are countless things I know nothing about. When I come across people talking about something I've never heard of, I feel ashamed and stupid. But not when I'm with Ethan. He makes me feel important and like I'm a part of this life.

We get straight to work. Not much talking taking place, just lots of chopping and lugging. We've been at it for about an hour when Ethan gets jack of the heat and takes his shirt off. I'm distracted by the sweat glistening on his caramel skin. It's hard to take my eyes off his contracting muscles as he continually heaves the axe above his shoulder before thrusting it down on the log. Pieces of wood shards fly everywhere as he rips through the wood in one swipe.

It's this vision of him that I take to bed with me that night and many nights after. He stirs something inside of me that is bursting to get out. I never feel this way around John, nor do I dream of John in the same way. While asleep, I long for Ethan to caress my skin. I can feel the heat from his fingers as they draw near. Then I wake up filled with guilt. How can I think of another man this way when I'm in a relationship? John is such a sweet person who seems to care for me deeply. We're perfectly suited to each other as we both understand the life our parents planned for us and the way we're meant to behave. I should feel blessed, not bound.

The next day, Ethan and I are given another list of chores. This time Del needs us to drive to Newcastle to pick up some grain she's ordered from overseas. It means I'll be spending the better part of the day confined to the cab of the ute, alone, with Ethan. A chore which suits me just fine. I can think of at least a million worse ways to spend my day but not many better ones. The first hour or so of the drive we engage in light-hearted chit chat about frivolous things like television shows and movies. Since living with Del, I've been binging a fair bit, trying to make up for the years of being isolated from the outside world. As I have very little experience in this area, I'm highly focussed on Ethan's description of plotlines and character development. Some of the movies he outlines with such passion and detail, I can almost imagine having seen it myself.

'You really haven't seen any of these?' he asks.

I'm pretty sure he doesn't believe me when I tell him that my parents had to approve anything I watched, and the list was extremely short and restrictive. We had a television in the house, but my parents favoured religious programs and so I didn't bother with it much. I tend not to tell people about my inability to watch all the latest programs and movies for fear of seeming even more weird than I already look.

Sometimes it's just easier to pretend like I understand what people are talking about. But with Ethan, it's hard for me to hide that part of myself. He makes me feel so at ease and unjudged when I'm with him.

'So, tell me what it was like living in your house growing up?'

'Huh?' His question catches me off-guard.

'What were your parents like?'

'Terrifying,' I blurt. 'I mean…not terrifying…that's not what I meant.' My heart races with panic. 'Terrific…yeah…terrific, that's what I meant.'

'Freudian slip.' Ethan laughs.

'What?' I'm a little frazzled and have no idea what he's referring to.

'You know, when you accidentally say something weren't supposed to but you really mean. Like a glimpse into your subconscious. Your true feelings.'

'No. It really was an accident. I would never say such a horrible thing about my parents,' I say, attempting to recover.

'Calm down, it's okay, we all do it. I'm not going to tell anyone what you said. Think of me as a vault. What you say with me, stays with me. Okay?'

I don't know what to say.

'Here, let me start,' he says, placing his hand on my leg and giving it a light squeeze. 'My parents were heroin addicts.'

'What?' His words knock the wind out of me.

'My birth parents. Not Del, silly.' He giggles awkwardly. 'Del's the one who saved me.'

'Saved you?' I feel lost.

My heart starts racing. I'm not sure I'm ready to hear what he has to say because I don't know how I'll be able to comfort him.

He takes a deep breath and continues. 'I was really young so I don't remember everything, but there are some things that I'll never forget. My parents would get high a lot and there were many nights when they wouldn't make any dinner. I used to get really hungry. And sometimes the pain was so bad, I'd go to them and ask for food but it only made them mad.' His voice starts to shake. 'They had padlocks on all of the kitchen cupboards that they told me were to make sure that I wasn't stealing food. But there was one large cupboard that they kept empty and when they got really mad at me, they'd lock me inside.'

'How horrible,' is all I can say as tears stream down my cheeks. The thought of him as a young boy being so scared and unloved is confronting and makes my childhood seem like paradise. Guilt and sadness fill me.

'Sometimes I'd be in there for hours.' As he continues to tell his story, he never once takes his eyes off the road. 'One night, after I'd been in the cupboard for about an hour, my parents got into an argument. My dad was yelling so loudly that I started to feel safer in the cupboard then being out there with them. The yelling didn't go on very long. The gunshots were the last thing I heard.'

I don't know whether to look at him or stare at the road. I don't know what to say or what to do. I'm crippled by his story and my heart is aching for him. All I want to do is reach out and hug him and tell him that he's safe, but he's like a statue driving the ute determinedly along the highway. There is no emotion on his face.

'I don't know how long I was there after it went silent, but it was Del's face I saw when the cupboard opened. She had the face of an angel. She simply scooped me up in her arms. The moment she hugged me I finally knew what safe felt like.'

'She has the healing touch of Jesus,' I mutter without realising it.

'Oh my god.' Ethan bursts out laughing. 'Don't you ever let her hear you say that!'

My cheeks burn with embarrassment.

'Oh, hey,' he says, squeezing my knee again. 'I didn't mean to upset you. I want you to feel like you can talk to me. You and I have a lot in common. We've both been saved by Del.'

I find his comment confusing. 'Del isn't saving me from anything. She was forced to take me in after I killed my parents,' I blurt.

'What did you say?'

'It's my fault my parents are dead,' I say with a sob.

'That can't be true.' His tone is soothing. 'It was a car accident. You're not responsible.'

'I wished they were dead,' I confess, tears pouring down my cheeks. I'm so consumed in my grief I don't even notice that Ethan has stopped the car.

'It's okay,' he whispers, rubbing my back. 'I wished mine were dead too.'

I lift my head to face him. 'You did?'

He nods.

'But my parents weren't really that bad. They just wanted the best for me. They wanted to protect me from all the evils in the world.'

'That sounds really nice,' he says softly. 'Tell me more.'

'They believed that living your best life under the eyes of God, helping those in need and being a pure person are the key to the afterlife. They believed it was their job to teach me how to be a good person and not be swayed by those who live the way of the devil.'

'Did they have a lot of rules?'

'No more than other parents I would imagine.' I find myself defending them.

'Huh,' Ethan mutters. 'Mine only had one. Don't tell me you're hungry.' He lets out a bitter laugh.

'How can you joke about that? You were in a terrible situation.'

'Yes, I was,' he says firmly. 'But I didn't know any different. To me, it was normal and everyone lived that way.'

'My situation wasn't the same,' I snap, finding his implication slightly offensive.

'All I'm saying is that sometimes we don't know our options until someone else shows them to us. If Del hadn't come that day, I would have been carted off to a foster home and ended up a number in the system,' he explains. 'If your parents were still alive, what would happen to you if you strayed off the path they mapped out for you?'

His question makes me feel uncomfortable, like he's baiting me. I know I can't answer him. I am not permitted to talk about the laws of our church with an outsider. I want to tell him that I'm still bound to the path. That I'm still under the control of the elders and I'm struggling with the guilt of knowing that I've already strayed. To think about all the things I've done that are against their teachings makes me feel sick.

'Something tells me you've been locked in your own cupboard,' he says quietly.

'It's more like a movie,' I whisper.

'What?'

'My life is more like a movie. Like what you were describing earlier. I felt like I was watching my life unfold before me. Like the storyline was already decided and I have no control over how it ends.' I finally let go. The words seem to flow out of me like a deep exhale bringing with it a wave of relief. 'But that night I changed things. By wishing them dead and sending them off angry in the car, I altered my path and I don't know what to do.'

'Maybe that's why you've ended up with Del. She's not your typical foster parent, you know.'

As he wipes the tears from my eyes, I begin to feel a sense of relief. Like things are going to be okay. Ethan returns the ute to the road. I take a deep breath and sit back in my seat as I exhale.

For the rest of the trip, we sit in a very comfortable silence.

Chapter 21

It's the evening before Ethan is due to go back to Sydney. After finishing dinner, Del suggests that Ethan and I do the dishes together.

'I'm going to have an early night,' Del announces. 'My aching bones are longing for a good night's rest.' She kisses us both on the cheek before slipping me a sideways look. 'Enjoy your evening. You both deserve it.' She winks then leaves the room.

After the kitchen is clean, Ethan offers me a drink as we sit by the fire.

'I seem to recall you are partial to whiskey,' Ethan says as the flames flicker in his eyes.

He hands me an ice filled glass and sits next to me on the lounge. I sip the amber liquid hoping to calm my nerves. Nerves that I don't understand. I have no reason to feel nervous around him. We've just spent almost every moment of the week together. It's just that, in the flicker of the fire light with him sitting so close to me, I can barely breathe.

We sit in silence, staring at the fire, listening to the crackling of the wood. As I finish my drink, Ethan pours me another. I'm feeling more comfortable in our silence. In our rhythm. Watching the flames dance around the room and on his face, I feel a stillness I haven't experienced before. I feel at home.

That night, in my dreams, I experience my first kiss.

I awake to the whistle of the kettle and the smell of sizzling bacon wafting through the house. It's a bit of a struggle to convince myself to vacate the warmth of the sheets and get my slightly sore and tired body up and moving. After slipping into my ugg boots and wrapping up in my snuggly dressing gown, I make my way down the hall. I can hear Ethan singing the INXS song he played for me earlier in the week.

I stand in the doorway and watch him strike a pose at each pause while continuing to stir the scrambled eggs. His hips jerk to each side underneath navy flannel pyjama leggings. The sight makes me giggle.

'Are you demonstrating the slick moves of the Sharpie gang?' I tease.

He turns to face me and with a quick flash of a smile, breaks into a series of erratic moves across the kitchen floor. At one point, he's slightly bent over with his arm moving up and down like he's pumping water from a well while shuffling his feet, lifting his knees and moving backwards. My giggle explodes into laughter that starts to hurt my ribs.

Ethan grabs my hands and pulls me onto his makeshift dance floor, insisting I try it out for myself. My pathetic attempt results in the two of us crashing to the floor in a heap of laughter.

'What exactly are you two cooking in here?' We both stop and look up at Del. It's only a moment before she starts laughing at the sorry sight of us.

'I think we may all need a day of rest,' Del announces as we sit down for breakfast. 'Ethan why don't you stay another night and enjoy this beautiful place without having to do any work.'

She really wants a day to read a book and suggests that Ethan and I go for a hike or have a picnic by the river.

Ethan agrees in an instant.

'I'd been wanting to hike up to the top of the northern boundary. How about we take the quad bike to the edge of the paddock and walk up from there?'

'Sounds good,' I say, an underlying wave of butterflies churning up my insides.

While I clean up the breakfast dishes, Ethan packs a picnic for us. As he doesn't know how long it will take us to hike up there, he thinks it's best to be prepared. He even packs a rug into the daypack so we have something to sit on that will protect us from the scratchy long grass.

After Ethan straps the daypack onto the quad bike, he puts himself in the driver's position, leaving me enough room to sit behind him.

'Best to put your arms around me,' he says. 'Safer that way.'

My heart picks up its pace as I hop onto the bike and put my hands lightly on his waist.

'That won't do,' he says, grabbing my hands and pulling them around his chest.

'You've got to hold on tight.'

So that's what I do. I hold on as tight as I can, resting my head against his back, listening to the thumping of his heart.

As we take off on our adventure, his heartbeat is drowned out by the revving of the bike's engine. But in my mind, I can still hear it. My veins course with exhilaration and excitement as my grip on Ethan remains strong. I swear it only takes a second to reach our destination and I'm stricken with sadness. I try not to make my sulking too noticeable as I slink off the back of the bike. Knowing that we have a return journey ahead of us brings me a little solace.

We set out on our hike up to the tallest point on Del's property. Ethan tells me how he loves to seek out the highest points he travels to in order to get a good idea of what the place really looks like.

'I reckon to get to know a place you've gotta see it from above,' he says as he leads me through dense bushland. As we get higher, the trees become thinner and easier to navigate through. 'Regrowth,' Ethan comments. 'This place would have been stripped bare at the turn of last century. They used to ringbark the trees to make room for cattle or use it if they needed the wood to build.' He drags his hand along the bark of a medium-sized eucalypt. 'Pretty amazing to think of what this place would have looked like before the white man came.'

What I learn about Ethan as he talks me through the hike, is how connected he is to the land. Not just his connection to farming and cultivation, but his connection to the plants and animals. His passion to become a lawyer isn't just to help farmers but also to protect the land from being destroyed by human nature. He's unlike any boy I've ever met before. He has a beautiful balance of masculinity and sensitivity that I find alluring. I spend most of the day listening to him and learning about the world outside of Gloucester. A world I so desperately want to explore. There's just something about learning about it from him that makes me want to explore it all with him.

That evening Del joins us for a drink by the fire and tells us stories of when she was 'young, wild and free', as she explains it, before she got married. To me, her life is like a children's storybook, full of colour and creativity.

'I remember going to the very first Mardi Gras in Kings Cross. It was insane,' she recalls. I, of course, have no idea what she's talking about, but I'm not willing to admit it. Instead, I continue to listen intently hoping she'll reveal enough details to help me understand. 'I'd never seen anything like it. I mean, I'd been to many protests but this was something else entirely. Having friends who are part of the LBGTQ community, it was important for me to stand alongside them in their fight for equality.'

I still have no idea what she's going on about and the look on my face must be a telltale, as Ethan pipes up with a little insight. 'She's talking about the gay community. There was a time when same sex relationships were illegal.'

'Oh, sorry, dear.' Del turns to me. 'I should've explained better. The very first Mardi Gras was all about raising awareness of the lack of equal rights for the community, but instead, it turned into a night of police brutality and more public prosecution of an already dehumanised group of people.'

'It sounds horrible,' I say, unsure of how I feel about the conversation. My brain is working overtime, filled with the words of my parents. They taught me that homosexuality is a sin. There is absolutely no room for that kind of behaviour within my church and when it's talked about, the statements are always laced with venom and hatred.

'Disgusting', is how my parents referred to it.

'Crazy, isn't? To think that it was a crime to love someone.' Del shakes her head. 'It was such a sad time to see this amazing, colourful, charismatic, creative group of people ridiculed and treated like sub-humans. It lit a fire in me and I continued to help in the fight for their rights. It took too long, but it finally happened.' I can see a tear in her eye. 'It's important that us privileged folk work hard to help lift up those who are trodden upon by the ignorant masses.'

I know she's not referring to me directly, but it's hard not to feel that way. I'm one of them. I'm one of the people who've been raised under a shroud of beliefs cast upon me by my parents. I bow my head in shame. Shame for my parents and those in my church. Del's story rattles inside me as I begin to realise that the people I call family, are among those who cast judgement on others.

'Hey now,' Del whispers in my ear. 'Are you okay?'

I don't know how to answer. I fear if I open my mouth, I'll be sick.

'You're not responsible for how others behave,' she says softly. 'You are only responsible for your own actions.'

I bury my head in her chest. She squeezes me tight. A rush of whiskey fills my head and things start to blur.

'Well, I think that's enough for tonight, eh Sara.' She smiles. 'How about I help you to bed?'

Her offer is greatly appreciated and I'm pretty sure I'm asleep before I hit the pillow.

Chapter 22

The long days of physical work in the brisk autumn air and evenings of whiskey have taken their toll and Ethan is long gone before I make my way to the kitchen in the morning.

'He had class today, so he left early,' Del says as I enter. 'He didn't want to wake you.' Although she doesn't really need to explain, I'm happy she's told me and even happier that he thought of me before he left.

'I need to head into town today to pick up a few things. Interested?'

Relieved to know it would be another day of rest, I happily agree to keep Del company.

It's been a little while since Del and I have had some quality alone time together and I'm looking forward to it. I love spending time with her. She always makes me feel special and important. For the majority of the drive into town, she asks me about John. For some reason, I'm now finding the topic of John a bit tricky and a little weird to discuss with her. It's almost like I'm betraying her. Don't get me wrong, she's not said or done anything to make me feel like she doesn't like him. I just get the feeling she likes the idea of me and Ethan better. Possibly because she's told me how special she thinks I am and how she hopes that Ethan will end up with someone like me.

'You have a tender nature about you that is endearing,' Del had said to me one afternoon a couple weeks earlier. 'You're an old spirit.'

At the time, I had no idea what she was talking about. I'm as naive as they come. My parents had made sure I knew very little about what happens in the world outside of our house. And even though I'm taught about history and things at school, my parents had somehow planted a seed in me that has stopped me from understanding it. The teachings all seem like big fairy tales set in a Godless world where men fight for greed and power.

But the more time I spend with Del, the more I'm beginning to see things differently. She lives in a world where people make choices without praying for the right path to choose. A world where it's okay to be around people who think differently than you, who believe differently than you, and who live differently than you. Whether she believes in God or not, something has brought our paths together at a time in my life when I'm struggling to find my direction and understand my position in the world. Del sees something in me that she calls an 'old spirit' and I see something in her that makes me believe I can achieve anything.

Other than picking up some chook food and stopping by the cattle agent for a quick chat about outstanding payments, the only other place on Del's list is the bank. I've never been in a bank before. Father always said it was a place for men's business, so when we arrive outside the building, I freeze in my tracks. Del has her hand on the front door before she notices I'm no longer at her side.

'You comin'?'

I meekly shuffle up behind her and follow her in through the big glass door. I expect to be walking into a vortex filled with the buzzing of telephones and the chattering of men in suits. But instead, the place is still and quiet. There's a short queue of people lined up towards a counter where two women are serving. Not only are women working here but there are only women with their children in the queue. The thud of a rather large rubber stamp causes me to grab Del's arm.

'You okay?'

'Yep.' I swallow, too scared to tell her the truth.

I'm terrified. I feel like I'm going to be struck down by the wrath of God for disobeying my father. It's like he's looming over me with disapproval.

As Del moves up in the line, I stick really close to her, my hand still gripping her arm.

'It's okay, love,' Del whispers as she pats my hand.

Although her words are comforting, there's a part of me that isn't going to feel completely safe until we are outside of the building. It's not that I haven't broken my parents' rules before, it's just that there's something about this place that makes me uneasy. It's so cold and sterile and full of people barely talking to each other.

It's eerily kind of like being in a church building, hence my fear of retribution.

We finally get to the counter after what feels like forever, and I wait at the side while Del completes her transaction. As I'm looking around the room, taking in all the details from the dark red carpet to the brown polyester chairs, Mr and Mrs Vale walk in. They seem to have an air of royalty about them as Mr Chapman, the bank manager, comes rushing to greet them. I know he's the bank manager because he's one of the few people my father would take time out to talk to if we ever came across him in the street. And my father would always point out the fact that he was the bank manager as if it was a really important thing for me to know.

'Mr Vale, Mrs Vale lovely to see you again,' Mr Chapman says, shaking Mr Vale's hand. 'Would you like to join me in my office?'

'Oh, not me, Mr Chapman,' Mrs Vale said. 'Business talk is no place for a woman.'

Although the comment is made to Mr Chapman, Mrs Vale's eyes are locked in on Del as she says it.

Del just so happens to be finishing up at the counter and is turning to leave. 'Come on, my dear,' Del says, offering me her arm. 'Our business is done here,' she emphasises just loud enough for everyone in the room to hear.

As we walk by the Vale's, Del pauses briefly. 'Always a pleasure to see you, Arthur and Margaret.' And we continue on our way.

Although I don't turn to see Mrs Vale's expression, I can feel her eyes burning a hole in our backs.

'Some people are so rude,' I hear Mrs Vale say as the door closes behind us.

'Indeed they are,' Del says to me as we walk to the ute. 'Some people think their shit doesn't stink.'

We both break out in laughter. Del always knows the best way to relieve the tension.

Chapter 23

Returning to school for the final term of the year is both exhilarating and terrifying. Part of me can't wait for the end of high school, while the other part is nervous because this term will determine whether or not I'm eligible for university.

On the first day back, Ms Davis tells me that we'll know by the end of the week if I'm able to sit the exams. When Friday finally arrives my chest is tight and my stomach is full of knots. It's crazy to think that eight months ago I had no idea what I was going to do after school, and now I'm seriously considering furthering my education and leaving Gloucester. Just to be sure that I don't chicken out, Ms Davis and Mr Charles helped me complete a few university applications before the end of last term.

I take a deep breath and head to Ms Davis's room. We agreed that I would continue to come to school in term four to study. I'll be the only year twelve student at school, given that we're all free to study at home before the exams start in a couple of weeks. But that doesn't worry me. In fact, I'm looking forward to it because it means there are less people around to judge me.

Tension continues to build as I approach the door. I take a deep breath before I enter the room that holds my destiny. Ms Davis is standing in the middle of the room waiting for me, along with Mr Martin. The sight of him makes my knees quiver and I struggle to approach them.

'There you are, Sara,' Ms Davis beams. 'We were just talking about you.'

I try to swallow, but my mouth is far too dry.

'Yes, Miss Johnson,' Mr Martin says in his usual monotone way. 'It seems that I was mistaken about your ability to sit the exams. According to your teachers, you have met all the requirements, and therefore, you are eligible.'

Without another word, he leaves the room. The moment the door closes behind him, Ms Davis bursts out with excitement. 'You're in!'

'Oh wow! How? How did you change his mind?'

'Well, had Mr Martin actually spoken with the head teachers, like he said he did, he would have known that you were keeping up with all the class work.' Her face is glowing with the biggest smile I've ever seen. 'All your teachers got together and insisted that he sign off on your work.'

'Wow,' is about all I can manage to say.

I'm not used to people standing up for me. Being the weird kid and the odd one out is all I've never known at this school, so to think that all my teachers rallied for me is hard to comprehend.

'All your hard work has paid off. None of them can ignore that.'

'Thank you,' I say.

'My pleasure,' Ms Davis responds as she pulls me in for a big hug.

During my bus ride to the Edwards' house that afternoon, I let myself fantasise about going to uni. I picture myself living on my own, making my own decisions about everything, and not worrying about the church group finding out. So long as I'm living in Gloucester, there is no way for me to truly be free. Del made a promise to the Edwards that she would make sure I went to their house every Friday night. If I decide that I no longer want to go, I'll be putting her in an impossible situation. I know that Del will support me with whatever choice I make, but I don't want her to be forced to break her promise.

If I go to university, far away from Gloucester, I can no longer be forced to attend, and I'll finally be free. I'm certain that wherever I end up going won't be like Gloucester and that the gossip won't feed back to the church group. They won't be able to find out everything that I'm doing. The thought of having the freedom to discover what it is that I'm actually interested in instead of being told what I have to be interested in is almost unfathomable. Even though living with Del has introduced me to a completely different world, I'm still bound to the rules of the church. I may break a few of them from time to time, but at the end of the day, I'm still terrified of being banished.

Even though I know that I have to seek approval from the elders to leave to attend university, I'm not going to let it stop me from imagining what it would be like. My thoughts shift to Ethan. He once mentioned eating take-away from a restaurant that served food from Thailand. It sounded so exotic and spicy. When he spoke about how much chilli was in the food and how his eyes welled up, it was kind of funny but exciting. I wonder what it tasted like. There's a Chinese restaurant in town, but my parents always refused to eat from there, saying something about how they used dog meat instead of beef. I'm not sure where they heard that from, but they were so convinced that every time a dog went missing my father would make a comment about it.

'*The Asians must be running a new special,*' he would say while my mother laughed.

It was usually said in the company of other members of our church, who also seemed to think the comment was funny. But it never really sat right with me and always made me feel uncomfortable and embarrassed. It made me wonder how people who live in the light of the Lord could be so judgemental of others. Thinking of it now makes me feel physically ill.

When John arrives the next morning, Del beats me to the door.

'It's so lovely to see you, John,' I hear Del say as I enter the lounge room. 'Why don't you stay and have a cuppa; you're not in a hurry are you? It'd be wonderful to catch up.'

Even though John has been coming by most Saturdays for the past few months, Del hasn't really spent that much time with him. I usually greet him at the door and say goodbye to Del before she gets a chance to come to see him.

John is incredibly shy around people he doesn't know and I can see the hesitation in his eyes.

'We really should get going,' I interject, trying to give him an out.

'Oh come on, Sara. There's no need to be in such a hurry,' Del says as she gestures for John to come inside.

'It's alright, Sara.' He smiles awkwardly. 'We've got time.'

'Excellent,' Del says and leads us to the kitchen.

I can tell by the look in John's eye that he's hoping the conversation won't delve too deeply into his future hopes and dreams. Although I've told him that Del isn't like the other adults in our lives, I don't think he actually believes me. That's the thing about being raised in the type of environment we have been, adults are the people you fear the most. And for John and I, who've always been a little on the outside, adults are also the people you trust the least.

'So tell me about yourself.' Del starts the conversation boldly.

'Um,' John spurts.

'John works on his parents' farm,' I pipe up.

'I'm sure John is capable of speaking for himself,' Del says as she passes John and me each a cup of tea. 'Now, John, what was it you were going to say?' She leans in with curiosity. Her interrogative techniques are making me uncomfortable and all I want to do is grab John by the arm and pull him out of there.

'Um, I'm not really sure,' John finally manages to say.

'It's okay, dear,' Del says as she places her hand on his forearm. 'You're still young. No need to have any major life plans at your stage.'

I can't tell if she's being mean or showing genuine care. I mean she's never really said anything bad about John, but I know she's not interested in the fact that I'm dating him.

"Okay, that's enough,' I blurt as my discomfort gets the best of me.

I grab John and pull him towards the front door.

'Hey there, Sara,' Del calls from behind us. 'There's no need to be rude.'

'I'm not the one being rude,' I bark back at her.

'What's got into you? I'm just trying to make John feel at home here.'

'Yeah, Sara,' John comments. 'What's wrong?'

'I just think that it's time to go,' I say and proceed out the door, pulling John behind me.

'Sara,' John says, pulling back against my momentum.

I let go of his arm and storm out.

He follows me. 'Sara, stop!'

I ignore him and jump into the car. I'm so angry, I'm not sure if I'm going to scream or cry. As John gets into the driver's seat, I bury my face in my hands.

'What was that all about?' he asks.

A wave of shame rushes over me and my eyes explode with tears.

'Hey, it's okay,' John says calmly as he starts the car.

After we're off the property, I sniff back my tears. 'It's just that I didn't want you to feel like you had to explain yourself to her.'

'I didn't feel that way.' His tone is gentle. 'Del's a really lovely person.'

'But she was interrogating you.'

'No she wasn't.' He remains calm.

'Yes she was,' I snap. 'She's just like my mother.' My voice is getting louder.

'All adults are the same. They want to control us.'

John pulls the car over to the side of the road. My anger doesn't cease. Instead, it intensifies.

'She sounded just like her. The way she judged you. The way she disapproved of you,' I spit.

My head fills with the voice of my mother and I'm thrown back to a time when John had come by our house to pick up something for his father. It was a couple of weeks before the accident. I remember my mother inviting him in for a cup of hot chocolate and some of her freshly baked Anzac biscuits. My mother had an agenda, just like Del did, except she wasn't really interested in what John wanted to do with his life, she simply wanted to know all the latest gossip about his family.

'I hear your sister's having a baby.' If there was one thing my mother lacked, it was tact. John shifted in his chair. 'It's just that Kim, Mrs Harris's daughter, the one that works at the medical centre, said your sister came in for an appointment and brought her husband along.'

Mother stopped for a moment waiting for a reaction from John, but he just sat there in silence, looking only at his teacup.

'Surely, she's pregnant, why else would her husband be there?'

Still nothing.

'It's okay John, I won't tell anyone.' She softened as she patronisingly patted his hand.

'Isn't your father waiting for you,' I broke in, trying to throw him a lifeline.

'Huh?' he muttered.

'Didn't you say your father wants you back home by ten-thirty?' This was in the early stages of me testing out my ability to lie, so I remember encouraging myself to stay strong and not let my voice waver. I also hoped that he would quickly pick up on it and help me with the convincing part.

It took a moment for him to catch on, but once he did, he bolted up from his chair. 'That's right, I almost forgot,' John said sharply. 'You'll have to excuse me, Mrs Johnson, I don't wish to keep my father waiting.'

'Of course not John,' was the only response she could give. To disobey one's father was like an act against God, himself. She'd been preaching that one to me since the day I was born.

A few days later it came out that Karen had suffered a miscarriage at sixteen weeks. She'd been having trouble with the pregnancy since the beginning, and the doctor had recommended she wait a little longer before sharing the news. Karen and her husband were at the medical centre that day for a follow-up appointment to determine if she'd be able to fall pregnant again. I found out from my mother. She didn't ever apologise or even offer condolences to John, she simply remarked to me how she figured Karen was pregnant and perhaps if she had been more open with the church group about it, she would never have lost the baby. My mother's lack of compassion was sometimes hard to swallow.

As the memory ripples through my mind, John places his hand on mine.

'It's okay,' he says, trying to console me.

'I'm sorry.' Throwing my arms around him, I bury my face in his shoulder.

'Del's nothing like your mother,' he whispers. And with that John lets it drop.

After having some time to cool down, I know that I was completely out of line and owe Del a huge apology. That fact that John lets it all lie is one of the things I like most about our relationship. He knows that when I'm ready to talk I will, just like I know that about him.

We find a shady spot by the river for our picnic. John's mum had filled a basket with sandwiches and cakes, which we enjoy in comfortable silence. It's a lovely afternoon with the sun highlighting the smooth stones resting on the bottom of the riverbed. Birds come and go by the edge of the water, stealing a quick drink before taking flight again. Every so often I catch a glimpse of a fish or two making their way upstream. Although I'm not really interested in knowing the intricate details of each animal species, I can easily waste countless hours watching these amazing creatures go about their business.

I'm completely enjoying the beauty around me and have very little concept of how much time has passed. I'm quite content with my front row seat to nature's spectacular show.

'I'm gay,' John blurts.

The words rip through my head distorting as they go.

'What?' I turn to face him.

'I'm gay,' John says again, without dropping his gaze.

I don't know what to say. I mean, I know what the words mean but I don't know what they mean to me.

'You're the only one I've told. You're the only one who'll understand.' He shifts, finally dropping his eyes from mine. 'You know, because of your relationship with Georgia.'

'What?' I have no idea what he's talking about.

'Your girlfriend, Georgia.'

'My girlfriend? What do you mean?' I'm baffled by what he's suggesting.

'That's why you understood why I needed you to cover for me, right? So, my parents didn't know that I was in a relationship with a guy?' John attempts to clarify his own confusion. 'You knew, right?'

I have no idea what to say. Clearly, we had misunderstood each other somewhere along the line.

He starts to retreat, packing up the lunch with his head down.

'I shouldn't have said anything. Let's just forget it.'

The drive seems to take place in a surreal state of static motion as John's words continuously repeat in my mind. I'm stuck in a cloud of confusion that makes it near impossible to notice anything that's happening around me. By the time the fog starts to clear, I'm alone on the front porch and John is long gone. He barely even stopped to let me out before he took off.

His words ripple through my thoughts and I try to grasp onto what happened.

I hadn't thought about Georgia in months. I've been so busy with school. Which is interesting considering how important she had been to me. She came into my life at a time when I felt so alone and alienated from my peers. She opened my eyes up to a world outside of my family and church group, a world I didn't even know existed. I felt things with her that I didn't understand. Maybe it was an attraction or maybe it was an infatuation. I haven't really thought about it or what she meant to me.

She's my first love, that I know. But I'm unclear about what type of love it is that I felt for her. She represents a freedom I long for but am too afraid to reach for. And now she's gone, and life continues for me as it had before but with a different coloured light shining in the background. I'm able to see things I haven't noticed before. I'm feeling things I haven't felt before. Georgia opened me up. That's what John had seen.

And now he'd shared something with me that we both knew will never be accepted by his family. It's our belief that God only sanctions relationships between a man and a woman. Anything outside of that was an abomination with a one-way ticket to eternal damnation. John trusts me with not only his deepest, darkest secret but his life. If I tell anyone about what he confessed to me, it will mean he'll be banished from his family. No one can ever know, which means I have no one to talk to about it. The funny thing is, I'd be able to talk to Georgia about it. I pull my mobile phone out of my bag and the selfie she took of us the day she left pops up on the screen. A tear rolls down my cheek as I touch her face.

'I miss you,' I whisper. My heart aches. 'I wish you were here.'

Chapter 24

It's clearly awkward for both John and me when we inevitably come across each other the following Friday night. He completely avoids eye contact during the service and doesn't go outside during the collection. Instead, I find him sitting in the kitchen with some of the women busying themselves around him as they clean up from the meal. I sit next to him, but he pretends not to notice.

'I had a lovely time on Saturday.' I try to break the tension by letting him know that his secret is safe.

My tactic seems to be working as he turns to look at me. I greet his gaze with a smile. His reaction remains sombre, but I insist on holding my grin until either my cheeks spasm or he cracks.

A moment later, he returns the gesture and I'm able to release my aching face. We start talking about pointless things until Del shows up to collect me.

'How are things going with you and John?' she enquires shortly after we start the journey home.

When I went to her to ask for forgiveness after treating her so badly when John was over, she told me I had nothing to apologise for and that was that. We haven't spoken about it since, nor about John.

'You seem to be getting very close.'

Lying to my parents was something that I had to master in order to continue to live in their house. And even though I know I don't need to with Del, when it comes to John's secret, it's not my story to tell.

'He's so wonderful, Del,' I say with enthusiasm, to keep her off the scent. 'We went for a lovely picnic by the river. Everything was perfect.' This lying thing is something I've become really good at.

'Oh.' She sounds surprised. I suspect it has something to do with her desire to see me spending more time with Ethan. 'That's nice to hear.' Her words are encouraging, but her tone suggests something else.

'Don't you think he's right for me?' I push, hoping that maybe she'll admit her bias against John.

'Um…'

'Why not? Do you think I deserve someone in my life who's nice to me?' I continue to charge.

'Of course I do, Sara. I'm just not sure—'

'He's right for me?' I cut her off. 'You mean like Ethan would be?'

I can feel anger brewing inside of me. I'm so sick of adults making decisions about my life and the thought of Del making plans for my future is really putting me off.

'That's enough, Sara,' she says sternly. 'That is not what I meant. You're free to make your own decision about your life and who you want to spend your time with.' Hearing her words makes me feel bad for my outburst. 'Far be it from me to tell anyone who they should be in a relationship with. Having been on the receiving end of that playing card, I won't wish that upon anyone.'

'Sorry,' I mumble in shame.

'How about we shift this mood and play some music, what do you reckon?' Del says, tapping the volume button on the retro car-stereo to let the sounds of rock and roll fill the ute.

I spend the rest of the ride home listening to Del sing at the top of her lungs, mostly getting the lyrics right.

Chapter 25

Mrs Vale has asked me to help with the CWA canteen at the Harris's annual bull sale. It's an event that has been taking place for decades, and for many farmers across the state, they simply must attend. The Harris bulls have an impressive reputation with a long-line of direct lineage to prize beasts, and for many farmers, it's worth the drive. For Gloucester residents, it's the social event of the year. One that you want to be seen at. In the past, I had been expected to sit in the shed with my mother and the other women. It was important to my mother that we were seen there together.

But this time, I will be at the CWA booth serving the hungry farmers and cattle truck drivers before the auction starts and won't be joining the rest of the women until the official activities are underway. The booth is flat out from the moment we finish setting up until the auctioneer calls for all the bidders. I'm exhausted by the time I'm able to sit down on a haybale and am enjoying my rest when Trish Harris approaches me.

'CWA ladies workin' you too hard?' Her question is laced with a sting of sarcasm. 'I don't know how you do it, hangin' out with all those old biddies?'

We both know that my acceptance into the CWA cohort is uncharacteristic based on my family's lack of historical connection to the community, and despite her last name, she's yet to be included. It may appear that she thinks the whole thing is lame, but in actual fact, it's like a rite of passage. One that has been bestowed upon me, the weird kid, and not her, a Harris descendant.

Choosing a spot beside me, Trish makes herself at home.

'Is John here today?' she asks as if it's a proper question, but like everything else, it's rhetorical.

'I haven't seen him,' I respond, knowingly playing her game.

She knows John is here. He's the heir of one of the largest cattle stations in the Gloucester region, not to mention the additional properties his family holds in Tamworth.

'Is everything okay between you two?'

And there it is, the real reason she's decided to take time to talk to me. I've been a little on guard from the moment I spotted her sashaying towards me in her RM Williams jeans held in place with an oversized shiny silver belt.

Trish was in John's year at school and it's clear she feels she has more of a right to be seen with him than I do. She comes from old Gloucester blood and has been raised to believe that certain families are meant to be connected. She acts as though she should be the one to marry someone like John instead of me. I'm an outsider. Not from a royal Gloucesterian bloodline. She's always been dismissive of me and I'm never really sure how to respond to her.

'You can talk to me,' she says quietly as she puts her condescending arm around me. 'It can be hard to hold a relationship together with a guy like John.'

I'm not sure what she's implying. Does she know John's secret? My heart begins to flutter. My mouth goes dry.

'I know what it's like to date an older guy, always wondering if you're giving him all he needs.'

I feel a mix of relief and discomfort. I shift in my seat causing her to remove her arm from my shoulder. Instead of engaging, I simply stare at my feet, hoping she'll just go away.

'There you are, Sara!' John's voice is like an angel sent straight from heaven. 'I've been looking everywhere for you.' He comes over and sweeps me up in a big hug, almost knocking Trish off the hay bale.

'Hi John,' Trish pipes up. 'It's so good to see you.'

As John releases me from his bear hug, she nuzzles her way closer to him.

'Nice to see you too, Trish.' He dismisses her as he grabs my hand and pulls me to his side. 'I have something I want to show you,' he says, keeping his attention focussed to me. 'If you'll excuse us, Trish.' He doesn't even wait for her response before he pulls me out of there. 'You okay?' he asks as soon as we are out of earshot.

'Yes, thank you,' I whisper, still a bit shaken.

I've never been good at talking with people I don't know very well, especially people who make me feel like I'm less important than they are. Trish has a way of shrinking people when she walks into a room. She's also very good at getting people to disclose information to her without realising it. It's knowing all these things about her that got me so tongue-tied.

'It looked like she was giving you a hard time. You looked like you needed rescuing.'

'She was asking about you. It caught me off guard. I wasn't sure what to say.'

'What did you say?' His question is laced with nervous concern.

'Nothing. Then you showed up.'

Satisfied with my answer, John releases my hand. We slip into silence, something we normally both feel comfortable in, but not this time. Our unfinished business is sitting between us like a giant elephant, yet neither of us are in a position to talk about it. We both know it can't happen here, surrounded by virtually the entire community, but we both know the discussion needs to happen soon.

'How about we head to the beach?' he suggests, finally breaking the deadlock. 'Maybe we can grab some dinner?'

Regardless of our seemingly impossible situation, he's still one of my favourite people in the whole world and I'm no match for his pleading eyes.

'Alright then, I think it's about time we got out of here.'

Chapter 26

During the drive to the coast, John fills me in on the auction, reliving each sale with as much vigour and excitement. His impressions of the auctioneers are hilarious, complete with over-dramatised gestures.

'Gordon got so worked up during the final sale, I thought he was going to blow his top.' John laughs. 'As the auctioneer got closer to the end of taking bids, he nearly climbed over the top of the gate. I think he was trying to get closer to the bull.'

Gordon is a farm hand on John's family's farm and regularly assists them at auctions. He had his eye on one of the beasts and was determined to win the bid. I can picture his ginger mullet flailing behind him as he shakes back and forth on the gate yelling his bids. I laugh so hard it brings tears to my eyes.

John pulls up next to the beach and we get out for a walk. It's a lovely spring afternoon and the sun is low in the sky, casting brush strokes of pink and mauve across the clouds.

As we make our way along the beach, John squeezes my hand.

'Sara, you are my favourite person in the world and I love spending time with you,' he says.

'I love spending time with you too.' It's true. I always have fun when I'm with him and he makes me laugh. 'You are definitely one of my favourite people.' I smile at him.

'I'm happy to hear you say that,' he says softly as he slows his pace. 'I was thinking that maybe we should get married.' His delivery is so casual it takes me a moment to comprehend what he's suggesting.

I stop, unsure of what to say. John continues walking until he finally notices I'm no longer at his side. As he walks back towards me, I stare at him completely confused. 'Why would you want to marry me?'

'Why wouldn't I?' he questions back. 'We have fun together. We like a lot of the same things. You make me laugh. I make you laugh.'

As he lists all the things that we mean to each other, I begin to see his point. He takes my hands and squares his shoulders to mine.

'It would make my parents extremely happy,' he says.

'But would it make you happy?' I ask, already knowing the answer. *How could he ever be truly happy with me? There would always be something missing.*

'I love you, Sara,' he says, the intensity of his words reflected in his eyes. 'You know me better than anyone else. You're my best friend. Aren't you supposed to marry your best friend?'

While I stand there listening to him trying to convince me, I start thinking about Ethan. I know that I love John. He's right. He's my best friend, but he doesn't make me feel like Ethan does. If my parents were still alive, they'd never approve of me dating anyone outside of the church. Especially someone like Ethan, who's grown up with the freedom to make his own choices in life. And even though I no longer need their approval, I still need to follow the same principles in order to remain part of the church group. But my options to meet another man that will meet the approval of the elders is much better than John's. His parents will never permit him to be in a relationship with another man, let alone a same-sex marriage. He could never truly be himself.

After several minutes of silence and deep thought, I tell him I need time to think about his proposal. He says he understands and that there's no pressure. He tells me he wants me to really consider the option and what it will mean for both of us. What he's proposing is not only marriage but the chance for us to live our lives as we want without ever having to let the elders know. We'd have the best of both worlds.

As we continue our walk along the beach, he talks about moving away together to his family property in Tamworth where people don't know us and we can be ourselves without being under the watchful eye of the elders. I can tell he's put a lot of thought into it and worked out all the details in his head. All he needs is for me to agree. I'm his ticket out of this life.

During his continued sales pitch to me, we walked into town to grab a bite to eat. 'We can move right after you finish your exams. You can go to uni there and I can support you while you get your degree,' he smiles before taking a bite of his pizza.

'You've got it all figured out, don't you?' I remark, flashing him a cheeky smile.

'Before I ask you officially, I'll need to talk to my parents and ask for their permission from the elders,' he says as if the decision has been made.

'John, I don't know what to say. I need time to think about it. It's a big decision.' Panic is rising within me and I feel like things are moving far too quickly. My head starts spinning.

'I know, I know. Sorry, I'll stop,' he smiles. 'How about we talk about horses?'

Chapter 27

I have extremely restless nights trying to figure out what to do. I'm eighteen years old, and although I have very little concept of what getting married actually means, I'm pretty sure I'm supposed to be in love with the person. Not that I have any idea what that actually means. What has become clear to me over the past year is that love is not simple. It's complicated and multi-layered. It's not that I don't love John, I do, so it might not be totally wrong to marry him. He's nice to me and treats me well. *What more is there to look for?* I wonder.

But then there's Ethan. When I think of him my whole body tingles.

My tangled mess of thoughts continue rushing through my mind across the rest of the weekend and stay with me on the bus to school on Monday morning. This is not the kind of distraction I need before starting the HSC exams. I try to focus my thoughts on the English exam I'm about to take. The best way I can think of taking my mind off things is to think about Shakespeare and his unique way of commenting on history through his plays.

'Shakespeare offers a view of society that cuts right across the class system,' I say aloud, knowing the noise of the bus will drown me out. 'His plays present all kinds of characters, from lowly beggars to members of the monarchy.'

My attempt to distract myself is futile. Thoughts of John keep seeping in. I can't shake thoughts of how hard it must be for him to be stuck in a world that doesn't allow him to be who he wants to be. I want to help him get free, but I don't know if marrying him is the answer. But he's offering me a chance to leave Gloucester and try something new. Something just for me.

My mind wanders to Georgia. I think about how much I loved her yet I couldn't bring myself to go away with her. I stayed behind for John, and now he's asking me for help and I'm hesitating. I decide to put my conundrum on a metaphorical shelf until I can speak to Del. She's been married, so she can probably offer some advice. Besides, I suppose I should let her know what's going on. If I do decide to marry John, I want her to be involved.

After shelving the decision, I'm finally able to clear my mind of the matter and refocus on my pending exam. I head straight to the hall and find Ms Davis waiting for me.

'How are you feeling?' she enquires.

'Nervous,' I admit.

'You'll do great. Just remember the tips I showed you. Take a deep breath, relax, and take your time. You can do this.' She gives me a reassuring smile.

Her final words of encouragement fill me up as I make my way to a desk. It's been a long time since I've sat in a room with other students. There are groups of them in clusters dotted around the hall. The noise of their conversations echo around the hall.

The girl sitting next to me looks nervous too, keeping her head down while she unpacks her pencil case from her backpack. I don't recognise her. Maybe she's new. I watch as her loose curls brush the edges of her face. A face I'm struggling to see fully. I'm so enchanted by her movement I don't realise I'm staring until she looks back at me, revealing her freckle peppered cheeks.

I smile at her. 'Hi, I'm Sara.'

Her face screws up a little like she doesn't understand what I'm saying. I repeat myself and add in a little wave.

'Are you talking to me?' she asks.

'Yes.'

'Oh, sorry,' she says, brushing the fringe from her brown eyes. 'I'm just not used to people talking to me. I've been here three weeks and you're the first.'

'They're all too caught up with themselves to notice anyone else,' I remark. No one understands her situation better than me.

She laughs. 'I'm Jessica.'

Mrs Becker enters the hall and calls the room to order, telling us the exam is about to start. She proceeds to hand out the test papers. My brief encounter with Jessica is enough to settle my nerves. I'm able to greet Mrs Becker with a smile, which she returns as she places the exam face-down on my desk.

'Good luck,' she whispers.

My brain is so exhausted by the time I roll out of the two-hour English exam, I blindly follow Jessica to the senior centre. I haven't set foot in the place since the end of last year. I feel like an alien in my own school. I don't even know where to sit. Thankfully Jessica has been practising her own routine for the past few weeks, so I simply follow her to a corner of the room.

'Glad that's over,' Jessica says as she sits down and takes her lunchbox from her bag.

'Me too.' Letting out a deep sigh, I sit down beside her. 'English is the hardest one for me.'

'Same,' she says with a smile. 'The essays suck.'

'Definitely.'

As I take out my own lunch, I decide it's best to change the topic.

'So, where are you from?' I start. One thing I learned from Georgia is that it's okay to ask people about themselves. I was raised to not ask questions and to just sit quietly until spoken to. Georgia taught me that kind of passive behaviour is no way to make friends and she's right.

'Melbourne,' Jessica answers. 'This place is a big change from my last school. There were fourteen hundred students there.'

I've never met someone from Melbourne before. A million questions rush to my mind making it difficult to figure out which one to ask first.

'What's it like in a big city?' is what I settle on.

'You never been?'

I shake my head.

'To Melbourne or a city?'

'Neither.'

'I've never really spent time in a small town.'

It may seem a little strange, but our vastly different hometown experiences make us feel somewhat connected. We agree to share with each other all the information we know about the places we grew up in.

For me, it's like watching a movie as Jessica describes all the alleyways filled with little restaurants and cafés. When she speaks about the art galleries and museums, I'm entranced. She seems so worldly. So cultured. So refined.

'How did you end up in Gloucester?'

'My dad works for a mining company and he's been transferred here for the next few years. He usually just goes away to work, but this time my mum decided she wanted to come along. Try something new. Something quiet.'

'I think she found it,' I joke and we both laugh.

The excitement of making a new friend fills me up for the rest of the day and I feel completely elated by the time the bus drops me off, I virtually skip my way off the bus. I've been distracted with school stuff that I haven't thought once about John until, of course, I see Del.

'How did you go?' she asks the moment I open the ute door.

'Not sure I want to know.' I slump into the seat.

'I bet you did better than you think.'

I want to stick with my plan of talking to her about the situation with John, but I'm really in need of her tenderness. I decide to wait until we're back at the house.

Once we arrive, she goes straight into the kitchen to start preparing dinner. I join her under the guise of fixing myself a snack. As I fumble around the room, I start up a bit of small talk, asking her about her day. She happily chats away, telling me all about the house cleaning and laundry dramas. By the time she finishes, I'm sitting at the kitchen table with some vegemite on toast. She has her back to me as she carries on preparing dinner. I take a deep breath and decide it's time.

'Del, how did you know you were ready to get married?' The question barely leaves my lips and she's spinning around on her heels.

'Why on earth would you be asking me a question like that?' Del asks sharply. 'You're eighteen years old, there's no reason for you to be thinking about marriage.'

Her reaction puts me off slightly and I'm not sure how to continue. 'I'm just curious,' I say, trying to keep my voice light.

She comes and sits down next to me. 'Has something happened to make you wonder?'

'No,' I lie. 'It's just, I was thinking about my parents and how they got together. It made me think about how relationships form.'

'How did your parents get together?' Her tone softens.

'I've only heard the story from my mother's side. She told me that he was the best-looking guy in the church and that all the girls wanted him.'

'Is that how you see John?' Her question is valid.

'I'm not sure,' I confess.

She sits back for a moment, taking a deep breath before she returns to preparing dinner.

'I was very young when I got married,' she begins. 'And to be honest, if I had to do it all over again, I wouldn't have gone through with it.'

'Didn't you love him?'

'It's not that I didn't love him. I mean, of course I loved him. It's just that the concept of getting married when I was your age, was more of an expectation than an option.' I know exactly how she feels. 'But these days, girls have more choices and don't have to get married if they don't want to.'

In all my life, I've never heard someone say something like this before. Marriage, in my world, is an expectation. To think that there is another way is so foreign to me.

'Love comes in many forms. It's beautiful and the more you have in your life, the more it fills you up,' she says, gesturing with a potato peeler in one hand and a half-peeled potato in the other. 'But passion. Now that's rare.'

I pause for a moment, trying to work up the courage to ask my burning question. I take a bite of my toast telling myself that once I finish, I'll ask. My mouth is so dry it's like swallowing cardboard, so I tell myself that I should get a drink first. I put my plate in the sink and go to the fridge. After I finish my glass of milk, I've no more excuses.

'Del?' I start.

'Yes dear,' she responds, absentmindedly.

'How do you know the difference?' I finally blurt.

'The difference of what?' she asks without looking up.

'Between love and passion?'

There I did it. I finally got it out there.

Del stops what she's doing and turns to face me.

'You just feel it,' she simply says, her face lighting up with a huge smile.

Chapter 28

I'm woken up by a noise at my window. It sounds like hail hitting the glass. I turn on the bedside light and sit quietly for a moment trying to determine what it is. There's no wind. Everything is still. Then I hear it again. It's a pebble being thrown against my window. It scares me half to death. My heart is pounding. I work up the courage and go over to have a look. I see a moonlit John just below the verandah. He waves for me to come out. I sneak out the front door and I meet up with him near a tree.

'Is everything okay?' I ask.

'My parents know,' he says, his eyes red from tears.

'What?'

'Mr Brown saw me outside the movies with my ex-boyfriend and told my parents. He said he'd seen us holding hands. My parents confronted me about it. I didn't deny it, so they kicked me out. Told me that I was no longer their son and locked me out of the house.'

'Oh John, I'm so sorry.'

'They've left me with nothing. No car. No money. Nowhere to go.' His eyes are filled with panic and fear. 'So, I'm leaving and I want you to come with me. You're the only one who understands me.'

I don't know what to say.

'We need to go now,' he insists, grabbing my hand and pulling me away from the house.

'But I'm in my pyjamas,' I say, trying to pull back.

'It doesn't matter. We'll sort it out when we get there,' he says, dragging me to a car.

'Get where?'

Instead of answering me, he opens the passenger door and pushes me in.

'Where did you get the car?' I ask as he climbs into the driver's seat. Everything is happening so quickly I'm unable to move.

John continues to ignore my questions and drives off. He hits the gravel on the main road and speeds up. He's going so fast round the winding bends I'm sliding sideways in my seat. I clutch the door handle to try to stop the movement, but my attempts are futile. John doesn't seem to notice as he clenches the steering wheel and continues to stare straight ahead.

'Slow down,' I plead, but instead he speeds up.

I'm terrified, holding on for my life. My heart is racing and tears are streaming down my cheeks. There's a crazed look in John's eye which is accented by the eerie yellow glow of the high beams.

'They'll never accept me. I need to find a place where I can be me,' he murmurs, increasing the speed even more.

My heart pace quickens as the odometer needle passes one hundred and thirty. The frequent unmarked twists in the road beg for a maximum speed of ninety, but John doesn't seem to care.

'Look out,' I yell just as a kangaroo bounds out in front of the car.

John swerves trying to avoid it, but he's going too fast.

My head fills with the sound of squealing tyres. My nose with the smell of burning rubber. The car spins around several times before it finally flips onto its side, scraping along the road. My head bangs against the door. Everything goes dark.

I awake, drenched in sweat, and shaken to the core. I sit up in bed trying to determine if what I've just been through really happened or is just a dream. Images of John's crazed eyes and the speeding car flicker through my mind like the hazy images of a silent film. I rub my eyes. It's just a dream. *Everything is fine*, I attempt to reassure myself, trying to return my thoughts to reality.

Glancing at the clock, I notice it's time to get ready for school.

What a way to start day two of exam week, I think. Taking a deep breath, I make the difficult decision to leave my bed.

While in the shower, I try to focus on my pending maths exam, but visions of John's terrified face crowd my brain. Pushing back the feeling that his destiny rests in my hands, I make my way directly to Jessica the moment I arrive at school hoping to find refuge in a light-hearted conversation. I find her sitting in our spot eating an apple.

'Morning.' She smiles before crunching into her shiny red snack. I flop down beside her. 'You okay?' she enquires.

'Rough sleep,' I sigh. 'Hoping the exam is an easy one.' I attempt to laugh.

My need for distraction must be pretty obvious as it doesn't take her long to launch into a story about her former life in Melbourne. Soon I'm focused more on her and less on my impossible decision about a fake marriage with John. Moments later the school bell denotes the start of my second HSC exam.

When the school day finishes, I make my way to the line of buses parked out front. But before I reach my bus, I notice the coloured ute parked across the street with Del leaning against the bonnet. I head over to her.

'Aren't you a sight for sore eyes,' Del says as she gives me a desperately needed hug. It almost feels like she needs one as much as I do. 'I've had a shocking day. I'm in need of an ice cream and a few moments by the river. Care to join me?'

I don't know how she knows exactly what I need, but her showing up right then, offering some time out from the world, can't come at a better time.

I'm most of the way through my creamy, chocolate treat, enjoying our mindless chit chat, before I decide it's time to bring up the topic of John. With Del sitting on the river rock next to me, I begin to unravel the tangled mess of my emotions. As the torrent of words flood out of me, Del simply stares at the rippling water as it rushes over the mossy rocks.

'What should I do?'

She seems entranced, fixated on the water, not moving a muscle. I start to wonder if she's heard a word I've said. Or maybe she's mad at me for not talking to her about this sooner. Stuck on the latter, I decide I'll explain my delay in confiding in her. As I open my mouth to apologise, she lets out a long sigh.

Turning her eyes to mine, she says, 'Honey, I wandered down the path of doing what was expected of me and it almost killed me.' Even though she's already told me about her marriage and the reason she left her husband, she's never gone into much detail about why she got married in the first place. 'I was not much older than you when I got married,' she begins. 'It was what was expected of me. My parents' grand plan for my future. They wanted to make sure that I would be taken care of.' Her face morphs with disgust. 'Taken care of, ha! It never occurred to them that I could take care of myself and that perhaps I didn't want to get married, have children and be chained to the stove.'

I try to picture Del as a kept woman. It's so far from the type of person I know her to be.

'They never thought to ask me what I wanted,' Del remarks after taking another bite of her ice cream. 'When I look back on it now, it seems so simple. If I'd been given the opportunity to spend time figuring out what I wanted to do with my life I would have moved here years ago.'

I smile to myself realising that Del and I have a lot more in common than I thought. I find comfort in knowing that even though her childhood was just as confining as mine was, she's been able to follow her own path.

'Sara, you're eighteen years old. You've hardly had enough time in this life to see what options are out there for you.' Her tone is laced with a tinge of seriousness. 'How can you be expected to make a life-defining decision at your age? Hell, I can barely be expected to make one at my age!' Her humour returns. 'Trust your gut, honey. Something is telling you that this isn't the right fit otherwise you wouldn't be asking anyone else's opinion. If this is what you really wanted, you'd just know.'

We sit for a while longer enjoying each other's company and the remaining morsels of our ice creams. Our silence is drowned out by the fluid sound of the water tumbling over the rocks. There is something about sitting here with Del that makes me feel so at peace. Del has a way of bringing a calm to my storm. A way of clearing away the fog that riddles my thoughts. I take some time to ponder what it is that I want. There is no doubt in my mind that I love John and that I want him to be happy, and I know these feelings are mutual. But Del's got a point. Something about this situation just isn't right.

My conversation with Del is enough to get me through the rest of the week. I've made my decision and have told myself that I'll talk to John about it after my final exam. During our next Friday night together, I keep the conversation light and suggest that we get together for dinner the following weekend to celebrate me completing the HSC. He thinks it's a great idea and suggests that we head to the beach and enjoy our meal with a view of the ocean and the sand under our feet.

It's moments like this that make my decision so difficult. On one hand, John is such a thoughtful person who really listens to me. While on the other hand, I know he will never be physically attracted to me and that our love will never go beyond friendship.

When I arrive at school on the Friday of the final exam, Ms Davis is waiting for me. The moment I see her, I start to wonder if something has gone wrong. Maybe they've taken back my approval to sit the exams and all this work has been for nothing. My heart skips a beat and my palms begin to sweat as I slowly approach her.

'Don't look so terrified,' she says with a calming smile. 'I'm just here to wish you luck on your final exam.'

I exhale a huge sigh of relief.

'There's no need for you to come to my room today. It's your last day here, so just enjoy the time with your fellow classmates.'

I can see a tear in the corner of her eye and I can't help but throw my arms around her.

'Thank you for all your help,' I whisper, trying to hold back my own tears.

'No matter what happens, I just want you to know that I'm so proud of you.'

Tears of joy flow from us both as we come to terms with our monumental achievement.

'I couldn't have done it without you,' I say.

'Nonsense,' she says, wiping her eyes. 'This was all you.'

And just like that, my time in Ms Davis's care is over. And once I complete this last exam, so is my high school career. I never thought I'd feel sadness about leaving this place, but given how this year turned out, I'm finding it hard to say goodbye.

When it's all over, I board the bus for the last time beaming with pride at my own accomplishment. When I get to the Edwards' place, I get straight to work helping Mrs Edwards get everything organised. Knowing what she needs done, I'm most of the way through the set up when she comes across me in the lounge room.

'Excellent job, Sara. Your mother taught you well. You are going to make an excellent wife.'

Her comment washes over me as I'm still high from my own sense of achievement. I smile graciously and proceed to finish my task. I can't wait to celebrate with John, so I keep busy, biding time waiting for him to finish up his work on the farm.

As time slips by, the lounge room starts to fill with people and there's still no sign of John. It isn't until Mr Edwards takes his customary place in the middle of the circle that I start to think John isn't going to show. My excitement turns to concern. My concern to fear. *What if he's decided to leave town without me? What if he got sick of waiting for me to make up my mind?* As my fear shifts to panic, I hear the front door open as Mr Edwards announces the birth of our newest elder.

Calm tones of acceptance rise up and fill the room as John enters. As he makes his way towards his father, his eyes remain focused on the floor in front of him.

'Let us all acknowledge the rebirth of our brother John and accept him as a wise leader of the faith,' Mr Edwards proclaims as he lays the sacred cloth around John's shoulders. The congregation murmurs in response.

I've seen these ceremonies numerous times in the past. It's how our community celebrates the transition from childhood to adulthood. For the men, it means they are now permitted to take part in the monthly elder meetings. It's where all the decisions are made about our community and where our laws are upheld. For the women, it means you're now permitted to take part in the preparation of the food. But ultimately, it means you are ready to marry. I nervously shift in my spot.

'John, may you take pride in the honour of entering manhood and follow Jesus on a new path of righteousness and devotion.'

I keep my head down as is expected of all the women, squeezing my eyes tight as Mr Edwards rattles through the rest of the ceremony. I try to imagine what is going through John's mind. He hasn't mentioned anything about this to me. Surely, he's known about this for weeks, but he hasn't said a word. *Is this the true motivating factor behind his marriage proposal?* I can't help but wonder. Now that he is accepted into the community as a man, he'll be expected to take a wife and start a family. By doing so, he'll be able to move away and start his own community if he sees fit. This is a big deal. *Why hasn't he said anything?* I begin to doubt our closeness. Maybe he isn't the man I think he is. How can he keep something like this from me?

Once the official ceremony is over, John remains the centre of attention for the rest of the evening. There will be no chance for us to slip away to the back step, not now nor ever again. He will now be expected to remain with all the elders until the end of the evening. I tuck myself further into my corner and watch as he makes his way through the crowd of congratulators. I'm hoping to catch his eye. To get a brief peek into his thoughts. He can't hide his feelings from me. His eyes always give them away. But as he goes from one person to another, he never lifts his gaze. He never once looks for me in the room. So crafty is his plan, he manages to avoid me completely and I find myself on my way back to Karamea without so much as a moment to speak with him.

Chapter 29

As I lie in bed staring at the chips in the yellow-tinged ceiling paint, I can't help but rethink everything. For weeks I have struggled to make a decision, filled with worry about hurting him. And now, I lie here feeling hurt myself. He says I'm his best friend. The closest person to him in the whole world. The only one he can be himself with. The only one who truly understands him. Yet when faced with one of the biggest moments in his life, he doesn't speak one word about it to me. The disappointment fills my throat as tears roll down my cheeks. Hugging my knees to my chest I try to squeeze away the pain until I finally fall asleep.

My stomach is a series of knots that seem to twist tighter as Saturday morning turns into afternoon. As time creeps on, closer to when I expect John's knock on the door, I'm consumed with my own thoughts. Last night continues to feature as I scramble to make sense of what is happening. I know that the men in our church are never expected to reveal all of their thoughts and plans to the women, but I thought John was different. He convinced me that we are connected by our desire to break free of our smothering world. I've allowed myself to get swept up in the belief that he's my ticket out of here. Maybe I missed something. Perhaps he's given me a hint, but I've been so caught up in my own emotions that I haven't noticed. But the more I search my memories of our moments together, the less hope I have of finding something.

I feel foolish. I planned to share my good news with him and to tell him that I'm ready to move onto the next stage of my life with him. My crazy dream of going to university no longer seems impossible and he's the one person I can't wait to talk to about it. But he's shut me out and I'm bursting. Sharing the news with him is different than telling Del. Even though Del's been super supportive, it's just not the same.

I take to dusting every nook and cranny in my room in a futile effort to distract myself. But instead, I berate myself for my stupidity.

'I can't believe I actually considered marrying him,' I lecture myself in front of my stuffed bear, Paulie. 'I mean, I was willing to help him keep up appearances so his family wouldn't disown him.' I'm starting to get a little worked up, dusting more frantically as my speech pace quickens. 'I'm such an idiot! I was willing to put his needs ahead of mine, to make sure he was going to be okay. But what about me?' I question as I pick up Paulie and shake him in frustration. 'At what point does it become about what I want? What I need?' I collapse in a heap on my bed, letting the tears flow freely from my sleep-deprived eyes.

I awake to a brisk knock on my door. Not realising I've fallen asleep, I'm a little disoriented when Del enters.

'Are you okay?' she asks gently. 'I haven't seen or heard from you much today and I was getting concerned.'

'Sorry,' I mumble, rubbing my eyes. "I'm a little out of sorts.'

'All that stress from the exams is finally coming out.' She smiles and sits next to me on the bed. 'It's good to let your body rest.'

'What time is it?' I ask.

'Almost three. When's John coming?'

'Should be here soon. I best jump in the shower,' I declare, dragging my weary body out of bed.

'Good idea.' She stands up next to me. 'Might help liven you up a bit.'

Once I'm locked inside the bathroom, I take a moment to assess myself in the mirror. Del's right, I look like a corpse with my pale skin and black bags under my eyes. I get into the shower. The warmth of the water is barely noticeable against my numb body as I mindlessly go through my shower routine. I close my eyes in an effort to escape myself, but it makes little difference.

After I get dressed, I make my way to the kitchen table where Del's enjoying a cup of tea and reading a book.

'John was made an elder last night,' I tell her.

'Oh,' she says, putting down her book.

'I had no idea. I had no warning.'

'He didn't tell you it was happening?'

I shake my head.

'Are you okay?'

'I don't know. I thought we told each other everything.'

'Oh honey,' she sighs. 'It's not part of human nature to tell everyone everything.'

'But he should have told me about this.' I can feel my anger rising. 'It affects me.'

'What do you mean?' she enquires. And rightfully so. I really haven't told her much about how our church group works. Not only am I not permitted to talk about it with people outside the group, it's even harder to explain it in a way that doesn't make me sound crazy.

'Being an elder means that he'll now be expected to get married.'

'I see,' she says. 'And you're wondering if that's why he's asked you if you'd consider it.'

I nod and place my face in my hands.

'Do you doubt how he feels about you?' she questions, softly.

I don't know how to respond. Having not shared John's secret with her, I'm finding it difficult to navigate my way through this conversation.

'Is it possible that he has different motives for wanting to marry you?' Her question isn't what I expected and I'm not sure what she means. 'There are lots of different kinds of love in the world and all of them are special and beautiful. Unfortunately, not all forms are understood by everyone.' I lift my eyes to meet hers. My tongue is tied and I'm unable to respond. *How could she know?* I wonder. 'Other people's ignorance is no reason to get married.'

As I open my mouth in the hope of words finding a way to come out, I hear a car pull up outside.

John's arrival sparks a combination of nerves and confusion. I'm worried Del may say something to him that will make him believe that I've revealed his secret. While at the same time, I'm trying to work out how Del knows. *Maybe he said something to her,* I suggest to myself as I go out to meet him on the verandah. I figure it's the best way to avoid interactions between Del and John.

Thankfully, John's just as eager to get on our way. He pops in his favourite forbidden CD and cranks up the volume. His singing blurs in the background of my thoughts as I wrestle with our impossible situation.

There is an awkwardness between us. We avoid speaking long after we arrive at the beach. Time passes as we sit side-by-side facing the ocean. As I squish my toes in the sand and inhale the sweet burning smell of salty seaweed, I try to reconcile everything that has occurred over the past few weeks. I know that he wants an answer, but I'm not sure I'm ready to give one.

He turns to face me and asks, 'Will you be my wife?'

Taking a deep breath and closing my eyes, I respond, 'No.'

Despite my efforts to explain that I do truly love him and that he is my best friend, nothing seems to make a difference to the expression on his face. He holds a look of pure sadness. Of utter despair.

'There is something else out there for you,' I say. 'I know that deep down inside you understand why I can't marry you.' His eyes remain vacant. 'More importantly, I know you understand why you can't marry me.'

My words finally cut through enough for him to raise his gaze to mine. I hold my breath hoping he will speak. But after a moment, he disengages, seemingly lost forever. The drive back to Karamea is extremely long and deadly quiet, complete with an ice-cold chill in the air. He doesn't even look at me as he pulls up out front of the house, nor as I get out of the car. I try to move slowly enough to give him time to speak, but not a word escapes his lips. He leaves me standing in the grass as he drives away, not once looking in my direction.

Grief sits like a boulder in my stomach. I hate to see him so sad. My shoulders are slumped as I enter the lounge room to find Del sitting, waiting for me.

'Do you want to talk about it?' she asks quietly.

I shake my head and tell her I just want to go to bed.

I don't even bother to take off my clothes nor do I even get under the covers, I simply collapse in a blubbering mess. I'm so lost in my own misery that I don't hear the phone ring and Del startles me when she enters my room.

'Mrs Edwards is on the phone.'

The thought of having to talk to her right now makes me feel physically ill, but I know I have to. I drag myself into the kitchen to pick up the receiver.

'With your mother in heaven, I feel it's my duty to teach you a few lessons she may not have had the chance to do, God rest her soul.' Her passive-aggressive tone is so much like my mother's, it's as though she's possessed. 'John tells me you turned down his marriage proposal.'

'Yes, ma'am.' I decide it's best to keep my answers short.

'Can you explain why?' she demands.

'He doesn't love me,' I say before I can catch myself.

'And who's fault is that?' she berates me. 'You've had everything handed to you on a silver platter and yet you choose to throw it all away, you ungrateful child. You should think yourself lucky that we even permitted him to ask you. Do you think you deserve better? Do you think you are better than all of us?' Del is standing close enough to hear the tone but not the words. She reaches out to hold my hand. 'You seem to have this misconception that your future is your rite of passage. That you know better than the elders. Your mother always said you were a little self-righteous. Well let me tell you something, little girl, you have no idea what it's like in the real world. Satan has soldiers everywhere waiting to tempt you. Waiting to recruit you into his army.' I'm numb to her words. It's nothing I haven't heard before from my own mother, but all I can think about is John and how he must be feeling.

As I stand with the phone to my ear and my head hanging with shame, listening to Mrs Edwards regurgitate a lesson on how to live my life in the warm light of God's eyes, my ears begin to fill with the rolling roar of the ocean.

Closing my eyes, I'm able to smell the salt of the sea and the warmth of the sun on my face. My shoulders drop as I drink in the moment and imagine wiggling my toes in the sand. I can feel the corners of my mouth lifting as I try to elevate myself out of this moment.

'You should be grateful that we've continued to welcome you in our home. Without us, you'd have nothing. You'd be nothing.'

Del grabs the phone from my hands. 'That's quite enough, Mrs Edwards,' she says sternly. 'She's done listening to you and your god-fearing babble. Good-bye.' And with that she hangs up the phone and wraps her arms around me. 'She doesn't know what she's talking about. She's so caught up in her own version of the world, she can't see outside of it.'

'Thank you,' I whisper.

Chapter 30

It's hard to find the motivation to get out of bed. I know I need to get up, but I find myself physically unable to. I've been watching the clock since the early hours of the morning knowing full well that I need to face the day, but it hasn't helped.

Del has agreed to take me into town so I could check on John. Just like my family used to do, the Edwards also attend a mainstream church on Sunday, and I know John will be with them. As much as I dread having to face his parents, I really wanted to see how John is doing. The whole time I was trying to decide whether or not to say yes to John, I haven't given much thought to how his parents would react. Without my parents around, I suppose there's a part of me that believes that I can have a say in who I marry. But given Mrs Edwards's reaction, it seems that's just simply not the case.

Maybe John's right. Maybe getting married is the only way forward for both of us. Maybe he can see how I need him as much as he needs me, something that I'm only now starting to realise.

Maybe I made a terrible mistake, I think as my heart sinks. *Maybe if I tell him that I was wrong he'll still want to marry me.* I convince myself that this is the answer. If I go to John and say I'm sorry, then everything will be okay, and his parents will forgive me.

'I'll tell him I'll marry him,' I declare to Paulie.

A wave of happiness sweeps over me as I finally emerge from my bedroom. Del offers to take us out for breakfast after we go by the church, so we can just jump straight into the ute.

We arrive at the church just as the service is ending. It's the first time I've been here since my parents' funeral. The old wooden structure that used to be a monument of strength for me now seems small. Some of the church's power was stripped away almost a year ago when I had to walk inside to say goodbye to my parents. Having been raised to believe that death is a rite of passage as you complete your journey back to Jesus, I still struggle to understand why my mother and father were called upon at the same time. I suppose that makes me selfish, to think about how their deaths have impacted me and left me alone in this world, but it's a feeling I just can't shake.

In spite of the memories this place holds, I'm determined to find my path back to John. My eagerness to see his face when I tell him the good news motivates me to jump out of the ute. I can hardly contain my excitement as I watch the parishioners pouring out of the front door. As I get closer, I spot Mrs Edwards and knowing he'll be close behind, I make my way towards her. I believe with all my heart that she will forgive me the moment John and I are reunited. So consumed with my plan for a future with John, I don't see the redness in her eyes until after I finish asking where he is.

I'll never forget the look on her face. It will haunt me until the day I die. I can only describe it as pure hatred. We stand locked in each other's gaze until John's father joins us.

'How dare you,' he sneers at me as he sweeps his arm around his wife, pulling her out of the way. 'What do you think you're doing?' I can feel his anger as he towers over me.

'I just wanted to talk to John,' I try to explain.

'You have no business being here.' His tone is low and full of venom.

'I'm sorry. I didn't think…' I sputter.

'Course you didn't think,' Mrs Edwards spits from behind her husband. Her words pierce through me. 'It's your inability to think of anyone else but yourself that's caused this.'

'I didn't mean to.' My voice shakes. 'I just want to talk to John. To straighten everything out.'

'It's too late.' Her scream turns to tears, as Mr Edwards pulls her away.

'What?' I call after them as they head to their car.

I've always been taught there is always time to ask for forgiveness. Confusion cripples my thoughts.

'John took his own life last night,' I hear Del say from behind me. 'He's dead.'

I don't know what happened after that. In fact, there is a huge chunk of time when I can't remember a thing. As the days pass, I find out that after dropping me off, John called his mother to let her know that I turned down his marriage proposal. He also told her that he wanted some time alone and that he'd be spending the night in a motel room in town. But instead of going to the motel, he went to the farm and parked his car in the small shed near the cattle yards about a kilometre from the main house. He closed the shed door, returned to his running vehicle, and rolled down the windows. His father found him the next morning when he went to get some oil for his tractor. As he left no note, the blame has fallen squarely on me, having been the last one to see him alive.

Surely you must know something, people ask me. *Something must have happened*, they persist.

Although I'm shrouded in a cloak of shock, I know exactly why he did it and it makes the weight of my part in it even heavier. But no matter what people say or how many times I'm asked, I will never tell them the truth. I loved John and I will take his secret to my own grave.

The hardest part now is figuring out his funeral. It's clear that my relationship with his parents is strained and the only way I'll be permitted to attend is if they allow it. This has become a very tricky situation, which could result in my banishment from the church group – something I really don't want to face. If I leave the group, I'd prefer that it's my own decision, not one forced upon me. And I'm not ready to make the choice.

So, I need to make this right. I need to fix it. And seeing how Mr and Mrs Edwards don't want anything to do with me, I know my only option is to go to John's sister, Karen.

Due to the circumstances of John's death and it being considered a sin, I know it's going to take some time for the elders to decide on a suitable way to bury him. All of our teachings indicate that he should be sent away and burned, with no one to acknowledge his passing. Given he's not only the son of an elder but also a recently appointed elder himself, the decision will be more complicated. The best angle I'll work is making sure the blame shifts to me. If the elders consider his suicide a revenge death, then it can be sanctioned, as it's a recognisable justification in the bible. In order to show it was a revenge death, an external motivation for his actions needs to be proven.

By reaching out to Karen, I'll play into the Edwards' belief that John ended his life due to the fact that his destined soulmate – me – rejected his marriage proposal.

I send her a text message asking her how she's doing, but she doesn't respond.

I send another two days later, but still nothing.

By day three, I'm left with no choice to dive straight in.

I feel John's death may have been at my hands. I text, my heart pounding in my throat as I wait.

Explain. Her response is sharp and short.

I caused him shame by not allowing him to fulfil his duty as an elder. Typing the lie makes it hard to breathe, but I know the only way the elders will give John the burial he deserves is to believe that I caused him irreparable shame and that his only path to retribution was to return the act of harm towards me.

As an act of violence against one another is a sin. I push the thought process further and hope that she catches on.

After a few moments, she types back…*his only means of revenge was to harm himself.*

If this works, the elders will determine that I must attend the funeral to ensure John's act of revenge was not in vain.

By the end of the following day, I receive the message from Karen that I'm hoping for.

You are expected at the funeral. She writes, followed simply by the date, time and place.

I'm glad that my parents aren't alive to be dragged into this vortex of shame I'm about to walk into. I will be required to sit at the front of the church during the service so that all those who speak in honour of John can direct their pain, anger and hurt at me.

The day of the funeral. I am numb. I'm thankful that the service will ensure he rests in peace and I'm ready to accept my punishment, but my heart aches for John. I wish I could have another moment with him. A chance to tell him how much he meant to me. A chance to take it all back. Taking a deep breath, I suck back my urge to curl up in a ball and cry floods of tears until there is nothing left inside of me. I want so desperately to mourn the loss of my best friend but my emotions have no place at John's funeral. I will not be permitted to speak nor cry. I will be expected to sit there and take everything that is said to me, at me or about me, to ensure John's retribution is served. The only way I can think of to survive this day is to crawl deep inside myself and hide away.

'Are you sure you want to do this?' Del asks during the drive to the church.

'I have to.' I've explained the situation to her. A situation she has no issues telling me she doesn't understand. I know that she'll never be able to comprehend all the rules of my religion and that she's just looking out for me.

When we arrive at the church, Del goes for a walk. I'm to wait in the ute until I'm summoned and it's best she's not with me. Even though I've told her she doesn't need to stick around, she insists on being there when it's over. As I sit there, alone, in the increasing heat of the ute, I close my eyes and imagine John is sitting next to me.

'There's nothing stopping us from taking off and leaving this place. I could hot wire this puppy and drive us to Queensland. We could go visit Georgia.'

The sound of his voice in my head causes a tear to roll down my cheek. 'I should have said yes,' I say.

'Wouldn't have been good for either of us,' his words whisper next to me. 'There was no way out for me, but you've still got a chance. It's not over for you.'

More tears stream down my face, cooling my burning cheeks.

'Are those for me?' John asks. 'There's no need for that.' He reaches out to wipe the tears away.

'I'm so sorry,' I whisper as I feel his hand touch my face.

'Nothing to be sorry for kiddo.' He flashes his eyes at me – one azure and one emerald. 'Looking like a choirgirl. She's crying like a refugee.'

And just like that, he makes me laugh. Only John could be able to find a place for a Cold Chisel lyric in the middle of an impossible situation.

'I love you,' I say.

'And I, you,' he says. 'Don't let them take you down. Stay strong. You can do this.'

The knock on the window makes me jump and John disappear. It's time. I'm to walk into the church by myself, passing all the mourners, and take my place in a chair strategically placed next to the coffin within the eye line of the pulpit. As I walk towards John's body hidden within the polished wooden box, I can still hear his voice in my head. Determined to honour him and make him proud, I take each step with purpose and ignore the comments and snickers thrown at me as I pass by.

'Don't let them take you down.' His strength fills me up and carries me to my seat.

And there I sit for an hour and a half while each person takes their turn praising John before casting virtual stones at me.

I let each one break apart and wash over me while John's words play on loop in my mind.

When it's all over, I take a deep breath and exhale all the hate and anger I've absorbed, but before everyone is excused from the service, Mr Edwards returns to the pulpit. The night before I spent hours going over the service in my head. Although I've never attended one like this before, I've been well-versed in how they go. At this stage, all the mourners should be leaving me alone in the church to serve my penance, after which, I will be permitted to return to the church group, albeit in some form of isolation. But what happens next, I'm not expecting.

'Sara, it's time for you to stand,' Mr Edwards states in his formal church leading voice. I do as I'm told. 'As you've brought shame to yourself, the memory of parents, and your church family, the elders have decided you are no longer welcome as part of the congregation.'

His words pierce through me. And just like that I'm ousted. Banished.

'Now you must leave. Say goodbye to no one. Just go,' he says without emotion, staring straight ahead and not so much as a glance in my direction.

On his command, I turn and make my way down the aisle. My knees begin to quiver and my heart pounds so hard I fear it'll leap out of my chest. This time, as I pass the members of my church family, instead of casting words of disapproval they simply turn their backs to me.

Once outside the church I can no longer keep the strength in my legs and I collapse on the grass. I feel as though my whole world is crashing down around me. Like I've lost my grip and I'm falling endlessly. A dark cloud engulfs me.

You've brought shame to yourself, the memory of your parents and your church family, Mr Edwards's words reverberate in my brain.

I'm baffled. I honestly believed that by casting myself upon the proverbial stake that I would avoid banishment. I mean, I knew the risks of admitting fault but I thought that I'd get away with a period of isolation and punishment.

'What kind of God sends a child's family away?' I shout to the dark cloud around me. 'Why have you abandoned me?'

I've lost my best friend, the only one who'd be able to pick me up. I've let him down. I've let both of us down, and now it's too late. No matter how much I hope or pray, I can't undo what has happened. I'm alone with nowhere to go and no one to care.

I open my eyes as a light drizzle of rain starts to fall on me and I find myself sitting by the river. As I watch the water flow along the rocks, I think of Del and the time we've spent together in this very spot.

'I can sit here and wait for a miracle or I can take control of my life,' I say to the little fish swimming below me. Thoughts of Del motivate me to get up and start walking. 'I don't care how long it takes. I'll make it there eventually.' I head towards Karamea House.

My determination overshadows any thoughts of reality and I take little notice of the state of my clothing. My rain-soaked cotton dress sticks to my body, clinging like a wet towel, and my feet slosh around in my flat shoes. It feels like hours have passed since I was at the church and the warmth of the afternoon is starting to fade. But the concept of time means nothing to me and I continue on my journey with no concern over how long it will take to get there. As I walk along the country highway I've travelled by bus almost every day this year, I'm guided by the moonlight. The wind rustles across my body causing me to shiver, and I pretend there aren't blisters rupturing on my ankles. I have no idea how much time has passed but my legs are beginning to struggle and can feel myself starting to fade. I spot the old Rookhurst schoolhouse as it's lit up by a large stream of light approaching behind me. It's as though a spaceship has come down from the heavens. I stumble, struggling to keep upright. The sound of the engine grows louder and the light comes closer, blinding my ability to see. Fear takes hold and I start to run. But instead of making a full stride, I collapse and everything goes dark.

Chapter 31

I wake to the chime of the doorbell. I must have overslept. Unsure of where I am, I slowly open my eyes taking in the familiar sights of my room on the top floor of my parents' house. I breathe an enormous sigh of relief and squeeze Paulie tight. *It's all been a dream.*

Taking several moments to cherish my surroundings, I slowly get out of my soft, warm bed and make my way downstairs. Taking each step one at a time, not wanting to take anything for granted, I meander down the staircase and float into my mother's kitchen.

So surreal is the moment that I see John sitting at the dining table, I can't stop myself from shouting his name. But as he sits there chatting with my parents over a cup of tea, he doesn't seem to notice me. None of them do. I run to the table where they all sit, yelling his name and theirs with tears of joy rolling down my cheeks, but all of them act as though I'm not even there.

Their conversation is sombre and the mood in the room is limp. They seem to be talking about something that makes them very sad. My mother is wiping tears from her cheeks as my father caresses her hand.

'Has something happened?' I ask, but no one responds.

As I get closer to them, I notice that my mother is clutching a photograph. It's one of John and I from the rodeo. I smile as I remember how much fun we had that day, but I'm the only one feeling joy as John proceeds to offer my parents his condolences.

'Sara was a beautiful person and I thank God every day that I was lucky enough to be her friend,' John says.

A sharp pain strikes my heart and the room goes dark.

When I awake again it's dark and quiet. Very quiet. I'm alone and have no idea where I am. The only sound I can hear is the frantic beating of my heart.

I try not to panic. To give my eyes time to focus in the dark. To try to make sense of where I am. I know I'm in a bed and that there's something familiar about the smell of the room I'm in.

As my eyes come into focus, I sit up to have a better look around.

My heart skips a beat as I notice someone sitting in a chair in the corner. They wake up as I gasp. 'Sara,' the familiar voice rumbles around the room. 'You had me worried,' Ethan whispers as he makes his way towards me. 'How are you feeling?' he asks as his beautiful brown eyes come ever so close to mine.

I try to speak but my mouth is like a desert.

'You're dehydrated,' he explains, handing me the glass of water from the table beside my bed. 'Have a drink.'

I've heard of water being called the elixir of life but it's at this moment that I grow a special connection to the phrase. It's the best tasting, most refreshing glass of water I've ever experienced.

'I bet you're hungry,' he says. And with a simple nod from me, he tells me he'll be right back.

This time I have no intention of closing my eyes and running through another cycle of dreams. I'm determined not to go back to sleep. I sit there for several minutes hoping this scenario is the real one.

It's not until my eyes fall upon Del coming through the door that I know for sure that I'm safe. As Del sweeps across the room, I can hear the shuffle of her feet across the floorboards.

'It's time to let a little freshness into your lungs,' she announces as she pulls aside the curtains and lifts the window. A gentle stream of cool night air slips into the room as Del comes over to my bed. 'And it's no good sitting here in the dark,' she says as she clunks the switch on the bedside lamp. 'You gave us quite a scare,' she whispers, the light illuminating the concern in her eyes. 'How are you feeling?'

'Like I've been hit by a bus. How long was I out?' I ask as she helps me up to a sitting position, fluffing the pillows as she goes.

'Been almost twenty-four hours. I'd been pondering as to whether or not to call the doctor. I wasn't sure you'd be with us by morning.'

'What happened?' I ask, trying desperately to piece together the fragments in my jumbled memory.

'After you left the church you collapsed on the grass,' she tells me. 'I got you to the ute as quick as I could and hightailed it out of there. You were moaning and groaning all kinds of things on the drive home. You've been in and out of sleep ever since.'

'I've been banished,' I admit, the shame causing me to hang my head. 'I have no family.'

Placing her hand under my chin, Del raises my face to hers. 'We're your family.' Her tenderness warms my heart as the pain of being banished streams out of me. Tears flowing freely. She wraps her arms around me and says, 'It's okay honey, you're home now.'

'Wakey, wakey eggs and bakey,' Ethan announces, coming into the room with a wonderful smelling plate of food. 'I figured as you've been asleep for such a long time that you'd be in the need of some brekky.' Wiping the tears from my eyes, I thank him as he places the plate on my lap. 'Surely the thought of my cooking isn't that bad,' he smiles. I laugh, the sting of embarrassment burning my cheeks. 'Looks like you're out of water. I'll get you some more,' he says, graciously changing the topic as he excuses himself from the room.

'Why don't you tuck in. He's been dying to cook for you ever since he got here.' Del smiles.

Without having to find the words, Del just seems to know what I need and she doesn't push me for information about what happened. I eventually tell her in the days that follow and although she doesn't cry, I can see a little glistening in her eye.

When I moved here after my parents died, it was only meant to be temporary. A part of me believed that I would end up at the Edwards'. And now that will never happen. But with Del, I've never asked if I could stay, it's just assumed that I will. She's already made me a part of her family and looks at me as one of her own. She's become more of a mother to me than mine ever was.

Chapter 32

Being released from the obligation of the church is something I've only really fantasied about. I've dreamt about what it would like to be free from the expectations and the judgements. Free to explore new things and new places. Free to make my own decision and my own mistakes. But waking up this morning with the reality of my banishment sinking in, I start to panic.

Things weren't supposed to end up this way.

Having convinced myself that I could swindle the elders into letting me off with only a mere punishment, I was blind-sided by their decision to cut me out completely.

It was pretty obvious, I scold myself.

I should have known what the outcome was going to be. If there's one thing I'm certain about, it's the rules of my church. Everything is black and white. There is no room for grey, or colour of any kind.

I let myself wallow for a little longer before I finally drag my drained body out of bed. I really should be looking at the positives, like Del and this house. Karamea has been more to me than just bricks and mortar, it's been a refuge from the chaos of my life. And Del has taught me what acceptance and love really look like.

As I make my way to the kitchen, I begin to shed the shame of my old life to let in the light of my new one. It helps to see the pair of smiling, happy faces waiting to greet me.

'Good morning, darl'.' Del comes at me with a much-needed hug.

'Hungry?' Ethan asks after waiting his turn for an embrace.

'Starving.' I grin.

'Why don't you have a seat and I'll bring you a plate,' he offers.

Moments later, the three of us are sitting together at the table enjoying a feast, complete with freshly brewed tea.

'You know what day it is, don't you?' Del asks.

The question catches me off guard. Things have been such a blur over the past few weeks, I really have no idea.

'The results are out.'

I stare blankly at her.

'The HSC results,' she says.

'Oh, right.' I'd completely forgotten.

'Shall I grab my laptop?' Ethan offers.

'Absolutely,' Del responds.

'I'm not sure it'll be anything to get too excited about,' I say.

The idea of having my failures broadcast across the breakfast table is making me feel uneasy.

'Don't be silly, Sara,' Del says, "I'm sure you've done well.'

Ethan returns to the table and places his laptop in front of me. 'Here, you just need to log in.'

My mind goes blank as I stare at the Department of Education login screen. It's asking for my school email address and password, but for some reason, I can't remember what either are.

'You okay?' Ethan enquires.

'Uh…yeah,' I mumble.

More time passes.

'Are you sure?' Ethan asks again.

'I just can't seem to remember…'

'I know what will help you,' Del says as she gets up and leaves the room.

Seconds later she returns with Paulie, my stuffed bear, sitting it down on the table in front of me.

'Sometimes we just need a little comfort.' She winks.

I grab Paulie and give him a tight squeeze. I close my eyes. Taking a deep breath, I tell myself that it's time to embrace my future. After returning Paulie to the table, I place my fingers on the keys and log in.

It takes me a few minutes to work my way through to the results, but as soon as they are revealed, my heart stops.

'What does it say?' Del asks.

'Yeah, come on, don't leave us in suspense,' Ethan insists.

I'm in too much shock to move my mouth, so I spin the screen towards them instead.

Del and Ethan lean in to read the screen. Ethan scrolls through, murmuring to himself.

Del looks at him, then at me, letting out a squeal. Her face erupts in a huge smile as she leaps up from the table.

'You did it,' Ethan shouts and joins Del on his feet. 'You rocked the HSC.'

Even though I can see their excitement, I'm still numb from the news. I don't think I ever truly believed that I could do it. I mean, I know that Ms Davis was confident, and that was incredibly inspiring, but given the way my life has been going so far, I was quietly pessimistic.

It turns out her faith in me was well placed and that I do have the ability to learn and retain.

'You know what this means, right?' Del asks, pulling me up from the chair. 'You're going to uni.'

'Don't skip ahead. I haven't been accepted anywhere yet,' I say, solemnly.

'Oh, don't be such a downer,' Ethan says. 'It's time to celebrate. How about some champagne?'

'Sounds perfect,' Del agrees.

Roughly two weeks later, I start receiving responses from the universities I applied to months earlier. The first one comes from the University of New England offering me a spot in all the degrees I requested. Shortly after I receive similar news from the University of Wollongong.

'The Illawarra is a stunning place to live,' Del says when I tell her about the latest offer. 'I lived there for a brief period of time.' Her eyes glaze over as she gazes off into the distance.

I wait patiently for her to tell me more, but she seems to be reliving a few memories that are making her smile and giggle quietly to herself.

'Should I leave you alone?' I say with cheek, trying to break her daze.

My comment catches her attention and her cheeks flare a rosy red – not something I'm used to seeing happen with Del.

'Oh my,' she coos, placing her hands on her cheeks. 'I got lost there for a moment.'

'Anything you'd like to share?'

'No, dear, you won't find it that interesting.'

'Sounds like Wollongong should sit at the top of my list.'

I take a moment to search the location on my phone. If I'm going to live there, I may as well have a look to see what it has to offer.

While I'm scrolling through 'things to do' in the region, I receive an email from Bond University. My heart skips a beat. It's the one in the Gold Coast. The one I applied to one day when I was thinking about Georgia.

I click on the message, holding my breath.

As my eyes read the words, *Congratulations*, butterflies fill my stomach.

'*Do I?*' I wonder as my fingers linger over the Instagram symbol.

I push the icon to reveal the red highlighted message bubble that I've been ignoring for months. I keep telling myself that Georgia has cut all ties and is no longer interested in her former life and those from it. But the truth is, she's sent me at least a dozen messages that I'm too scared to open.

'*Maybe it's time,*' I try to convince myself.

I close my eyes, my finger hovering over the link.

'*You can do this,*' I encourage myself.

But I can't. Instead, I close the app, put my phone on the bench and head outside for some fresh air.

Chapter 33

Christmas was always a huge deal in my parents' house, being the only day of birth we ever celebrated. To them, the birth of Jesus was one of the holiest days of the year. We never acknowledged the more commercial traditions of Santa Claus and his trusty reindeer, nor the idea of overeating and gift-giving. For my parents, December 25 was observed with a near-full day of prayer sessions, with breaks only for a share in a humble meal comparable to what Joseph and Mary would have been able to afford during the time of their son's immaculate conception and birth.

At Del's place, it's a completely different story. For her, Christmas is all about being with the ones you love, sharing good food, lots of laughter, and most importantly, spending time together. And although she's made it clear that she doesn't expect a gift from me, I can't resist. I've never bought a present for anyone before. It wasn't the thing to do in my family but this year, I can do whatever I want.

I tag along with Del on her trip to Forster to take care of a bit of business before the holidays hit. Telling her I need to look for something, I slip away while she heads into the bank. I don't have a lot of money, but I have a good idea of what I'm looking for and where to find it. I head to the homewares section, hoping to find just the right thing for Del. It doesn't take me long to find it.

The moment my eyes fall upon it, I know it's the perfect gift. It's the most colourful tea pot I've ever seen and it absolutely screams Del. Just looking at it makes me think of her brewing her favourite blend before settling down to read her book in the evening.

With that sorted, I move onto my more difficult task of finding something for Ethan. It needs to be just right, but I have no idea what that is. With Del, it's easy, she loves tea and her old pot is chipped, so a new one makes sense. But with Ethan, he doesn't seem to need anything.

I meander through the shopping centre, moving from one place to another, and then I see it. It's like a shiny beacon calling me over to the men's clothing section. There it stands hanging on the end of a t-shirt rack, fully in black with the large distinctive red bold Gothic font highlighted in yellow, complete with a lightning bolt synonymous with AD/DC. I know he'll love it.

With a smile plastered on my face and a sense of elation in my step, I make my way to the checkout counter only to be stopped dead in my tracks.

At first, I hear her voice then seconds later, she's standing right in front of me.

I haven't seen Mrs Edwards since the funeral over a month ago and the sight of her fills me with dread. She's chatting with Mrs Cameron from our church, but their conversation halts when she sees me. Together we're frozen in a moment of silence that seems to last forever. I hold my breath, not sure what to do.

As her eyes connect with mine, there's a brief flash of acknowledgement before she turns to Mrs Cameron and continues talking, quickly walking away.

After having seen this woman at least once a week for my entire life, she's now like a complete stranger. I'm left feeling numb.

'Can I help you, Miss?' The store attendant's words snap me back to reality. 'Are you wishing to purchase those items?' And with the nod of my head, I'm back.

Christmas morning at Del's is full of surprises and new experiences. First of all, she doesn't go to church, so I figure we'll be able to have a little lie in, but I'm wrong.

It's not much past five in the morning when I hear Ethan bellowing *Jingle Bells* as he marches up and down the hallway.

'Come on, ladies,' he hollers. 'Get your lazy butts out of bed. It's Christmas.'

His excitement is infectious and I gladly rise from my slumber to join him in the kitchen.

'Merry Christmas,' he says as he greets me with a big hug, lifting me off the ground.

Although it's hard to take him seriously in his gaudy festive t-shirt and similarly disturbing boxer shorts, it's the reindeer antler headband that's the most distracting. The bells dangling from his antlers tinkle as he bounces around the kitchen. I've never seen someone so overtaken by Christmas spirit.

As I stand there in awe, watching him prepare breakfast crepes, Del comes up behind me.

'He's like this every year,' she says, smiling. 'Ever since he was a boy. You'd think he would have outgrown it, but, huh, what do you do?' Del shrugs her shoulders and goes over to receive her Christmas hug from him.

There is nothing for me to do but watch Ethan sing and prance around the kitchen making breakfast. He's already set the table, holly wreath embroidered napkins included, and the kettle is on the boil. So, I sit in the corner of the kitchen with a nice hot cup of tea, completely entranced by the performance in front of me.

After breakfast, Ethan insists we move to the lounge room for some present opening before washing the dishes. He declares himself as honorary Santa, shuffling Del and me to sit on the lounge.

'And what's this we have sitting under the Moon's Christmas tree this year?' he says in a silly, deep Santa-style voice. 'Why it's a present for the lovely Del,' he states as he delivers the gift I got her.

I hold my breath as I watch her carefully unwrap the present. 'Don't want to rip any of the beautiful wrapping paper', she says.

She gasps as she unveils the teapot.

'Oh my word. It's the most beautiful thing I've ever seen. I absolutely love it!' She leans over to give me a hug.

It's at this moment that I understand what the joy of gift-giving is all about. I haven't spent a lot of money. It's not fine china or a popular brand of kitchenware, but none of that matters to Del. She just tells me it's one of the greatest gifts she's ever received because it came from me. People talk about the 'art of gift-giving' or it being 'the thought that counts', but none of that has had any meaning to me until today.

It's not long after Del opens her second gift, one from Santa, that Ethan hands me a small box shaped gift. The wrapping paper is covered with prints of Santa wearing sunglasses and holding a surfboard. I love it so much I don't want to open it. The image makes me think of the ocean, which is present enough for me.

'You realise there's something inside, right?' Ethan teases me.

'Oh, leave her be,' Del pipes in. 'You take your time, honey. Enjoy the moment.'

I read the label on top: *To Sara, Love Del.*

Another smile graces my lips. I'm holding my very first Christmas present, and I'm determined to savour every moment of the event in my mind.

Following Del's lead, I carefully unwrap my gift. Under the paper is a white box. Inside the white box is a bit of red and green tissue paper protecting my first ever Christmas ornament. There's something about the plastic Santa with a red sack slung over his shoulder and a big grin on his face that reminds me of Del.

After we've unwrapped everything and the room is littered with bits and pieces of colourful, festive paper, Ethan approaches me with a small parcel wrapped in red paper, tied up with gold string, resting in the palms of his outstretched hands. He's abandoned his Santa shirt for the AC/DC one I've given him, and as he gets closer with that amazing smile on his face, my heart skips a beat.

'The last one's for you. It's from Santa.' He winks.

My hands quiver as I remove the paper to reveal a small blue velvet box. I pause for a moment trying to catch my breath. It's a box I've seen before. It was a few years ago, when my father bought my mother a gold necklace and pendant after one of their really big fights. I remember the fight so vividly because my father had literally pulled their bedroom door off the hinges. He was so angry. It was one of the scariest nights of my life. The next afternoon, he returned home with a box just like this one. My father would often present my mother with a gift of flowers as an apology after a fight. But this one was so bad he came home that day with jewellery.

'Come on, dear,' Del encourages. 'Open it.'

Lifting the lid unveils a gold chain with a delicate diamond encrusted moon hanging from it.

'Let me help you put it on,' Ethan offers, gently taking the box from my trembling hands as tears roll down my cheeks.

He kneels down in front of me and removes the chain from the box.

'It's just a little something to remind you that you're a part of our family,' he says as he leans in and places the chain gently around my neck, kissing a tear from my cheek as he moves away.

'I think that's my cue,' I hear Del say as she leaves the room.

'It's beautiful,' I say, choking on a whirl-wind of emotions.

'Not as beautiful as you,' Ethan says, placing his lips upon mine.

My whole body tingles from head to toe. My heart is nearly pounding its way out of my chest. In this moment, something changes. It's like Ethan has unlocked a chest hidden deep inside of me. If this is what Christmas is all about, I think I can get used to it.

Chapter 34

I feel like I'm floating. Ethan and I spend the next few days together, doing odd jobs around the property, cooking, playing cards, ending each evening cuddled up on the lounge. Del seems really happy about the situation. Every so often she makes a comment about how her family is finally perfect.

With the Christmas festivities over, we move on to planning a New Year's eve party. Del invites pretty much everyone she knows from Sydney to come up and camp for a few days. Ethan invites several of his mates and encourages me to invite Jessica for a few nights. Ethan and I pick her up during one of our trips into town. I can't wait to see her. We've got so much to catch up on.

I'm so excited I find myself talking non-stop to Ethan the whole ride in.

'How about two of you go to the café for a milkshake while I pick up the things we need?' he suggests.

'Really? Are you sure? I mean, I'm happy to help you with the errands…' I deliberately trail off hoping he insists I spend time with Jessica instead. Which he does because that's just the kind of guy he is.

'I think it's best if the pair of you get the gossip out of your system before I'm stuck in the car with you for over an hour,' he smiles.

'You are the best,' I say, wrapping my arms around his neck and planting a kiss on his cheek.

'Yes, I am, aren't I?' he responds in his cheeky tone.

After we load Jessica's stuff into the ute, she and I decide to walk to town and send Ethan on his way.

'Wow, he's really cute,' is the first thing Jessica says after Ethan has driven away. 'What's the story with the two of you?'

She doesn't waste any time getting straight to the point, which I expect after Ethan gives me a goodbye kiss. And I don't waste any time filling her in on all that's happened since the last time I saw her.

When I show her the necklace, she almost cries.

'That's so sweet.' She places her hand on her heart. 'So romantic.'

'I feel so comfortable when I'm with him.'

'That's really great. I'm really happy for you. You deserve it.'

We head into the café and order our drinks before sitting at a table outside. As I look out across the main street, I start to think of John. Tears swell in my eyes.

'Are you okay?' Jessica places her hand on mine.

'My relationship with Ethan is so different from my one with John,' I sniff. 'John and I were really close and talked about everything. He truly understood me and what it was like for me growing up. I don't talk about it with Ethan.'

'He doesn't ask about it?'

'No.'

'Do you guys talk about John?'

I shake my head.

'Does that worry you?'

'I don't think so.' I don't really know how to explain what I'm feeling. My heart aches when I think about John and I feel so guilty. Talking about it will only make it worse.

'What things do you talk about?'

'He reads a lot. He tells me about it. Teaches me stuff.'

'I bet he does,' she grins. 'Older boys have more experience.'

Her cheeky tone helps lift my mood.

'Is he a good kisser?'

I blush. 'I think it's time to change the topic. Why don't you tell me what's been happening around town.'

We're all caught up on the latest gossip by the time Ethan collects us and the conversation during the drive is all about his cute, single friends that are on their way up for the New Year's party.

By the time we get back to Karamea House, it's early evening and a few people have already arrived. Among them is one of Ethan's mates, Paul, who's already made himself at home – tent pitched, barbecue on and beer in hand.

Paul greets us as we arrive on the verandah with bags full of groceries. 'Great to see you, mate, I can see why you've been spending so much time at this place,' he says with a smile, 'surrounded by such beauty.' The way he winks at Jessica and me makes both of us blush.

With an awkward giggle, we escape into the house. Buzzing from the high of the brief encounter, she and I start unpacking the food while talking about meaningless things, like if we think it's going to cool down overnight.

Ethan enters the kitchen with the last bag of the groceries.

'Don't you take much notice of Paul. He's a bit of a player,' he cautions Jessica. 'A bit of a lady's man, if you know what I mean.'

He grabs the snags, a beer, kisses me on the cheek and returns to the verandah.

After all the food is placed in its rightful place around the kitchen, Jessica and I get to work preparing a few salads. Pretty soon, the fleeting moment of Paul's flirtatious way is a distant memory.

We're most of the way through the preparations when Del appears. She's been busy getting all her guests sorted and has come to check on the kitchen activities after knowing everyone is settled.

'I must be the luckiest woman alive to have such creatures as the pair of you in my life,' she raves as she sweeps through the kitchen.

Once we establish that all the finer details have been organised, she offers one last chance for her additional service.

'We've got it covered,' I say, with a sense of pride in having taken onboard all the things she's been silently teaching me over the past year.

I'm determined to show her the same kind of graciousness and hospitality she's given me. After I present her with an ice-cold glass of chardonnay, she succumbs to the role of hostess and attends to her guests, who are already well on their way to relaxation, watching the sunset over this beautiful place.

Jessica and I stick together throughout the night, not only helping serve the food but also cleaning up.

For me, it's a pleasure to be able to give back a little of the kindness that Del has shown me. For Jessica, I think it's a chance to escape from the country life that her parents have unwittingly cast her into and return to that 'city feeling' she's been longing for. Even though we are knee-deep in bushland, the people around us definitely bring a 'big city' vibe.

I haven't seen Ethan much over the course of the evening. He's been busy with his mates and I'm not wanting to intrude. I'm happy to just hang with Jessica. Social situations make me nervous. I'm not quite sure what I'm supposed to do in a crowd of people I don't know. Hanging out on the fringe suits me just fine.

After the food is done and the kitchen is relatively tidy, Jessica and I decide to escape to a quiet place off the side of the house to check out the stars with a mostly full bottle of red wine.

'Now this is the type of country life I could get used to,' Jessica announces as she takes a big swig from the bottle.

'I could think of worse ways to spend an evening,' I say, taking the bottle for myself.

We erupt in laughter.

'Is it a joke that can be shared?' Ethan's voice comes from out of the dark.

'Depends on who's asking,' I respond with a witty tinge of sarcasm. A trait that I've picked up since spending more time with him.

Without any warning, his lips are on mine. I get so caught up in the moment, the rest of the evening seems to melt away.

With New Year's Eve day comes a whole new group of people, with their tents dotted across the yard around the homestead. Their bodies fill the kitchen and spill out onto the verandah. The whole place is a buzz with chatter, laughter, and the smell of good food. Ethan is busy collecting firewood and hanging out with his mates, while Jessica and I do what we can to help Del. But with all the other hands available, we seem to be more of a hindrance than a help, so we escape the crowds and go for a wander.

It gives me a chance to show her around the place a little and also find out what happened last night. I was so swept up in my make-out session with Ethan, I lost track of her. All I know is when Ethan and I finally came up for air, she was gone.

During our walk, we settle into a chat about nothing in particular. We speak about things like how pretty the trees are and the interesting way it appears like the rocks have just been scattered around the place.

After a little while, I can wait no longer and get straight to the point.

'So, did you have a good time last night?'

Her cheeks flush red far quicker than her lips can answer, 'It was nice.'

'Nice?' I question, stopping to face her. 'Is that all you're going to tell me?'

'Paul suggested we go for a walk while the two of you were busy and it was nice,' she repeats, still revealing nothing juicy.

I opt for a moment of silence and continue to stare at her, hoping she'll break.

'What?' she asks, finally breaking the standoff. 'Nothing happened. He was a complete gentleman. He asked me about myself and I asked about him. We walked back to the fire and that was it.'

'Was there a spark?'

'Course there were sparks, we were near a fire.' She flashes a cheeky grin then starts walking again.

'I knew it,' I grunt, following after her. 'Something did happen.'

'What about you and Mr Sydney Uni?' Jessica retorts, using the nickname she gave Ethan months ago when I started talking about him at school, a lot.

'It was nice,' is all I give back and the two of us burst out laughing.

When we return to the homestead, the party is in full swing. The air is wafting with the guitar wail of rock music and the charred scent of barbecue. As we approach the crowd, Ethan spots us and yells out, 'It's about bloody time ladies. Grab yourselves a beer and let's get this party started.'

Paul has already made his way to the esky and has the bottles open and ready for us as we reach the crowd of people standing around the fire.

'Come on,' Paul says as he puts his arm around Jessica and manoeuvres her over to where he'd been standing.

I stand alone, awkward, not quite sure where to go. I start nervously drinking the ice-cold beer in a feeble attempt to calm down or at least seem busy. With all of these people, Ethan and Del's people, I'm not quite sure where I fit. Del's been really good, introducing me to everyone when she can. But she's been busy in the kitchen preparing food and catching up with all her friends and I don't want to be in the way.

It's a bit the same with Ethan, I think it's best to leave him alone with his people. And I've been fine with that until now. Jessica's been my anchor. My person to hang with, but in a flash, she's gone and here I stand, alone. It's like being at school. It's like being the one no one wants to be seen with. I feel naked and vulnerable.

My nervousness takes hold and I continue to suck back the beer, closing my eyes hoping the moment will pass quickly.

'Geez girl, you thirsty?' Ethan's words shake me from my daze. 'At this rate, you won't make it to midnight.'

I open my eyes to his handsome face close to mine.

'Now, will you get over here and meet my mates,' he insists, wrapping his arm around my waist. 'They're beginning to think I made you up.'

As we walk over to the crowd, his arm firmly connected to me, I begin to feel a sense of belonging. When we get to the group, Ethan introduces me to everyone, and just like that, I'm a part of the crowd.

The rest of the evening is spent chatting and laughing around the fire. We're all having such fun, we've lost track of time. Thankfully, Del saves us from missing the stroke of midnight, and for the first time in my life, I experience a traditional countdown. For me, it's more than just the start of a new year, it's the start of a whole new beginning for me. As I stand with a group of people, who feel like friends, it feels okay to let go of the turbulent year that brought grief, tragedy, and despair.

Ringing in the new year comes with a warmth of excitement for the future, as I can see a path towards my own happiness and a sense of deservingness. The count reaches one and everyone yells 'Happy New Year'. The celebration continues as we all move around sharing kisses and hugs like one big happy family. After making the rounds, I find myself with Ethan.

'Happy New Year, beautiful,' he smiles. 'I hope your year is full of new adventures.'

'Happy New Year.' I wrap my arms around his neck and plant a long, lingering kiss on his soft lips.

Chapter 35

Once the new year celebrations are over, there's no slacking off for Ethan and I. Dell puts us straight to work across a range of jobs that need doing on the farm. She has a vision for the place and is wasting no time getting things underway.

'I can see people coming here as a place to seek refuge from the evils in the world,' she explained to me one day when we were tending to the vegetable garden. 'It's so peaceful here that you can reconnect with nature. Become one again with the earth.' She appeared to be speaking to the fist full of soil as she let it slowly fall back to the ground.

'It's safe,' I added.

'Yes, Sara.' She smiled. 'It's a place where people can feel protected.'

I love it when she talks about her vision of what Karamea House can be. She often speaks about opening up the rooms to welcome in anyone who needs a place to recharge, restore or regain their inner strength. It's exactly what it did for her and what it's slowly been doing for me.

Before she can consider opening the place up for others, there's a lot of work that needs to be done to prepare the property, and especially, the house. It's very old and in dire need of renovation.

But the reality is, Del simply doesn't have the finances to pay for it right now. So we work, bit by bit, fixing up whatever we can with whatever materials we can rustle up from other people's discards. A lot of properties in the area set up a rubbish pit on their land, so they don't have to lug large items into the town landfill. Upcycling is something Del is passionate about and she isn't shy about asking those she meets at the cattle sales if it's alright for us to have a rummage around in their pits to see what we can find.

'You'd be amazed at what people throw away,' Del says to Ethan and I as we pile into the front seat of the ute one Sunday morning.

She's made arrangements to check out the MacGregor's rubbish pit and is taking us along to do the digging. It isn't just a coincidence that we are heading there on the one day of the week that the entire MacGregor family is away. Both Del and Mr MacGregor agree it's best for her to show up while his wife isn't there given Del's reputation, thanks to Mrs Vale, and Sunday is ideal as the whole family is at church.

It seems like a lifetime ago that I spent my Sunday mornings at church with my parents. I'd like to say it took me a long time to get used to not going, but it was as easy to dismiss from my life as the Friday night rituals. There was a time when I felt that I'd be lost without the security of my church family, but I've come out the other side just fine. I'm experiencing a new sense of belonging. Now my Sundays are spent looking for diamonds in the rough or any scraps of building materials that we can use at the house. It's more of a spiritual journey than I ever experienced in the eighteen years I spent with my church group. This offers me a sense of freedom. The chance to learn more about the world and the different kinds of people in it. But most of all, I'm getting to know myself better.

Looking through the items that people discard gives you a bit of insight into their lives, or at least an opportunity to fantasise about what type of people they are. Often during the several weeks that we spend going from property to property, I make up my own little mini-series in my mind about what kind of conversations took place before people like, Mr and Mrs King bought the distinctly 1980s black and red paisley lounge suite that now sits abandoned on the top of their broken-down whitegoods.

'It's all the rage in Sydney,' Mrs King would have said to Mr King on their way into town,' I imagine.

As the fashion has changed, I suspect that Mrs King will have requested a new lounge suite. Heaven-forbid her household decor be labelled as 'so last season'. Instead of being stuck with a lounge suite that is no longer socially acceptable, what else is there to do but pitch it into the rubbish hole. And lucky for us, as it's an excellent find. The thing is in pretty good nick and will spruce up the front verandah nicely.

One Sunday, after picking up a few wooden chairs from the Turner's property that will come in handy when extra people came by, Ethan suggests we head to the beach for a fix of saltwater spray and fish and chips. Originally, we were just going to have a look at what the Turner's pit had to offer then make our way back home, but Ethan reckons the day is far too perfect to waste.

Having been raised in a family where the mere thought of doing anything on impulse was considered a sin against God, being able to experience a spur of the moment alteration to our plans is quite liberating. Despite my initial tinge of anxiety about the sudden change of plans, the excitement of veering left overtakes me. From the moment Ethan turns east instead of driving safely back to Karamea, a surge of energy races through my body. It's so overwhelming, I wind down the window and let the rush of warm summer air run across my face. Closing my eyes, I embrace the sense of freedom as the tears run down my cheeks from the wind pelting my face. It's almost like a cleansing of my ingrained hesitation to experience anything new.

So much has changed in the past few weeks, the weight of my life-governing rules is starting to become a distant memory. After months of trying to imagine what it would be like to be in total control of what I did with my time, how I dressed, what I ate, or who I spent my time with, it's finally happening.

Ethan and I sit on the beach with the sand between our toes until it gets dark. It's a few hours of pure bliss, watching the waves roll on and off the shore. For a while, it makes me think of John and the time we used to spend on the beach. Tears crowd my eyes as the salt-heavy air fills my lungs. Without a word, Ethan simply wraps his arm around me. I lay my head on his shoulder basking in the security and comfort he offers.

It's getting pretty late by the time we slowly start on our journey home. The drive is fairly eventless. There isn't much wildlife looking to play 'chicken across the road' and town is pretty much empty as we skirt our way through. A few kilometres out of town, I notice a woman walking slowly along the side of the road and insist that Ethan slows down. She's stumbling on and off of the bitumen. As the ute's lights cascade over her slumped back, she appears not to notice. Thinking it's an odd reaction, I suggest to Ethan to pull over.

'Are you okay?' I call as I get out. 'Do you need some help?'

No response.

I continue towards her calling out 'hello' to see if she'll stop but she continues on. When I catch up to her and place my hand on her shoulder, she turns to face me and my heart stops. At first the appearance of her battered and bloodied face sends a wave of fear washing over me, but it's the recognition of the woman beneath the swollen bruises that causes me to hold my breath.

'Oh my God, Mrs Vale, what happened to you?' I gasp.

She rambles something unintelligible as tears stream down her blackened cheeks. She seems quite unaware of who I am, but she does allow me to escort her back to Ethan, who is already on his way to meet us. We get her into the ute and, in silence, make our way to the safe haven of Karamea.

During the drive, Mrs Vale falls asleep. Ethan and I keep quiet so as not to wake her. When we pull up he whispers, 'Wait here with her, I'll get Del.' The thud of Ethan's door closing causes her to nearly jump out of her skin. She covers her face and pleads, 'Please, no more. I promise to never do it again.' Tears return to her eyes and her body quivers.

'It's okay, Mrs Vale. We're not going to hurt you,' I promise her. 'You'll be safe in the house.'

The sound of my voice seems to wake her from her daze and she turns to look at me. She squints through her swollen eyes trying to make out my face in the dim light. 'It's me, Mrs Vale, Sara Johnson.'

'Oh, Sara dear. You're not meant to see me like this,' she says, trying to hide her injuries from me. 'I must be in such a state.' She tries to straighten her clothes and fix her hair.

'You look beautiful as always, Mrs Vale,' I say with a gentle smile.

Del opens the door on my side. 'Margaret, darling,' Del says as she leans into the ute. 'You look like you could use a stiff drink.' Del reaches out for Mrs Vale's hand, which gives me a chance to slip out from underneath her. I almost knock Ethan over, lacking grace in my manoeuvre as I stumble onto the uneven ground. 'Come on now, let's get you into the house,' Del says, helping Mrs Vale out of the vehicle.

Ethan and I quietly follow the women into the house, still in shock from the unreal situation we've found ourselves in. Del ushers Mrs Vale to take a seat on the lounge and asks Ethan to pour all of us a whiskey.

Ethan does what he's told without a word with me on his heels. As soon as two are poured, I take them to Del. She places one into Mrs Vale's shaking hands, cupping her hands over Mrs Vale's to help steady the glass. 'This will help calm your nerves,' Del assures Mrs Vale, who seems like she has no idea what to do with the glass. 'Nice and easy, just a sip to start with.'

'He won't like it,' she mutters.

'He's not here,' Del says, again encouraging her to drink.

Mrs Vale closes her eyes and takes a sip. A moment later, she takes another slightly bigger one. The pattern continues until before long Ethan is refilling her glass. Halfway through her second glass, she starts to relax, allowing herself to sit back on the lounge. Del asks me to get a bowl with some warm water and cloth and soon Del is gently cleaning the blood and tears from Mrs Vale's face.

Mrs Vale finishes her second glass of whiskey while Ethan gets a pillow and I grab a blanket at Del's request. After we place the items on the chair next to the lounge, Del suggests we head off to bed, which we do without question nor a word to each other.

As I lie staring at the ceiling fan, so many questions race through my head. Each time I close my eyes, all I can see is Mrs Vale's bloodied face and terrified eyes.

Who could have done this to her? I think over and over. The idea that someone in town could be so vicious to someone so passive sends spikes of fear through my body. I mean, I know she can be a bit nasty with her tongue but I can't ever imagine her raising an angry fist. It's scary to think of what type of violence had left Mrs Vale looking so shattered. Then it occurs to me that maybe it was a car accident. That perhaps she'd swerved out of the way of a kangaroo, lost control and hit a tree. But we didn't see evidence of an accident before coming across Mrs Vale. Maybe she actually rolled down an embankment and that was why we couldn't see the car. Determined that was what had happened, despite knowing full well there aren't any embankments between town and where we picked up Mrs Vale, I calm myself into sleep. It's by no means a restful sleep, but it will have to do.

Chapter 36

Del's already in the kitchen when I get up the next morning. She takes little notice of me as I slip in and switch the kettle on.

'Morning,' I say softly, just to let her know I'm in the room.

She mumbles a greeting in return. Based on the glaze in her eyes, I suspect she didn't get much sleep.

'You okay?'

'Oh sorry, dear. It's been many years since I've slept on lounge. My old bones aren't used to it.' She flashes me a smile.

I should have known that Del would give up her bed just to make sure Mrs Vale felt safe and secure.

'Mrs Vale can have my room for as long as she needs,' I offer. I hate the thought of Del sleeping on the lounge in her own home.

She tells me that Ethan had already offered just before he left to pick up Aunty Bev. She holds knowledge of the medicinal plants and trees around the region and can help with Mrs Vale's healing process.

'The white fellas have taken away a lot of land where our bush medicine grows,' Aunty Bev explained to me one afternoon over a cup of tea. 'But if you know where to look, you can still find some.' I love it when she speaks about her traditions and the ways of the past. It makes me feel more connected to the land and gives me a better understanding of the plants and animals that I live among. 'The stuff out here is much better than anything you'll find in town. Much more potent. But you need to understand how it works and respect where its power comes from.'

The kettle whistles and I offer to make Del a drink.

'Why don't you make some breakfast,' Del suggests. 'Margaret will need a good feed.'

I happily set to the task, frying up some bacon and eggs to go along with toast made from the bread Del baked the day before. I'm determined to create the same kind of meal that Ethan delivered to me after my banishment. It had made me feel so welcomed and cared for, and I want to do the same for Mrs Vale.

Del gives me a hand in the kitchen. We've been working harmoniously in silence for a fair while before Del blurts, 'It was her husband.' Her tone is so sharp it catches me off guard. 'I suspect he's been doing it for years. Such an animal.'

Her statement causes me to freeze and my heartbeat to quicken.

Mr Vale did this? I think in disbelief, struggling to comprehend how someone so gentle could inflict so much pain on someone. Especially someone they love.

'Any man who lays a hand on a woman is a coward,' Del hisses. 'And to leave her for dead at the side of the road...'

As my mind swims with projections of Mr Vale attacking Mrs Vale, my hands tremble so much that I nearly drop the frying pan. 'How could someone do such a thing?' I question, mainly to myself.

'It's all a game of control,' Del says. 'It makes him feel empowered to dominate over her. But the truth is he's weak. A pathetic excuse for a man.'

I shudder as the sensation of fear ripples through my body. If I'm scared at the mere thought of Mr Vale attacking his wife, I can't even imagine what it's like for Mrs Vale. I feel physically ill.

'But she's safe now,' Del assures me, placing her hand on my shoulder. 'She never has to go back.' Her tone and touch are enough to push aside the wave of nausea. 'Did you happen to come across any bedroom furniture during your rummagings?'

Our discussion quickly changes to a plan for setting up the fourth bedroom of the house, which is basically a storage room. It isn't the first time the topic has been raised, but now we have the motivation to get it done. I suggest that Ethan and I go to visit Mr Holstein. He's the man everyone goes to if they need a bit of furniture or a little help during hard times. He's very discreet and keeps everyone's business to himself. We agree that I'll get the room set up for Mrs Vale as soon as possible.

Before Del takes a plate of food into Mrs Vale, she asks me to wait for Aunty Bev, so I find myself alone on the lounge. And it isn't a very wise place for me to be at the moment – alone with my thoughts. Visions of Mrs Vale being beaten swirl around in my head, but I can't bring myself to see the face of her attacker. Even though I have seen the horrific state that Mrs Vale is in, and I have no reason to think Del's wrong about who the perpetrator is, I just can't picture Mr Vale that way.

I have known this couple my whole life, and despite Mrs Vale being a little bossy to the people around her and sometimes a little mean to Del, she isn't all that bad. My mother always said that Mrs Vale has a good heart and that it's her passion to help others that drives some of her unorthodox behaviour. But Mr Vale, he's always been so gentle and friendly. I've never heard him raise his voice or say a mean thing about anyone.

My baffled thoughts must be written all over my face when Ethan and Aunty Bev enter the room.

'Trying to understand Newton's law of gravity,' Ethan jokes as he bends down to give me a kiss.

'Huh?' is about all I can muster.

'You okay?'

'Um, yeah, sorry, just lost in thought,' I lie. 'Hello Aunty Bev,' I say as I approach her for a hug. 'They're in Del's room.'

'Thank you, dear,' Aunty Bev says as she stands for a moment staring at me. 'Calm your mind, child. Sometimes the world is not how we first saw it. We must learn to adjust so it doesn't take over our thoughts.' With a pat on my shoulder, she leaves the room.

As I try to contemplate what the heck I'm meant to do, Ethan wraps his arms around me. 'How 'bout we go for a walk?'

After several minutes of listening to Ethan ramble on about the history of each rock we pass by, I finally start to relax. If there is one thing Ethan is really good at, it's knowing what to do to calm me down. He also usually seems to know when I do and don't want to talk about something, but on this occasion, he decides I need to talk about it.

'I know this is a lot for you to take in but we all really need to focus on Margaret and making sure she's okay,' he explains. 'She may not want to talk about what happened but she also might and you're going to have to try to handle that.'

I think I understand what he's trying to say. He thinks that I need to think more about what Mrs Vale is feeling and less about what I'm going through, but I'm struggling to navigate my way.

'This isn't about you, Sara, and you've got to find a way to get past it.' His tone is so blunt I'm not sure if I should be angry or hurt, but I know that I'm definitely offended.

At no point have I thought this is about me, but I have such a connection to the people involved it feels like it's happening to my own family. Ethan doesn't understand what I'm going through.

'You're just in shock,' he says while I continue to silently stare at the ground. 'Seeing injuries like that can throw you a bit.' I can feel a touch of anger bubbling in my belly. 'You need to grow up and not take it so personally.' His words sting and all I can see is red.

I stop dead in my tracks and turn to face him.

'You have no idea what you're talking about,' I snap. 'I grew up with Mr and Mrs Vale as though they were part of my family. My mother was very good friends with Mrs Vale and they spent a lot of time together, hence, I have spent a lot of time with her.' There are no more thoughts in my head, just words running out of me, fuelled only by anger. 'Yes, to see her in that state was a shock, but to find out that it was at the hand of one of the kindest, gentlest men I have ever known is incomprehensible to me.' I'm so fired up I don't take much notice of the look on Ethan's face, instead, I keep going. 'You don't know me. You don't understand my thoughts and feelings. How dare you say these things to me,' I hiss and spin on my heels to leave.

But before I can march off, Ethan grabs my arm.

'Good,' he says, turning me around. 'Now you're ready.'

'What on earth are you talking about?'

'That's the kind of anger we need.'

'What?' I am truly confused.

'What Margaret needs right now is an army of people to surround her, protect her, and make sure she doesn't go back to Arthur,' Ethan says. 'We all need to be angry about what he did, so we can make sure it never happens again.'

His comment leaves me speechless. I don't know what to think about the whole situation and it's making me crazy.

We start to walk back to the house in silence with my mind running loops of his words. Although I don't like his methods, I do agree with him. My anger is best placed on the man responsible for hurting Mrs Vale, no matter what type of person I think him to be.

And just like that something inside of me changed. My mother had placed the Vale's on a pedestal of how people should be, but it's been a ruse. All that prim and proper behaviour was just a veil masking who they really are. Visions of Mr Vale – no – Arthur – flood my head and I can see his face clearly as he continually hits Mrs Vale – Margaret. My anger falls squarely on him.

By the time we get back to the house the breakfast mess has been cleaned up and Del, Aunty Bev and Margaret are sitting in the lounge room.

'I don't want anyone to know about this,' I hear Margaret say as we enter through the kitchen. 'Arthur is a very well-respected man. I don't want people to think poorly of him.'

'Margaret, that is the most absurd thing I've ever heard,' Del says. 'Who cares about what people think of him. He's a monster. Look what he did to you.'

'I know he didn't mean to,' Margaret says. 'He's been under a lot of pressure lately and I probably did something he didn't like. It's my own fault, really...'

'That's enough,' Del snaps. Ethan and I watch as Del stands up and walks over to Margaret. 'There's no excuse for what he did to you,' Del says gently as she crouches down to face her. 'You are not to blame for this. He is.'

Tears fill Margaret's eyes as she hangs her head and gently sobs, 'What am I going to do?'

'You're going to stay here and heal, physically and emotionally,' Del insists, soothingly rubbing Margaret's back.

'Why are you being so nice to me? I've always been so terrible to you. I don't deserve your kindness.'

'Don't be silly, everyone deserves kindness,' Del declares as she stands up. 'I'll send Ethan to your place to pick up a few things for you. He can slip in while Arthur's at work.'

It seems as good a time as any for Ethan and me to make our presence known. 'No worries, Margaret,' Ethan says. 'I'm happy to get you whatever you need.'

Margaret wipes her face and attempts to tidy herself up, but it only causes her to wince in pain.

'No need to fuss,' I say as I approach her. 'You look beautiful,'

She smiles as much as she can, but the movement of her swollen face causes more tears. I pass her a tissue and kneel beside her. It takes all my strength to not cry alongside her. Instead, I summon up the anger I feel towards Arthur. Gritting my teeth, I take a deep breath and offer to join Ethan on the journey to collect

Margaret's things. I figure it might help put her mind at ease about having a stranger enter her house. I've been there many times over the years, so I have a pretty good idea where things are. I ask Margaret to tell me what she wants and I put together a list, along with other items Aunty Bev and Del also want from town. It's also the perfect opportunity for us to get some bedroom furniture sorted, so I suggest to Ethan that we hook up the trailer.

While Ethan is driving, I try really hard to keep distracted by focusing on a range of other things, mainly by chatting Ethan's ear off about superficial topics. If I stop and think about the fact that I am about to virtually break into someone's house, I might actually go into cardiac arrest. It hasn't really been so long since my world was shrouded in a very restricted, sheltered existence. A world where any decisions I attempted to make on my own, without virtuous guidance – which was basically my mother telling me what to do and how to think – would have led me straight to hell. As thoughts of my insubordination begin to surface, I'm surprised by the rush of excitement I feel creeping up inside me. Any pangs of guilt that are trying to find their way to the front are being defeated by the anger Ethan has unleashed in me.

I take the hit of adrenaline with me as we enter the Vale's house. Margaret gave me a key. It's weird to be in here alone. The place smells of polished wood, and the ticking of the wall clock echoes throughout the rooms. We go through the kitchen, which has been left in such a state it takes me aback. Never have I seen such a mess at the Vale house. Margaret always keeps the place immaculate. But her absence is obvious. There are dirty dishes in the sink and crumbs all over the benchtop.

Beyond the kitchen, near the back of the house sits the master bedroom. It's a part of the house I've never been in before, but Margaret's description of the layout helps us find our way. Ethan grabs the burgundy suitcase from the hall closet while I start to collect clothing items from the wardrobe. The room is dark and musty and the bed is unmade. I work hard to not disturb things I don't need to, collecting all the items on the list, including her favourite hairbrush and perfume.

After Ethan helps me fill the suitcase, we're on our way out when the thud of a car door closing stops us in our tracks. Frozen in the hallway near the front door, we desperately try to work out if the car is right out front or next door. There is a rumble of voices near the window at the edge of the house, but it's difficult to work out what is being said. Unsure of what to do next, we both stand there staring at each other. The thought of Arthur catching us in his home suddenly becomes very real. I squeeze Ethan's hand and try not to breathe. The voices get louder as they move towards the front door. Ethan pulls me towards the back of the house. I can hear the key twisting in the lock as Ethan places his hand on the back door handle. He goes to open the door but it's locked. In the panic, he's missed the deadbolt. I reach over him and switch the latch, allowing the back door to swing open. The clunk of Arthur's footsteps fill the house as we slip out the back.

Ethan closes the back door with as little noise as possible and we slump down below the window line. Hearts thumping, we scramble our way around the side of the house, cautiously checking to see if the person Arthur was talking to has gone. I can hear Arthur making his way to the back door. *His neighbour must have told him we were in there,* I think as we bolt to the ute parked across the road. As we're pulling away from the curb, Arthur appears at the front door. I lock eyes with him. I'm not quite sure whose are filled with more hatred, his or mine.

Chapter 37

The rest of our errands are a blur. Every place we go, we expect to run into Arthur, but thankfully he is nowhere to be seen. We get everything done as quickly as possible, leaving the trip to Mr Holstein's until last. His place is tucked up back of the industrial area, so we're pretty confident that Arthur won't be lurking around. Feeling a little more at ease, we jump out of the ute and head into the tightly packed storage unit.

'Hello,' I holler after not being able to see anyone when we first get inside. 'Mr Holstein.' I try again after getting no response.

'Oh, Sara,' I hear him say from behind a stack of tables. 'So lovely to see you.' I catch a glimpse of his white hair as he threads his way through the maze of furniture. Pretty soon I'm staring at his stunning crystal blue eyes and his smiling face greeting Ethan and me.

After introductions, I get straight to business. I really have no intention of us staying in town any longer than we need to. I've got to know Mr Holstein through my work with the CWA. He isn't a farmer, he's a humanitarian. He comes to the canteen at the end of every cattle sale to pick up the leftover food to take for those who are either homeless or who can't afford to eat. His shed of furniture works like an op shop, selling used, unwanted items to others who want them, with the money going directly to those in need in the community.

'I think I just might have something that will work for you,' Mr Holstein says as he encourages us to follow him into the abyss of furniture packed from wall to wall and floor to ceiling.

'How are we meant to get the stuff out of here?' Ethan whispers to me.

'You'll see,' I respond, flashing him a sweet smile. I'm looking forward to his reaction when Mr Holstein unveils his secret.

'It's right back here,' I can hear him say as he disappears in the darkness.

'How can he see anything back there?' Ethan questions.

I try not to giggle at his rising nerves. Usually, it's me getting anxious about things, so it's nice to see the shoe on the other foot.

'He knows exactly where everything is,' I say as I stop and wait.

Ethan follows my lead.

Then it happens. There's a bit of a clunk, a slight grunt, then the rattle of the roller door opening. Ethan and I are blasted by the flood of sunlight causing momentary blindness. I can hear Ethan's gasp as the dust particles become visible in the light. Once recovered, we head over to Mr Holstein.

'What do you think?' he asks.

Ethan is a bit stunned for a moment as he casts his eyes on the bedroom suite set neatly in the doorway for easy collection. With a quick inspection of the sturdy teak posted queen bed frame resting vertically against two matching bedside tables, Ethan and I are sold. Mr Holstein tells us there is a mattress in good nick near the front door, and after a quick chat about the price, we are loaded up and on our way home.

On the way back, Ethan and I agree that our near encounter with Arthur at the Vale house best remain between us as we don't want to cause Margaret any more angst.

When we get back to the house, Del and Aunty Bev are in the kitchen chatting over a cup of tea and Margaret has just gone into the bathroom for a much needed long, hot shower. It's the perfect opportunity for us to get her room set up as a surprise for her. Del and Aunty Bev help us pull the storage boxes out onto the verandah, getting it cleared out in a quick couple of trips. Then we work together to navigate the furniture into the room. Del and Aunty Bev make the bed while Ethan and I move the boxes down to the shed. We want Margaret to feel at home and not like she has put us out by her being here. The final touch is placing her suitcase of goodies on the bed, so her things are waiting for her in her new room. I greet her as she comes out of the bathroom, making sure not to startle her, and escort her to her surprise.

'We just wanted you to have a space of your own,' I tell her as she weeps.

'Thank you,' she whispers, wrapping her arms around me.

I've never had a hug from her before. She's not really the touchy, feely type. But that doesn't matter, I let her hug me for as long as she wants. I can feel her body slowly starting to release the years worth of tension that has built up inside her. When she's done, I leave her be, giving her time to collect herself before joining the rest of us.

Back in the kitchen, Aunty Bev is organising to get a few women together at her place.

'It's time for some women's business,' she says to Del. 'I shall bring the women together and we shall gather food for a feast.'

There is something incredibly exciting about the prospect of being invited into such a sacred circle. I've heard talk about the women's business before, but I really have no idea what it's all about. However, I understand that it's a secret gathering, for females only, as the men have their own ceremonies. Aunty Bev doesn't say much more about it before she leaves, she merely tells us what time to arrive.

'When the sun sits near the horizon, make your way to my place,' she smiles as she walks out the door.

I'm eager to ask more questions, but when Ethan enters the room, Del gives me a look that demands silence. *Men aren't allowed to know anything about women's business*, is what I hear her eyes say. They aren't to know where it's taking place or what's planned.

Knowing better than to ask about the weird silence, Ethan says something about heading to the pub later to catch up with a few mates he met at the cattle sales. It's pretty clear he can also read the look on Del's face. In fact, he must know it so well that he proceeds to make up some excuse about having to go into town early and is out the door before Margaret emerges from the bedroom.

'Thank you for collecting my things,' she says as the three of us sit in the lounge with a cup of tea. 'Did anyone see you or ask you why you were there?'

The question is fully anticipated. I know Margaret well enough to know she's concerned that her neighbours will be wondering what's going on. It won't take them long to notice that she isn't staying at the house. And based on Gloucester's rate of gossip, she knows that most of the town will have already made up their own version as to why.

'Not a soul around,' I lie. 'We got in and got out without a fuss.' I'm really good at this lying thing. I suppose I should be worried about the repercussions in the afterlife, but there is a big part of me that feels like this is the right thing to do.

Margaret has been through such an emotional ordeal that I can't bring myself to let her know that Arthur saw us and knows exactly where she's staying. The last thing I want to do was make her think she's unsafe.

For the rest of the afternoon, Del entertains us with stories of her childhood, growing up on a mango farm in northern Queensland. After a bit of time, Margaret starts to relax and begins to share stories of her own childhood, growing up in a fancy house on the north shore of Sydney. When Margaret talks about some of the places she used to go as a teenager, Del chimes in echoing familiar memories.

'I moved to Sydney in my late teens. Gee, we must have been in some of the same places at the same time.' And with a simple sentence, I watch the two women, who have been enemies since the day they met, find a connection.

I'm fascinated to watch as Margaret slowly sheds her veil of pretence and becomes a mere woman, almost like a teenager, getting to know Del on a whole new level. The bond that begins between them over the afternoon grows even stronger as the evening progresses. Although what happens later that night at Aunty Bev's house must always remain a secret among those who were there, what I can reveal is that Del and Margaret became as close as two human beings can be. Forever bonded by a series of unexpected, but perhaps, destined events.

The next morning there is new and infectious buzz filling the house. By the time I wake up, Del and Margaret are chatting away in the kitchen making breakfast together. As I slowly convince myself to get my lazy butt out of bed, I can hear their laughter amid the banging of pot and pans. The pair are cooking up a storm, both hungry from the night before and preparing a feast fit for kings and queens. Ethan is not long behind me as I emerge into the intense vibe of the kitchen.

'Morning sleepy heads,' Margaret greets us. 'Nice that you could join us. Why don't you lot get the table ready?' Her eyes are clear and her smile bright. She's so casual in the interaction I'm a little dumbfounded. Frozen in a moment of fascination at the continuing transformation I was witnessing the day before, it takes Ethan wrapping his arms around me to snap me out of it.

'Morning babe,' he whispers, kissing my ear. 'Looks like last night was precisely what the doctor ordered,' Ethan comments as we take plates and cutlery to the table. 'It would appear Aunty Bev has worked her magic.'

I can feel a rush of heat rise in my cheeks as moments of the night before flash through my mind.

'It was that good, was it?' Ethan jokes, flashing me his sexy smile. He knows full well I'm bound by secrecy and that I will never tell him what happened, but he insists on making me squirm. 'Did you learn any new tricks?' he winks.

'Nothing you'll ever know,' I say sarcastically, trying to ignore the sexual tension.

By this stage in our relationship, our intimacy hasn't gone much past kissing. Ethan has been very much a gentleman and has not made me feel like I need to do anything I'm not ready for, but I know he wants more. He's a few years older than me, has been in serious relationships, and is definitely not a virgin. But for me, all I can think about is how the act of sexual intercourse for any reason other than for procreation is considered a sin that will see me sent straight to hell. Despite the consequences being thoroughly ingrained in my psyche, there is a part of me that wonders what it would be like.

Georgia and I talked about sex after she told me she'd been pregnant. Her confiding in me about her experience made it easier for me to ask her a few questions about what it's like to have sex.

'It's no big deal,' she said one day during our walk home from school. 'It seems to make a guy happy. If Rodney was ever really mad, having sex was a good way to calm him down.'

After that discussion, the idea of having sex really didn't interest me and, of course, the whole time I was with John, intimacy was never really on the table.

Then along came Jessica with a completely different take on the topic.

'It can be so amazing with the right person,' Jessica revealed to me during a lunch period at school. She had a serious relationship before moving to Gloucester and seemed to know what she was talking about. 'If he knows what he's doing, it can really blow your mind.'

Although she never went into details, my imagination is pretty good at filling in the blanks. Especially when in Ethan's company. Just thinking of him is enough to make me tingle in places I never thought I could.

Being with him, in that moment in the dining room, with his luscious brown eyes flashing in my direction, my body is overcome with desire. Without putting too much thought into my actions, I barrel over to him and throw myself upon him. He greets me with matched intensity and I can feel his intentions as he presses his body to mine. We are deep into a very passionate kiss when there's a knock at the door. The startling bang is enough to kill the mood.

I open the door to find Scott Pulson standing on the other side of the screen.

'Hey Scott,' I say without even a thought that addressing a senior constable police officer so casually could be an issue. I originally referred to him as mister, as strictly taught by my parents, but the night he came to tell me about the accident, he insisted I call him Scott.

'Morning Sara. Just wondering if Del is home?'

'What's this about?' Ethan questions as he walks up behind me.

'G'day Ethan.' Scott's tone is friendly and warm. 'It seems Margaret Vale is missing and it's believed that Del may know something about it.' He continues to stand on the porch without attempting to come inside.

'She knows something about it alright, that bastard Arthur...'

'Ethan,' Del interrupts. 'Why don't you invite our guest in? Apologies Scott, it's lovely to see you. Would you like a cup of tea?'

'Thank you, Del,' he says as I make way for him to walk inside.

'Why don't you stay for breakfast, we were just about to sit down and there's plenty for everyone,' Del says, walking with Scott into the dining room.

'Oh dear, Mrs Vale, what on earth happened to you?' I hear him ask, clearly confronted by her appearance. 'Were you in an accident?'

We all take a seat around the table and after a few moments of silence, Margaret responds. 'It was no accident, Scott.' She starts slowly, describing just what happened the night before last. It's the first time that any of us have heard the story.

'Arthur had been at his Rotary meeting, as you know he's the president,' Margaret begins. 'He normally gets home around seven, but that evening he decided to stay a little longer to have a few drinks with some of the other members.' Watching Margaret rehash the most traumatic night of her life will stay etched in my memory until the end of time. As she explains to all of us how her husband of forty years had come home from the club drunk and full of anger, she displays an inner strength I admire. She retells how Arthur had been mad because his dinner was cold as he expected she should have known what time he was going to return.

'I had cooked a fish curry because his doctor had told him he shouldn't eat so much red meat, for his heart, you know. So, I'd asked Mrs Yates for a fish recipe and she'd given me one she'd seen on a cooking show,' she recalls with a dim spark of excitement in her eye. 'I had planned the timing perfectly, so it would be ready when he walked in the door just after seven as he always does. I had his plate on the table ready for the hot curry and a chilled glass ready for his favourite wine. I know how important it is to him to have his food ready the moment he comes in the front door and I pride myself in making sure his needs are met.' Listening to her speak about her relationship with Arthur makes me a little uncomfortable. I'm not quite sure why but there is something about what she describes that feels wrong.

'But when he didn't show up by seven-thirty,' Margaret continues. 'I decided it would be best to put the food away so it wouldn't spoil. I had planned to reheat it the moment he got home, but as it got later in the evening, I was struggling to stay awake and I fell asleep on the lounge,' she says as she hangs her head.

She sits there for a moment, her head down and eyes closed, breathing slowly. We're all captivated by her tale and none of us say a word while she takes a moment to collect herself. Del places her hand on Margaret's shoulder letting her know that she is still safe and among friends. Margaret takes a deep breath, raises her head and opens her reddened eyes.

'I don't know what time it was when he came home, all I heard was his voice. He was so angry. I was completely disoriented having been ripped from my sleep that I was unable to speak as he questioned me.' Her fear turns into anger as she continues to go closer to the heart of the story. 'He wanted his dinner and he dragged me in the kitchen demanding that I get it for him. I remember my hands shaking as I retrieved the plate of food from the refrigerator. When I told him what I had made his anger seemed to get more intense. He grabbed the cold plate of food and threw it against the wall, yelling *Are you stupid, why the hell would I want fish-fucking-curry?*' Unsure of what to do, I started to clean up the broken plate.' Her tone changes as she continues. 'His temper is something I'd got used to over the years of our marriage. And there have been plenty of times that I've been on the receiving end of an angry hand. But never before had it come in the form of a fist,' she swallows. 'He hit me so many times I lost count. And as my eyes blurred and my blood fell on the floor, I struggled to stay conscious.' Tears fill her eyes. 'When he was finished, he sat at the kitchen table with a glass of wine as I laid on the floor. I was in so much pain and unable to move or speak. He told me that my incompetence as a wife was embarrassing and how dare I make him so angry. Then he picked me up, put me in the car and drove me to the edge of town where he threw me into the grass.' She looks Scott in the eye and says, 'He told me that was where I belonged, with the rubbish at the side of the road. Then he left me.'

Scott sits quiet for a while, staring back at Margaret. Then he stands up and says, 'Right then, I guess it's time for me to pay a visit to Mr Vale.'

'What are you going to do?' Margaret's voice is quivering.

'Nothing you need to worry about Mrs Vale,' Scott says, placing his hand reassuringly on her shoulder. Then he wishes everyone a good day and leaves.

It's pretty clear that Scott went directly to Arthur and told him what Margaret said because it was only a few hours later that his car came barrelling up the driveway. As soon as Del catches sight of it, she goes for her shotgun and tells Margaret to go into the bedroom. Ethan follows Del as she makes her way onto the suspension bridge. I watch from the verandah as Arthur marches onto the bridge towards Del.

'You bitch,' he yells. 'What kind of rubbish have you filled my wife's mind with?'

Del lowers her shotgun, aiming it directly at his chest. 'Don't come any closer,' she warns.

'You lesbian whore. What are you tryin' to do? Convert my wife?' he slanders.

Ethan has not yet made his way onto the bridge but is instead watching closely from behind her.

'Get off my property,' Del hisses. 'You're trespassing.'

'You are holding my wife against her will and I demand you give her back,' he spits.

'Get off my property,' Del repeats but this time she cocks her gun.

'You crazy bitch. What are you going to do, shoot me?'

'The thought has crossed my mind,' Del says with a tinge of sarcasm.

Arthur hesitates for a moment, possibly contemplating whether or not Del will actually shoot him. Given one of the rumours about her is that she killed her husband, I suppose he thinks it's plausible and he begins edging his way back towards his car.

'You tell that ungrateful cow that she's no longer welcome in my house,' he yells before driving off.

Del keeps the gun pointed at him until his tailgate is no longer visible. Ethan makes his way up behind her and takes the gun from her shaking hands.

Del is visibly spent by the time we return to the house. Margaret emerges from the bedroom and gets straight to pouring drinks for everyone. Any plans to get work done around the property today are well and truly out of the question by the time the second round of drinks are poured. Instead, we decide to all share funny stories about ourselves or ones that we've heard about other people.

As the afternoon turns into evening, a fire is lit in the outdoor pit and the area around it is turned into a lounge room where we all lazily listen to more stories by the campfire. Ethan and I offer to make dinner, which ends up being very basic considering the amount of alcohol consumed. I'm fairly sure none of us will remember what we ate.

Chapter 38

The following morning, I awake to a knock on my door. Ethan sticks his head in to ask if I want to keep him company while he runs a few errands in town. Being a Tuesday morning, it's pretty quiet in town, which suits us just fine. After a quick stop for bread at the bakery and a few pieces of pork from the butcher, we make our way to the grocery store to get the rest of what we need.

Ethan and I are teasing each other, laughing and having a good time as we enter the store. Ethan wraps his arms around me trying to kiss my very ticklish neck and I playfully try to get away from him. I'm so caught up in the moment, I don't notice that Mrs Edwards has been watching us until we are literally face-to-face with her.

'Mrs Edwards,' I fumble, completely startled by her presence.

Ethan stays in his position, his arms still around my waist. 'Mrs Edwards, lovely to see you again.'

The three of us stand there locked in an awkward vortex of time, none of us quite sure of how to proceed. A wave of shame rushes over me. I can only imagine how she's judging my behaviour. Public displays of affection aren't permitted in her world. Given my banishment, I expect her to simply walk away as if she doesn't know me, but instead she continues to glare at me.

'Why don't I get started while you two catch up?' Ethan says as he lets go of my waist and bolts for a trolley.

The tension between the two of us must be difficult to be around.

'How are you?' I attempt to break the deadlock.

'How am I?' she fiercely retorts. 'How do you think I am?' she asks, although clearly not expecting an answer. Her voice is low, but her tone is venomous. 'My son's body isn't even cold and look at how you disrespect his memory.'

It takes me aback that she's speaking to me. The laws of the church are pretty clear. Once you disavow a member they cease to exist. For a brief moment, I wonder if she's softening to me, but then she continues.

'Is this why you didn't want to marry John? Were you too busy traipsing around with this heathen?' she hisses. 'I thought the elders were too harsh with their punishment on you, but clearly they saw you for what you are. A heartless tramp.' My knees are trembling and I'm not sure if they're strong enough to keep me upright much longer. 'Your mother was right about you,' she whispers as she leans in closer to me. 'You are a worthless piece of trash.'

Her words strike my heart like a thousand swords and I clutch my chest as she brushes past me on her way out of the store. My head is spinning and I feel sick. I have always struggled to know the image my mother had created of me in her mind. It was clear to me that she believed that I was hard work for her because I would question things and hesitate to follow commands. But how it was possible to have lived in her house for seventeen years and for her to have no idea of the type of person I am. What's worse is she told other people that I was a disappointment. Although it explains why she was in such a hurry to go to the Edwards' the night of the accident. It was a way for her to prove to the other elders that I wasn't worthy of being a part of the church family. Which means she thought I wasn't worthy of being part of their family. *How is that even possible?* I wonder. *How is it possible to hate your own child so much?*

To think that I have only known Del for a short period of time yet she welcomes me into her family with open arms makes me question my parents' ability to love me. Del seems to understand and accept me without me having to explain or prove myself.

My mother was always worried about what other people thought about her. She was on a mission to be elevated to a certain status in the community and would stop at nothing to get there. I had even witnessed times when she would talk down people she was friends with just so she could fit in with others. But I never thought she would have talked that way about me. Hurting others was not a concern of hers. My mother lacked a very important trait: empathy. And as her child, it was soul-crushing. Hearing that my mother didn't want me as her daughter, breaks my heart into a thousand pieces.

I'm struggling to shake my sadness as we return to Karamea. Ethan has been trying hard the whole way home to snap me out of it, but nothing is working. Despite knowing there is nothing I can do to change the way my mother felt about me and that my banishment from the church can never be removed, there was still a part of me that had hoped Mrs Edwards would eventually forgive me. Her words keep echoing in my head and her anger ripples through my body. Anguish fills me and it's hard to see straight. Ethan helps me find my way into the house and sits me down at the kitchen table. Then he disappears. I put my head down and sob. Every inch of my body shakes as tears pour from my heart onto the wooden table. A box of tissues is placed next to me. I grab several to dry my face and blow my nose. I'm a mess. I feel like I have nothing left: no family, no home, no future.

'Crying is a good way to cleanse the soul,' Del says as she gently places her hand on my back. 'Sometimes it's good to let it all out.' Her tenderness sparks another flood of tears and I bury my face in my arms. 'That's it. Let it all go.'

'I can never go back,' I say amid my sobs. 'I have no home. No family. Nothing.'

'Rubbish,' Del retorts. 'Nothing could be further from the truth. Look around you, my child and tell me what you see.'

After wiping my face and clearing my nose, I raise my head to face her. Through my blurry vision, I do what she asks and begin to look around the room.

'I see a kitchen' I sniff.

'Yes,' Del says. 'And what else?'

'Windows.'

'And what's outside the windows?'

'Grass and trees,' I say, still not entirely sure what she's getting at.

'Do you see anything else?' she asks quietly.

I turn to face her. 'I see you.'

'And I see you,' she responds, wrapping her arms around me. 'This is your home and I am your family.'

Despite how many times Del has said these words to me, this is the first time I really hear them.

'Genetics don't make family, Sara. Nor do bricks and mortar make a home. Knowing you can depend on someone and feeling safe where you lie your head, those are the things that we need to feel whole. You have all of those things here.'

As the words sink in, I'm overcome with a feeling of warmth. I've never felt so much love for someone or from someone before and it feels amazing. I want to stay buried in her arms for as long as she will let me, but Margaret comes bounding into the room.

'Come on you two,' Margaret says. 'It's time to go.'

'Go where?' I ask.

'You'll see,' Del smiles as she grabs my hand and drags me outside.

Ethan is already in the driver's seat with the engine running by the time Del, Margaret and I get onto the verandah. He's brought the vehicle up next to the steps and is signalling for us to jump in. Del offers Margaret the front seat before joining me in the back and pretty soon we were on our way heading down the steep hill to the side gate.

Margaret jumps out to open the large metal frame swinging it back towards the ute. Ethan drives through, Margaret closes the gate, latches it and gets back into the front seat. It's all a bit surreal to see her move so freely, with her hair left loose around her face. She's wearing an old pair of Del's jeans and a slightly oversized long-sleeved flannel shirt, tucked in of course. Never in a million years did I ever expect to see Mrs Vale, the most respected woman in Gloucester, wearing such an outfit. But it really suits her. And so does the smile she's been wearing quite regularly these days. It's such a beautiful smile.

As we head to the edge of the property it becomes clear that we're going to Aunty Bev's place. The pathway through to her house has undergone a bit of a renovation over the past few weeks, with Ethan and I spending many hours chopping, pruning and clearing a decent size road all the way through. It means that now we can easily drive a vehicle there, making late night gatherings less of an issue.

I can see the smoke of the fire as we get closer to her house. A tinge of excitement ripples through my body as I anticipate the amazing feed that will be created over that fire. I feel my own face transforming into a smile.

'That's better,' Del says to me quietly. 'You're much prettier with a smile.'

I blush.

'Let's get this party started,' Ethan announces, bringing the ute to a gentle stop. 'Everyone grab something from the back,' he says as he gets out.

'That's how you know you are part of the family.' Del smiles at me. 'When you're expected to help out.'

Del and I each grab a side of the esky and carry it over to the house. There are already about a dozen people congregating as Aunty Bev's son, Derek, turns a small pig on the spit over the coals. Knowing most of the people, Del and I say a quick hello as we continue to the house. Aunty Bev is busy in her kitchen organising the plates of food that have been brought by the others already sitting by the fire.

'Sara, dear, it's so lovely to see you,' she says as she stops what she's doing just to give me a hug. That's just always the way it is with her. She has this way of making me feel special.

'What can we do to help?' I offer.

'I think I'm right here, ladies. There's still a bit of time needed to cook the meat, so we best grab ourselves a drink and join in the fun.' Her eyes seem to twinkle as she speaks.

Out to the fire we go for a family gathering like none I've ever been a part of before. Not only is there good food, great conversation and lots of laughter, but there's a bit of storytelling, some live music and plenty of singing. It's the kind of get together I can get used to being a part of.

The next day Ethan has decided he wants to take me to a nice, romantic, secluded spot on the north-western edge of the property for a picnic. It's a place he's been talking about showing me for a while now. He'd mentioned it in the wee hours of last night, but I assumed he meant at some point, not precisely this morning. When I finally make my way into the kitchen, he's in full gear getting everything prepared and packed up.

'Bout time, lazy bones,' he teases. 'Bit hard to get out of bed this morning?'

'It was definitely a big decision.' I smile and kiss him on the cheek. 'I had to spend a bit of time discussing the options with myself before I came to the conclusion that it was time to greet the day.'

Neither of us drank much the night before, but we were out late. It must have been close to two in the morning when we finally convinced Margaret and Del to get into the ute. Although it isn't the first time I've seen Margaret let her hair down since moving into Karamea House, it still seems so out of character for her. But this person that is exploding out of her is amazing, exciting, adventurous, and completely unpredictable. She explains it to be like breaking out of a mould that she's been suffocating inside of for years.

'I'd created myself into what I thought other people wanted me to be. I'd become the type of woman you saw in the pages of *Housekeeping Monthly*, straight out of the fifties, and I was stuck there,' Margaret explained to me one afternoon.

'I didn't realise that I had lost all remnants of who I really am. I'd completely forgotten about the young woman I once was. The woman who had dreams and ambitions. I gave that all away when I met Arthur.'

Watching her transform from the woman I've always known her to be into the woman she had once always wanted to be, makes me feel like my own transformation is possible. She left her old life behind and the world hasn't ended. Her life isn't over. In fact, it's quite the opposite. It's like her life is finally beginning.

After asking Ethan if he needs a hand and being told it's all taken care of, I toddle off to the shower. When I was living with my parents, I was only allowed to shower a few times a week on certain days, which was dictated by my father. On my shower days, I was only permitted to have the water on for three minutes. Given the distance between the hot water system and bathroom, the majority of that time the water was cold. At Del's house, I'm free to shower when I want for as long as I want. Knowing we're on tank water, I still keep my showers short, but I revel in the freedom and the bountiful hot water. It's in this place that one of my former least favourite chores has been turned into one of my most cherished activities. I even sing. Sometimes so loud that Del and Ethan will be humming the tune for hours afterwards. This shower is no different and I spend five minutes under the hot water singing my little heart out.

By the time I emerge, Ethan has packed the saddle bag on his motorcycle. I slip on the back and wrap my arms around him tight. It isn't scary to be a passenger, I just use it as an excuse to lie my body along his. The sun is shining and I feel truly happy. As I press against his back while he cautiously takes me to a place he's chosen just for us, I realise that this is what romantic love feels like. And not only do I love him but I believe he loves me back. I feel so connected to him like we're meant to be together. My dreams are filled with visions of our future together. He is the one. I truly believe that.

When we arrive at our destination, I can see why he's chosen this spot. The view of the far-reaching expanse of bushland beyond Del's property stretching out in front of us is stunning. We set up our picnic and settle in, listening to the eastern whipbirds crack and the bellbirds snap. I'm at peace and feel content.

'You are beautiful.' He brushes the hair from my face. 'Every time I look at you it takes all my strength to not grab you and kiss you.'

'You're corny,' I say with a giggle.

'I'm not kidding,' he says, turning my face to his. He shifts himself closer to me and slips his arm around my waist. 'I hate the thought of going back to uni next week. It kills me to think I'm not going to see you every day.' My chest tightens as he stares intently in my eyes. I hold my breath as he says, 'I love you.' I lose myself in his kiss. His hands all over my body. His tongue intertwined with mine. The sound of desire in every breath he takes. Everywhere he touches sends a jolt of lightning through me. We shed each other's clothing and my inhibitions disappear.

'I love you too,' I whisper as I feel him inside of me. My body tenses, but his gentleness is calming. He kisses my eyelids and tells me that I'm beautiful. I feel safe. My pain passes, passion takes over, and we connect.

It's late in the afternoon when we start to make our way back to the house. Ethan thinks he heard a gunshot or two and suspects Del may have needed to chase off a dingo. As we come out of the clearing, we notice a cloud of dust lingering above the road indicating that either someone has just arrived or has not long gone. Everything seems fine outside the house. There's no sign of Del with her shotgun fending off wild dogs, so the panic to rush back diminishes.

Ethan pulls up next to the verandah and we unpack the saddlebag. Although, I must admit, there's a bit more kissing and fondling going on than unpacking. We can't keep our hands off each other as we clamber into the kitchen, giggling. I'm so happy. I feel like nothing can bring me down. We're so caught up with each other, it takes a while for us to notice Margaret's faint call coming from the lounge room. Ethan is the first to hear it and goes to find her.

I don't follow him. I'm putting the picnic rubbish in the bin when I hear him scream. It's so intense it causes me to run after him.

'Mum,' his voice cracks. 'Oh my god, what happened?'

Del is lying on the floor covered in blood and Ethan is trying to wake her up. He alternates from shaking her shoulders to trying to cover the gunshot wound in her chest. Tears are streaming down his cheeks as frantically he calls her name. I'm frozen, unsure what to do. Then I notice Margaret. Her eyelids flickering as she tries to call for help. She's covered in blood. I run to her side.

'I'm okay,' she whispers. 'You need to call for help.'

Taking her direction, I bolt to the other side of the room to where I left my mobile phone on the table. Then I see Arthur.

With shaking hands and a desperate attempt to avoid vomiting, I dial triple zero and put the phone to my ear. The voice on the other end tells me to be calm and to grab some towels and apply pressure to the wounds. I place one on Del and put Ethan's hands on top before I return to help Margaret.

'I should have been here,' Ethan grunts with tears in his eyes and anger on his lips. 'I should have been able to protect you.' He's rocking back and forth with a look on his face that scares me. It's full of rage.

The paramedic on the other end of the phone asks me what happened. I tell her that Del's been shot in the chest and Margaret in the stomach. When I try to describe Arthur's wound, it's difficult to get the words out. He shot himself in the head and there isn't much left of his face. The gun is resting near where he fell to the floor.

The ambulance arrives with the police not far behind. Ethan and I are sent outside while the teams work on Del and Margaret. Ethan is so mad that he's being told to leave Del, he starts fighting with the police. He's swearing and throwing punches. His behaviour is so erratic, I hardly recognise him. One officer physically restrains him, while another tries to calm him down. I try to comfort him, but he growls at me and tells me it's my fault.

'You brought these people into her life,' he hisses.

I can tell by the look in his eyes that something has been triggered inside of him. It's like he's returned to that little boy locked in the cupboard. I try to tell him that I'm sorry and that everything is going to be alright, but a police officer ushers me away to a seat on the other side of the verandah. A helicopter lands on the paddock and the paramedics rush Margaret over to it. Before long, she's gone.

More time passes and a second ambulance arrives. Still no sign of Del. I ask the officer what's taking so long but before he can answer, the paramedics rolled out a stretcher with a large, long black bag in the shape of a person on it. I know it has to be Arthur. I know he's dead. The paramedics return to the house and moments later they come out with another black bag.

Del.

I feel my world crumble around me. Ethan goes into the ambulance with her and before I can make sense of what's happening, they're gone.

The police keep asking me questions about what happened, but I have no information for them. I have no idea what happened. They offer to take me to the hospital in Newcastle so I can be with Margaret. I agree. I don't know what else to do. There's nothing for me here anymore. The vision of the anger in Ethan's eyes shoots daggers through my heart. I hope soon that he'll have a chance to think more clearly and will no longer blame me. My heart breaks for him and the flood of emotions that must be crowding him. As I slump into the back of the police cruiser, the events of the afternoon start to unfold. *How can it have gone from one of the greatest moments of my life to the worst?* Shame overwhelms me knowing the horrors I brought to this special place. *It's all my fault,* I sob quietly on the inside. My heart feels as though it's being ripped from my chest. I'm numb.

Chapter 39

The time that passes is meaningless and the next thing I know I'm in the hospital with a nurse telling me that Margaret is in surgery. He says something about damage to her internal organs and that she's lost a lot of blood.

'She should come out of this okay,' he says, trying to comfort me.

His positivity helps lift a bit of the tension from my body but it's only met with a wave of exhaustion. I can't hide my scattered state and I stagger. As he catches me, he kindly offers me a place to rest.

'She'll be in surgery for a few hours. It's a good idea for you to get some sleep.'

He shows me to a modest room with a small cot pushed up against the wall.

'It's a place we sometimes escape to for a quick nap during long shifts,' he says with a smile. 'It's yours for as long as you need.'

The idea of getting any actual sleep is futile. The moment I close my eyes, all I can see is the lounge room full of blood. The safe haven that has comforted me during the hardest year of my life is now the scene of a horrific crime. No matter what I do or how hard I try to think of anything else, it consumes my thoughts.

As I lie in the dark, attempting to escape the visions, I once again feel alone. The replay of Del being taken from Karamea in a body bag only brings more tears. It's all so surreal. I desperately long to see Ethan. To be there to comfort him. To feel his comfort in return. Thoughts of being intimate with him only hours before are crowded with his anger. I would give anything to be lying in his arms instead of alone in this hospital room. I keep opening my eyes hoping to wake up from this nightmare.

But when my eyes close, all I see is Arthur. The sight of his partially blown-off face makes me nauseous. I'm stuck in a cycle reliving the horrific moments after entering the house. I can't find a happy place to escape too.

It's pretty clear I'm not getting any sleep. Having no idea how much time has passed or what hour of the day it is, I decide to get up and check on Margaret. It's my vain attempt to find some good news to help calm my nerves. I search for the nurse's station and ask if Margaret has come out of surgery.

'Mrs Vale is in recovery,' the nurse in the blue top says to me. 'She's still under anaesthetic and may be out for a little while longer. Why don't you go to the cafeteria and get yourself some dinner?' she suggests. 'The kitchen's still open.'

She tells me it's nearly eight o'clock, but if I get there quick, I should still be able to get a warm meal. After being told how to find my way through this maze of a building, I'm on my way.

In my effort to distract myself, I let my thoughts shift to Ethan. I wonder where he is and how hard this whole situation must be for him. The police confirmed that Del was already dead when the paramedics arrived, and most likely before Ethan and I had even got back to the house. The bullet had pierced her heart and there wasn't anything anyone could have done to save her. Ethan was so angry. This whole situation must be dredging up memories of his childhood. My heart aches for his loss of another parent.

I get to the cafeteria just before they close and grab a plate of meat and veg. Finding a place to sit is easy as the place is nearly deserted. I pick a table near the window, but instead of eating, I play with my food. I cut the beef into interesting little shapes and make channels in the mashed potato for the gravy to run through. I'm considering stacking the beans into a tower when I spot Ethan on the street down below getting out of a police car. My heart skips. I'm so happy to see him. I can't wait to feel his strong arms around my body. I am so desperate for some comfort. For him to hold me and tell me that everything is going to be okay.

The moment I see Ethan enter the building, I push aside my plate and go looking for him. The anticipation of seeing him fuels me with a new found energy and my pace quickens.

As I round the corner at the nurse's station near Margaret's room, I catch a glimpse of his dark hair. I burst into a sprint.

'Ethan,' I yell.

He turns at the sound of my voice, but instead of greeting me with a smile, his eyes pierce my heart. His glare is full of hate. It stops me dead in my tracks. He says nothing before turning and going towards Margaret's room. I follow quietly behind him, too scared to make a sound. I know he was angry at me but I thought by now he would have realised that there was nothing I could have done to save her. That there was nothing anyone could have done. Surely the police told him the same thing that they told me. That she was killed instantly and no matter how quickly we would have entered the room, it was already too late.

Scott Pulson is standing outside of Margaret's room waiting for Ethan.

'How are you doing mate?' Scott asks, placing his hand on Ethan's shoulder.

I can see the tension Ethan is holding in his chest. He's fighting hard to hold back tears.

'Our preliminary investigation has given us a pretty good idea of what happened, but I won't be making my full report until I speak to Mrs Vale,' Scott explains.

'I understand,' Ethan murmurs.

'Are you okay to hear?' Scott enquires, respectfully.

Ethan nods.

'As far as we can tell, Mr Vale arrived at the house with a loaded gun.' Scott gets straight to the point.

'He shot Margaret first, then Del before turning the gun on himself. It happened very quickly.' As Scott runs through the situation in a very matter-of-fact way, I can see the emotion in his eyes. Gloucester is such a small town and he's friendly with everyone. He knows exactly who all the criminals are and I'm pretty sure Arthur Vale wasn't one he'd considered. He tells Ethan to let him know if he needs anything then he excuses himself, making up a reason for having to go. It's pretty clear that Scott is fighting back his own tears as he flashes a weak smile when he passes me.

I don't know what to do next. I desperately want to wrap my arms around Ethan and give him the comfort and security he always gives me, but I can feel his rage. I'm locked in a state of shock and bewilderment. The whole situation is so surreal. I keep hoping that I'll wake up at any moment. I pinch my arm to see if I can snap out of it, but all I feel is pain.

'I'm so sorry,' I say, placing my hand on his shoulder.

'You should be,' he hisses as he slips away from me.

He stands facing the door to Margaret's room, not once turning in my direction. After taking a deep breath, he walks into the room. I quietly slip in behind him before the door closes. I want to be near him, but I know it's better to be invisible. I find a spot in the back corner to slink into and wait, too scared to get any closer to him. I'm determined to be there for him. I know it's only a matter of time before he'll break down and our connection will be restored.

Margaret is resting peacefully on the hospital bed, tubes coming out of her into nearby machines. As Ethan approaches her side, her eyes begin to flicker.

'How are you?' Ethan whispers.

Tears gently rolled from her eyes. 'I'm so sorry Ethan,' she pleads. 'This is all my fault.'

'Shhhh,' he soothes as he holds her hand. 'It's okay. You need to rest and not worry.'

'She tried to protect me. To save me from him and he shot her.' Her chest begins to heave and the monitor next to her beeps in quick succession.

'This isn't your fault,' he says, calmly. 'I should've been there. I should've protected both of you.'

As I watch him comfort her and all I want is to be part of it. My insides are being torn apart. He must blame me for him not being there and I don't know how to fix it. After being so close to him earlier that day to now feeling like a leper in his presence is more painful than I can handle. The only thing I can do is leave.

I return to the cot and cry myself to sleep.

Sometime during the next day, Jessica arrives with her family. Scott had gone by their place to let them know what happened and to tell them that I was on my own. Ethan left not long after I'd quietly slipped out of Margaret's room and I have no idea where he's gone.

I'm sitting with Margaret, keeping her company while she drifts in and out of sleep when the nurse comes in to tell me Jessica is outside. She's standing with her parents near the nurse's station when I come out of the room. Jessica runs up to me and gives me a hug, asking me how I'm doing. Still feeling a bit numb, I tell her I'm okay. The truth is, I really have no idea how I am.

'You look like you could use a decent meal,' Jessica's mum says.

Jessica hands me a bag of my clothes and one of the nurses shows me to a room where I can have a shower.

A short while later, we're leaving the hospital. I haven't been outside for at least twenty-four hours or maybe even longer. I've lost track of time. As far as I can tell it's around midday. The sun is shining and has a typical sting of summer to it.

'Looks like it's going to be another warm one,' Jessica's dad says, trying to make small talk as we walk to the car.

It's not until we're driving out of the car park that I remember we're in Newcastle. Everything has been such a blur I haven't really taken much notice. I've not been here before and have no idea where we are or where we're going, but I really don't care. I just sit back and watch the unfamiliar streets roll by. Jessica shifts uncomfortably next to me, not really sure what to say or do.

'Did you hear about Mr Martin?' she finally blurts. 'He's gone. Moved to Victoria.'

It takes me a moment to comprehend what she's just said. Thankfully, she doesn't need me to join in the conversation, she's happy to continue on her own.

'There's a new principal and I hear it's a woman,' she says. 'Can you imagine that in Gloucester? A female principal. My god, their heads may well explode.'

'Are you serious?' I attempt to get lost in her distraction.

'Yep. Mum saw Ms Davis and she couldn't wait to share the good news,' Jessica's eyes twinkle.

Jessica's opinion of Mr Martin is about the same as mine. He didn't make her arrival at a new school as enjoyable as it should have been.

'There may be hope for that school yet,' Jessica's mum chimes in from the front seat.

'Hey now, Beth, not all men are stuck living in caves,' her dad pipes up. 'Some of us came out from under our rocks a long time ago.'

'Yes Thomas, you're very hip,' Beth says drily, causing us all to laugh.

Spending a few hours with Jessica and her parents gives me a chance to break out of my dark and dreary mindset. They all work hard to keep me busy with frivolous conversations over lunch and light banter during a leisurely walk along the beach. I haven't thought once about last night. That is until we arrive back at the hospital. The moment I spot the mammoth brick structure, my reality starts seeping back in.

'How's Ethan going?' Beth asks quite innocently, but the mere mention of his name opens the floodgates. 'Oh my god, I'm so sorry.'

'Are you okay?' Jessica asks, wrapping her arms around me.

I did not grow up in an affectionate family, so it never occurred to me that I would ever need human contact. I know what it means to be held by Ethan, and

Del has always made me feel safe when in her arms. Even Aunty Bev has this way about her when greeting with a hug. But the touch of others was not something I ever really thought would matter to me. When Jessica offers me her comfort and security, I melt. As I sob, she doesn't waver and continues to hold me until I'm out of tears.

'Come home with us,' Beth offers quietly from the front seat. 'You are welcome to stay for as long as you want.' I can hear the sincerity in her tone. It makes me think of Del.

I thank her for the offer, but so far, none of Margaret's family have shown up and I want to make sure she isn't alone. Thomas tells me that they have family in Newcastle they are staying with and that they'll come by each day until I'm ready.

After I get a hug from all of them, I make a quick stop at the bathroom to tidy myself up before returning to Margaret's side.

When I walk into her room, she isn't alone. Sitting beside her, holding her hand, is a young woman with gentle tears rolling down her cheeks. Margaret is mirroring the young woman's emotion as they quietly stare at each other. I'm not sure if I should stay or go. They haven't seemed to notice my entry and I don't want to interrupt them. After a moment, Margaret's gaze falls upon me.

'Oh Sara, there you are,' she says, saving me from my indecision. 'Come over here. I want you to meet my daughter, Annie.'

Daughter? I think. I had no idea that Margaret even had a child.

She's stunningly beautiful, with long amber hair and chestnut brown eyes. Looking at her is like stepping back in time to what I imagine Margaret to have looked like when there was still colour in her hair.

'Nice to meet you. My mother had been telling me all about you.' Annie smiles.

A million questions are racing through my mind and I'm struggling with which one to ask first. I finally decide to start with the simplest one when the doctor enters the room.

'We need to run a few tests,' he says. He tells us it's going to take a little while and asks that Annie and I leave the room.

We agree to go to the cafeteria for a coffee.

'I bet you have a million questions for me,' Annie says as we walk the hallway.

Her directness takes me off guard and I'm not sure how to respond.

'She never told you about me, did she?'

I can't find the words to express what I'm feeling.

'It's okay. I didn't expect she would,' she continues once we have our coffee and find a quiet place to sit.

What I can't comprehend is that I've known the Vales my whole life and never knew they had a child. No one ever talked about it. Annie looks to be in her mid-twenties, so I would have thought people in town would have known about her. Given the town's desire to keep up on all the latest gossip and my mother's pride in being on top of it, I can't figure out how I didn't know.

'I was sixteen the last time I saw her,' Annie explains. 'I never really went to school in Gloucester. My parents shipped me off to boarding school from a young age. Basically, as soon as I was old enough to be accepted. It's very much a British-thing. My father grew up in England. That's what his parents did with him, so it was important he raised me the same way.' She's very relaxed as she recounts her story. 'I'll be honest, it was the best thing they ever could have done for me. Living in that house was torture. Watching the way my father treated Mum was sickening. I suppose he decided to ship me off so there was one less witness to his evilness.' Her demeanour changes when she speaks of her father. Her tone lowers and her speech slows. 'The only time I'd see my parents was during the holidays, and let me tell you, it was horrible. My mum would try to play happy family and keep up appearances, but behind closed doors, my father was a monster. It was becoming unbearable to be around them, and one Christmas, I confronted my father.' Her relaxed manner starts slipping away as anger creeps in. 'He'd been drinking and while Mum was cooking dinner, he wandered into the kitchen to demand his meal. I could hear him from my room, so I came out to see what was happening. She was telling him that dinner wasn't ready yet and that she was sorry it was taking so long. It was only five o'clock, and as per my father's demanded routine, dinner wasn't expected until six. Mum was too scared to say anything. But I wasn't.'

She pauses for a moment and stares out the window.

'I told him what time it was and asked him to leave her alone. He turned to me and told me to shut up and that if he wanted his dinner at five o'clock then it should be ready for him. My mum tried to calm me down and told him that she'll have it for him in a few minutes. I could see her desperately trying to figure out what to feed him. She'd been making a pasta bake and she hadn't even cooked the pasta yet. The water was only just coming to the boil.'

She takes a deep breath.

'But a few minutes wasn't good enough for him. He wanted to eat that minute. So, he started to call her names. He told her she was useless and that he could easily get a new wife ten times better than her. He told her she was lucky that he put up with her. Then he grabbed the pot of boiling water and threw it at her.' Tears fill her eyes.

It's hard for me to believe what I'm hearing. I know Arthur was a monster, but to hear a story from so long ago and to know she was being tormented for so long is difficult to hear. I place my hand on hers and tell her that she doesn't have to continue, but she insists.

'I want you to know why she never told you about me,' she presses on. 'The water scalded my mum pretty bad and I needed to get her to the hospital, but my father was in a rage. He was yelling about the mess of the water on the floor in the kitchen, telling my mum to clean it up. When I went to her aid, my father told me to leave her alone, that the only way she was going to learn was to clean up her own mess. Something snapped in me and I grabbed one of the kitchen knives. Shaking, I pointed it at him and told him to leave her alone. He told me I was an ingrate and how dare I talk to him that way. I was frozen, unable to move. So, he left the room to go get another drink. I could hear my mum whispering my name from the floor where she laid. She told me I had to leave and never come back. She said if he ever hurt me, she wouldn't be able to live with herself. She told me where I could find a stash of money hidden in the garage and demanded I go. I pleaded with her to come with me, but she told me she couldn't. When we heard him coming back, she kissed me and begged me to go. That was the last time I saw her until today.'

Annie had found a stash of ten thousand dollars exactly where her mother had told her it was, along with a name and address of a woman in Newcastle. That same night, Annie hitched a ride to the safe house her mother had been planning to escape to. The woman, Katherine Jones, welcomed Annie in with open arms and told her she could stay for as long as needed.

'Knowing my mother had already been planning to leave him made me believe that she would be okay and would get out soon. As the years passed and she never arrived, I started to lose hope. Thankfully, Katherine was connected to Gloucester and I would get regular updates that my mother was okay. And when Katherine called me to tell me what had happened, I got on a plane as soon as I could,' she she says with a meek smile.

Annie finished high school and got an apprenticeship as a hairdresser. She worked at the same place up until a couple of years ago when she decided to buy her own business in Perth. She recently got engaged, and with the news of her father's death, she couldn't wait to tell her mum all about her fiancé.

A few hours later, we're all together again. Margaret apologises to me for not ever telling me about Annie. She worried that if she spoke about her then Arthur would want to find her. He had tried for a while after she first disappeared. He got the police involved and pretended to be devastated that she'd gone missing. The Gloucester community rallied around the couple and as time passed and hope faded for her return, it became a faux pas to talk about her.

According to Margaret, the narrative the town swallowed was that Annie had been abducted and was presumed dead.

'There had been a few unsolved cases of young women vanishing around that time, so no one questioned it,' she explains. 'After some time passed, people forgot, and things went back to normal.'

Gloucester is not only good at spreading gossip, whether it be truthful or not, it's also good at pretending certain things never happened. I guess that's why I never heard about the existence or disappearance of Annie.

Chapter 40

Seeing Margaret and Annie together brings a beautiful light into the room. When Jessica returns the next morning with her parents, I take them up on the offer to go home with them. I know Margaret is now in good hands and that I'm not needed anymore. Besides, they have a lot of catching up to do.

It isn't long into the drive back to Gloucester that my thoughts return to Ethan. I wonder how he's doing and if he's thinking about me. I assume he's gone back to Karamea. I'm desperate to see him but scared at the same time. The idea that he might not want to see me is terrifying.

'Del's funeral is tomorrow,' Beth disrupts my anguish. 'They're giving Margaret special clearance to attend. Her daughter will be bringing her.'

I'm speechless. I've been trying really hard not to think about Del. It's still too painful. My sleep is crowded with constant images of that afternoon and the only way I can get any sort of rest is to pretend that it was all a dream. For me, at night, Del is still alive and I'm trying to hang onto that for as long as possible. The reality is too much for my heart to cope with.

'I think we should get you a new outfit for the occasion.' Beth's offer breaks me out of my rut. 'Something colourful, don't you think?'

I start to imagine how Del would feel about a room full of people, dressed in black, mourning her. She used to joke about her funeral simply being a procession of people on Harley Davidson's arriving at Karamea for a kick-arse party and a huge bonfire. The thought of honouring her with a splash of colour makes me smile.

'Have you heard from Ethan at all?' Jessica asks quietly.

I shake my head.

'What is his problem?' she blurts. 'He has no right blaming you for what happened.'

'He's just angry that he lost his mother.'

'But you lost her too,' Jessica retorts.

I appreciate what she's saying but it gives me little comfort. The thought of having to face Del's funeral and Ethan on the same day makes me feel ill.

Jessica's mum tries really hard to cheer me up when we arrive at the clothing store. As we enter, she announces that we need something colourful to wear. She rifles through the rows of options making random suggestions, some more absurd than others. We all embrace the notion of light heartedness and begin putting on our own mini fashion show, each of us strutting around the store, critiquing each other's outfits.

The shop is filled to the brim with our laughter when Mrs Carson walks in. Her presence causes a bolt of silence to rip through the building. I haven't seen any of Margaret's CWA women since Ethan and I had picked Margaret up, bruised and battered, at the side of the road. Mrs Carson is dressed in a light green pant suit with her silver hair tightly twirled up in a bun on the top of her head. As I catch a first glimpse of her, I almost think it's Mrs Vale. The resemblance to Margaret's former self is remarkable, and a little disturbing.

With a tight upper lip, she walks over to Mrs McEwen at the counter asking to collect the outfit she's put aside for the funeral.

'It's very important to have the correct attire for such an affair,' she comments intentionally loud enough for us to hear. 'One must behave respectfully at such a dignified event.'

'So, you'll wear the red,' Beth speaks up, pointing in my direction. 'Jessica will wear the blue, I'll take the yellow, and Tom will have the green.'

'Great idea, Mum,' Jessica says. 'We'll be our own rainbow. Del would love it.'

Jessica is right. Del would love it. She would love the colour choices and the idea of arriving at her funeral as a rainbow. But most of all, she would love that we are making sure that the stuck-up percentage of the community are still being knocked down a peg. It's one of the best ways Jessica's family can honour her.

I'm physically ill the next morning and not sure I can make it through the funeral. I don't know if I can face Ethan and experience another moment of his hatred towards me. But most of all, I don't know how I'm going to say goodbye to Del.

Beth offers me something to help settle my stomach, but I can't even consider putting anything in my mouth. We have about an hour before we have to go, so I go for a walk. I make my way to the park, desperate to sit on the rock by the river where I sat and had ice cream with Del only a couple of months earlier. For her, the river was the place of solitude that offered a path forward when faced with a difficult journey. Returning to our spot helps me feel a little bit closer to her. As I sit where she once sat and shared a bit of her life story, I take a moment to reflect.

She trusted me and welcomed me into her heart with open arms. She showed me a new world outside of my sheltered existence and happily took me in when my parents died. I'd never met anyone like her. She was so free. She did what she wanted when she wanted. She never judged people even though they judged her. It was important to her to give people a chance before casting an opinion on them. And she always gave the best advice.

I wonder what she would say to me to help me face the day. What words of wisdom would she share to help me find my strength to face Ethan? Could she explain to me why he's so mad at me? Could she tell me what I've done wrong? I opened myself up to him and made myself vulnerable to him. I shared the most intimate moment of my life with him. I gave him my heart and told him that I loved him. I'd trusted him completely. And now, when we need each other most, he's shut me out.

I miss Del. I miss Ethan. I've lost my family all over again. It seems that once again, I need to find a new path forward. Del would tell me I could do it. She'd tell me that I was a strong, independent, beautiful woman who could take on the world. I want to have the strength that Del saw in me. I want to make her proud. So, I get up and walk back to Jessica's house, determined to turn this nausea into the strength I need to make it through.

The funeral is at Karamea House. It's perfect. Exactly what she wanted. No stuffy church. No dreary cemetery. She wanted a huge party to celebrate her life, and that's what she's getting.

Jessica holds my hand as we walk from the car towards the crowd. To my amazement, we aren't the only ones sporting an array of colour. In fact, there is very little black to be seen. Only the few rigid CWA members, who I assume are only attending for pure social etiquette reasons, are dressed in traditional attire. Seeing all the colour makes me smile. It's a testament to how much Del has impacted the community. Her personality was clearly infectious as they all stand there proudly honouring her. She made an impression on every farmer, business person and shop owner she'd come in contact with. Even Mrs McEwen is wearing purple.

'I thought I'd add another colour to your rainbow,' she tells me as I walk by her.

Aunty Bev has gone all out, sporting the most colourful dress I've ever seen. 'I figured she'd approve,' she says as she gives me a big hug.

We've been mingling for about ten minutes, and I still haven't seen Ethan. There are so many people there – a lot more than I expected – making it easy to remain lost in the crowd. It isn't until I hear his voice from the verandah that I finally catch a glimpse of him.

He looks so handsome in the multi-colour pants Del had bought him for his birthday this year, to go with the dusty yellow button-up shirt she'd got him the year before. He's asking everyone to gather around as the service is about to start. I want to run to him. How I ache to hold him, touch him and kiss him. But I stay put and try to keep out of the way.

'Thank you everyone for coming today to help celebrate the life of Del Moon, my beautiful mother,' Ethan says. 'Although her life was abruptly stolen from her, she wouldn't want us to dwell. She would want us to lift our glasses and get this party started.'

Everyone cheers and has a toast in Del's honour. He invites people to say a few words about her or share stories. Aunty Bev is one of them.

'Del was a strong, proud woman who loved her family,' Aunty Bev says. 'But her family wasn't just blood, she opened her arms to many.'

As she speaks, tears flow uncontrollably from my eyes and I long to be in Ethan's arms. Jessica puts her arm around me, which helps a little.

After the speeches are over, people begin to gather around the fire to share stories about Del. I go looking for Ethan. It's time. I need to talk to him. To see how he is. When I finally spot him, my heart skips a beat. I take a deep breath and bravely walk up to him.

He's with a group of people reminiscing about his mother. I decide to place my hand on his arm.

'Can we talk?' I ask when he turns to face me.

I feel like a stranger to him. He makes no attempt to greet me. He barely seems interested in the fact that I'm even here. But he does come with me.

Once we're clear of the crowd, I stop and face him. I hope that he'll reach out and grab me, hold me tight and not let go, but instead he just looks at me.

'What do you want?' he says, dismissively.

'To see you. To see how you are doing,' I plea.

'I'm fine, thank you.' He is so cold.

'Can I hug you?' I ask.

'If you want.' He lets me put my arms around him but makes no effort to reciprocate. 'Are we done?' he says while I'm still holding him.

'I love you,' I whisper. 'I miss you.'

He grabs my arms and pulls me off of him. 'I can't do this. I can't be near you, it's too much.'

He walks off.

My heart is shattered.

Chapter 41

After the funeral, Jessica's parents tell me that their offer to live with them for as long as I need is still open. I haven't made a final decision about where I want to go for university. Thoughts about my future have been a little derailed since the day we came across Margaret at the side of the road.

Jessica, on the other hand, has her plans all worked out, she's secured an amazing opportunity to study in London. A few days after I say goodbye to Del, I join Jessica's parents farewelling her as she boards her plane.

After Margaret fully recovers, she decides to move to Perth to be with her daughter. She feels like there isn't much for her in Gloucester anymore and that it's time she makes a new life of her own.

'I think it's time I figured out what I want to do with my life,' she tells me one afternoon when we meet up for a coffee. 'Maybe I'll go back to school, pick up a new trade. I always wanted to be a baker.'

'You'd be awesome,' I say. I'm excited for her. 'You always make the best carrot cake.'

'Thanks, honey.' She smiles. 'As Del always said, it's never too late to start something new.'

Margaret makes me promise that we stay in touch before we say a teary goodbye.

With Jessica gone, I feel a bit lost. I know I should be excited about getting out of Gloucester and starting a new adventure at university, but I can't help feeling like something is missing. I know I can't go backwards and bring my parents back or resurrect Del. I've come to terms with that. Even the fantasy I had about a future with Ethan is fading into a distant memory.

In the weeks after the funeral, I cry everyday – partly from the loss of Del and partly from the loss of Ethan. I waste hours coming up with excuses for his behaviour. I try really hard to justify his state of mind. I tell myself that he links Del's death with his memory his parents' murder-suicide. That he's reverted to that child in the cupboard, scared and alone.

But in time, my hurt turns to anger. He has no right to blame me or alienate me. No matter how difficult the situation, he should never have treated me the way he did. I'd given him my heart and virginity, and he discarded me like it meant nothing.

As the days continue to pass, I feel like I'm starting to lose my way. I still haven't made a decision about my future and I'm struggling to force myself to. I take a walk to the park and sit on Del's rock by the river. If I can't be at Karamea anymore, at least I have a special place I can escape to and remember her.

I'm just making myself comfortable on the rock when a message flashes on my phone.

'*So you coming to see me?*' It's from Georgia.

My heart flutters. Shortly after the funeral, I finally worked up the courage to look at her messages and respond with a meek, '*Hi*'.

We've been connecting ever since and she keeps asking me to visit her.

'*Sitting by the river,*' I respond, adding a playful emoji.

After all this time, she still makes me feel nervous.

'*You can't keep ignoring my question,*' she persists.

'*Hard to make plans,*' I deflect.

The idea of seeing her again is overwhelming.

'*What's stopping you? Still waiting for Ethan?*'

'*No,*' I respond quickly.

'*Whatever,*' she retorts with a cheeky emoji.

I hate the idea of her thinking that I'm still hung up on him, but I don't know why I keep avoiding her offer. My heart was so broken when she left. I would have done anything to have her stay.

But all my insecurities and fears are creeping back in. It's like no time has passed and I'm that scared, strange girl from that weird church group. I'm riddled with self-doubt.

'*I'll just be in your way,*' I type.

'*Not possible,*' She returns quickly. '*There's always been room for you here.*'

My heart quickens.

'*I miss you.*' Her words fluster me and can't get my fingers to work. '*No reasons left not to come.*'

She's right, I think as I jump up from the rock and start walking into town. My head is filled with visions of her face, her hair, her lips. My body tingles as I speed up my pace.

As I'm breezing through town, I spot Aunty Bev walking along the main street. She notices me at the same time and waves me over.

'Oh my dear girl, it's so good to see you,' she says as she wraps her arms around me.

I haven't seen her since the funeral. With her living outside of town and me not having a car, it makes getting together difficult.

'Got some mail for you at my place,' she tells me. 'Came a few days ago.'

She insists that I come back with her to collect it.

'Give us a chance to catch up.' She smiles as I walk with her to the car.

The drive back towards Karamea fills me with a range of emotions. There is a part of me that has been longing to go back, but I'm not sure I'm able to face the demons that now fill the place. Thankfully we don't need to go anywhere near Karamea to get to Aunty Bev's house. Her entry road is several kilometres away.

Aunty Bev is chatting away about things she's been up to and gives me a full update on all of her family. It's a big group, so it keeps her going for the entire drive. It doesn't worry me, though, in fact, I'm finding it soothing. I've really missed spending time with her.

'You get the fire goin' and I'll grab your letter,' Aunty Bev says before disappearing into the house with the bag of supplies she collected in town.

I make my way to the pit and get to work. It's interesting to think that a year ago I had little experience being near a fire, let alone knowing how to build one. The moment the flames take hold, a smile graces my cheeks and I'm overcome with a sense of accomplishment.

'The boys are on their way with some tucker for the fire,' Aunty Bev explains as she approaches with the kettle.

'Best get the billy on then,' I say, taking the pot from her and placing it on the wire rack over the fire.

'Looks like pretty important news,' she tells me as she hands me an envelope. 'Got a lawyer's name on it.'

Despite the letter being clearly addressed to me, I have not heard of the name of the person who's sent it. Aunty Bev is right. It's definitely from a lawyer, but not one from Gloucester. The return address is from Adelaide – a place I've never been. I remember at my parents' funeral someone mentioning that they'd lived there, but it was the first time I heard anything about it. My parents had only ever spoken as if they lived their whole lives in Gloucester.

I'm confused and not sure if I want to open it.

'Come on now. Don't leave me waitin' any longer,' Aunty Bev insists.

I reluctantly open it to reveal several sheets of paper bound together by one staple.

Dear Miss Johnson, the letter begins. *I am writing to advise you about the finalisation of the Estate of Samuel James and Hannah Elizabeth Johnson. As the sole beneficiary, the remaining funds will be distributed directly to you. Outlined in this document are the holdings and expenses of the Estate. Please contact my office to arrange the transfer of funds.*

'Sounds like your parents took care of you as they shoulda',' Aunty Bev comments. 'How much ya' get?'

I flip through the papers searching for an answer.

'It looks like around 250 thousand dollars,' I gasp.

'Sounds like enough to get you out of here.' She smiles.

I'm speechless.

'No excuse for uni now, huh.'

I shake my head.

'Just gotta make your choice.'

I nod.

'So wat ya gonna do?' Aunty Bev stares me dead in the eyes. 'Nothing here for you no more,'

'But you're here,' I say, softly.

'A young thing like you has no place hanging out with an old thing like me,' she laughs.

I stare at the paper, not sure what to do next. The money means I can go to whichever university I want and not worry about the cost. It means I can focus on my education and make plans for my future. I just don't know where to go.

If I choose Wollongong, I don't know anyone there and I can start my life the way I want. But there's a part of me that wants to be with Georgia. It's a longing that is tucked down so far inside of me, I've been able to ignore it. But the more I think about her, the more I want to see her. Her perfect face. Her shimmering blue eyes. Her glowing hair.

'Trust yourself,' Aunty Bev whispers. 'You know what ya want.'

Our moment is broken by the sound of a car coming up the driveway. Aunty Bev's nephews are about to arrive, so I pack the letter away and prepare for the party ahead.

The next morning, I catch a ride back into town with the boys. They don't have much on for the day, so they offer to take me wherever I want to go. They're under strict instructions from Aunty Bev to make sure I get moving with my decision.

She's right. It's time.

I ask them to take me to Jessica's house so I can collect my things. They wait for me outside while I say goodbye to Beth and Thomas.

When I return to the car, I ask the boys to take me to the train station. There's one coming around noon and I'm ready to get on it. After I promise to make contact once I reach my destination, the boys agree to leave me and I'm finally alone.

I pull out my phone to purchase the ticket. Once it's confirmed, I let Jessica know and ask her to update her parents.

Only one more thing to do before I leave Gloucester.

I open my message thread to Georgia and type, *'I'm on my way'*.

I hold my breath and close my eyes as I wait for her response. I'm terrified she's changed her mind.

The app pings.

'Can't wait to see you.'

About the Author

Anne Keen is an accomplished journalist, documentarian and a passionate storyteller. While working as a print and digital journalist in regional Australia, she began her path into documentary film making. Her first solo project, Undermining a Community was selected for the 2020 Far South Film Festival. Shortly after, she co-founded Treechange Films, which completed its first documentary in January 2021, Nanna Power: The Story of the Gloucester Knitting Nannas. The same year, the short film was selected for both the Melbourne Documentary Film Festival and the Far South Film Festival. In early 2022, Treechange Films created the short film, Kelvin for Screenworks' Fearless Films Season 3.

Born in Canada, Anne spent time as part of the newsgathering team at Global Television in Toronto, and Entertainment Tonight in Hollywood, as well as working in production on numerous films and television shows in North America before moving to Australia in 2000. She has a Bachelor of Media and Communications with a major in Writing and Publishing and a Broadcast Journalism diploma.